NO LOVE *Like Yours*

ORLINDA VALLEY

SERIES

BOOK TWO

DONNA R. MADDEN

Also By Donna R. Madden
The *More Than Enough Series*
More Than Enough
Your Love is Enough
You Are Enough
Orlinda Valley Series
No One But You
No Love Like Yours
No Place Like Home

This book is dedicated to
anyone who has ever struggled
to find the love of their life.
Keep searching.
You are meant to be happy, loved, and cherished.

NO LOVE
Like Yours

CHAPTER 1

JAMISON

There's nothing good about being a single dad with a five-year-old except for the ability to piss in my own bathroom without a wife nagging me to put the seat down, though, I'd do anything—even put the seat down every time—if I could hear Carly's nagging just once more.

After coming out of the bathroom, I put on my shorts and walked slowly to the kitchen, carefully navigating through shoes and toys on the floor.

A loud squeak scared the shit out of me. "Dammit." I kicked the dog's toy out of the way and woke up its owner—my seventy-five-pound pile of shaggy white fur. She picked up her squeaky toy and ran around my feet, ready to play.

"Seriously, Becca? The sun isn't even up yet." I patted her on her fuzzy head and attempted to step around her large body.

Her prancing around made getting to the coffee pot difficult. Luckily, I'd remembered to set it up and put it on a timer before I went to bed last night, so the coffee was waiting for me—one less thing to worry about in the morning. Nothing was as important as my first cup of coffee—well, there was something, but I hadn't had the opportunity for that in two years.

I finally danced around Becca, fixed my cup of life, and tipped it up. I leaned on the sliding door and could feel the caffeine make its way into my bloodstream and work its magic.

"Out you go, girl." Becca bounded out the door and ran around in circles, looking for that perfect place to relieve herself.

I shook my head and trudged into the living room to watch the local news and get my mind focused for the day.

I fell on the couch and glanced around the living room. Blankets and dirty clothes cluttered the area. The two overfilled laundry baskets were still in the corner of the room where I left them two days ago, and Becca's fur blew around like tumbleweeds.

This house was a wreck. Keeping up with work, my five-year-old, the dog, and the house had seemed simple when Carly was alive. She was perfect at everything. But now that she was gone, there doesn't seem to be enough hours in the day to get food on the table, let alone all the other things a parent needed to do to keep his child from looking homeless and neglected.

It'd been two years since she died. Two years of birthdays and Christmases missed. The good thing about time is that the pain you feel initially slowly dissipates and becomes something you can deal with. Yes, things get easier, but sometimes, I feel like a hamster in a hamster wheel. Always running and working hard, yet getting nowhere.

I watched the news for a bit. It was going to be a dreary day—fitting. It might rain, or it might not. To be a weatherman and be able to be wrong half the time. How awesome would that be! I sighed deeply, scrubbed the sleep from my face, and finished my coffee. I needed to hop in the shower and look more presentable before my family arrived.

A hot shower always seemed to wash away the doubt that filled my gut, and thankfully for me, it did the same today. I felt better as I put on jeans and a blue button-down shirt, with a white T-shirt underneath. I styled my hair with gel and brushed it back.

"Morning, Daddy." Darcie, my beautiful five-year-old daughter, walked into my room with her stuffed dolphin under her arm. Her auburn hair looked like a bird had taken up residence in it during the night.

My heart felt complete as soon as her sweet little voice hit my ears. "Morning, princess." I swept her into a bear hug and buried my face in her hair. She smelled like strawberry baby shampoo and lavender soap. Despite the shitty direction my life had taken, and the choices I never thought I'd have to make alone over the past two years without Carly, Darcie was the light at the end of the long, dark tunnel. My red-haired, green-eyed princess, whose eyes were shining with excitement and energy all the time, so much like her momma—was my reason for living. It was like someone knew I would need a ray of sunshine in my life and dropped her down from heaven.

"How did you sleep?" I whispered and dotted her face with kisses.

"Good. Daddy. Your face tickles," she squealed.

I chuckled and pulled away. "You hungry?"

"Yes, I'm hungry." She placed her palms on my face and held me close. "You look handsome today, Daddy," she said as she placed a kiss on my cheek. Her smile was wide and showed the hole where she lost her first tooth on Monday.

"Well, thank you, princess. You look absolutely beautiful your-self." I answered her as I danced her around the room, down the steps, and into the kitchen where my mother stood over the stove cooking eggs.

"Well, morning, Mom," I said as Darcie and I wrapped her in a hug. "I didn't hear you come in."

"Yeah, well, you were too preoccupied with this little darlin' here." Mom wrapped Darcie in a hug. "I was looking forward to getting kisses from Grammy's girl."

Darcie squeezed her grandmother tight and wiggled free from her grasp, and my mother's face became serious. "Jamison, baby, how are you doing?" She placed her hand on my cheek.

"Mom, I'm thirty-five." I knew that look. Her focused and serious look. I didn't want to deal with it right now. I wrapped her in a hug. "And your oldest. Technically, Rowan's the baby, then Bryson. In case you forgot."

"Yeah, well, I don't get to see Rowan every week. He's out saving the country and only needs me when his money's running low. Bryson and Darlene have each other, but you and Darcie need me." She pulled back. "Especially today." Her voice became soft and filled with emotion.

"I'm okay, Mom," I told her. I stared out the window at the yard and the weeping willow I planted after Carly's death. Carly loved weeping willows. I proposed to her underneath one by the Red River and planted this one in her memory. At the time, it was a great metaphor.

My heart constricted, but I didn't experience the normal pit opening and wanting to swallow me whole like I did this day last year. I was okay, or I had to be. A smile grew on my face. "I'm good, Mom. Better than last year."

"And that's how grief works. It slowly goes away. It may never totally be gone, but it becomes something you learn to deal with." She went back to the stove. "Now let's eat."

"Come on, Darce. Time to eat." I nudged her with my foot. She was lying on the floor, using the dog as a pillow. "Darce, honey, Becca's not a bed." Darcie laid on the dog all the time. Becca was such a sweet and calm soul and never seemed to mind. Her eyes were enormous as she just lay there, totally okay with being a jungle gym as long as she was getting the attention she desired. I rubbed the dog's head.

"Fine." Darcie patted Becca and gave her a peck on the face, then plopped in her chair as my mom placed scrambled eggs and toast on a plate in front of her.

"Daddy, are those my flowers for Mommy?" Darcie pointed to the pot of lilies I'd brought home last night.

"Yeah, honey. We're going to plant them under the tree right next to the ones we planted last year, as soon as we're finished with breakfast."

"Those are Mommy's favorites, right?"

A small lump formed in my throat. I took a sip of coffee to wash it down. "Yes, princess. I thought you'd like to make it a tradition to plant lilies around mommy's tree."

Darcie hopped into my lap and wrapped her little arms around me.

I didn't even see her leave her chair, but love radiated from her and calmed my aching heart.

"That would be great, Daddy. Do you miss Mommy? I miss Mommy. I'm like her, right?" Her voice was small and muted, and my throat tightened.

I swallowed and fought to control my feelings. I flattened her curls and looked into her green eyes. Today, they were green with gold specks. Like a meadow in the fall. "You are so much like her, princess. You have her hair and her beautiful eyes."

She smiled a tight smile and caressed my cheek. Carly used to do that same gesture to help calm me, and it still worked.

The front door opened. "Morning, everyone."

"Uncle Bryson's here," I told Darcie as I gave her a kiss, and she hopped off my lap.

"Uncle Bryson," she squealed as she ran off to greet her aunt and uncle.

"Hey there, you." He lifted her, spun her around, then placed her back on the floor.

Bryson, his wife, Darlene, and their five-year-old son, James, were here to help plant Carly's lily. Mom greeted them and took the kids from the room.

"Morning, Jamison," Darlene said as she wrapped me in a hug and placed a kiss on my cheek.

"How you doin, bro?" Bryson asked.

"I'm okay," I answered as we gave each other a hug and a firm pat on the back.

Darlene looked me in the eye. "You sure?"

"I'm doing good." I nodded and again did a check of my feelings. "I am. I still miss Carly like crazy, but I'm doing better than I was this time last year."

"Good. Carly would want that," Darlene said.

"Yeah, she would," Bryson said as he fixed a cup of coffee. We settled at the table, and I went back to eating my breakfast.

"Have you gone for your fittings yet for Kora and Kai's wedding?" Darlene asked me.

I popped an eyebrow. "It's only July. We have until October."

Bryson slapped his hand on the table and leaned back in his chair, his arms crossed. "That's what I told her. We have plenty of time."

"Right?" I agreed. "What's the hurry?"

Darlene rolled her eyes. "I was hoping you'd see the importance of it, Jamison." She wiped her hand in the air. "It doesn't matter. You should both grab Lance and get it done soon. It's never too early. The wedding will be here before you know it."

Thankfully, the conversation was interrupted by James running back into the room with Darcie close behind, and a smile filled my face.

Darcie had on a light green dress, her plastic princess shoes, and her hair was back in a ponytail. She was obsessed with everything princess, and I loved it when she dressed in her princess shoes. I hoped she stayed that young and innocent forever, but I knew that was wishful thinking.

"Ready, Daddy?" she asked.

"Absolutely, princess."

I picked up the lily, and we filed out the back door into the yard by the willow tree.

I kneeled on the grass, and Darcie joined me. "Why don't you do this?" I handed her the small spade.

Her eyes went wide, and she nodded. I helped her dig a hole next to the lily we planted last year. One lily every year.

"There," she said as she patted the dirt down. "A perfect flower for my perfect mommy."

I sat on the bench under the tree and pulled Darcie into my lap, her little hand in mine. "It's beautiful under here, Daddy."

"Yes, it is, princess. Your mommy would have loved this tree." The long branches touched the ground in spots. One day, it would be tall enough so the branches would surround the bench, providing shade during the heat and humidity of the summer. A perfect place to relax and for Darcie to remember a mother who passed away too soon.

We were quiet for a bit, and Darcie laid her head on my shoulder. I looked up, and Bryson gave me a tight-lipped smile.

My family was great. They never left my side those first days after I got the news that Carly had been involved in a ten-car pile-up on the interstate. I remember that day like it was yesterday. She had a day off and was spending it with her parents. If there was a silver lining at all, it was that Darcie was supposed to be there, but she woke up with a fever. My mom came over to watch her so Carly could still go spend some much-needed time with her parents. If it wasn't for her fever, Darcie would have been in the car as well.

I squeezed my eyes tight against the constriction of my heart. Losing Carly was awful, but if I had lost them both. . .

I wrapped my arms around Darcie in a tight hug. She was my life now. I needed to do everything in my power to make sure she didn't feel like she was missing out, but I also needed to make sure I took care of myself.

"Jamison." My mom's hand was on my shoulder.

I took a deep breath. "I'm good." I unwrapped Darcie and kissed her on the cheek. She jumped off my lap, and she and James ran across the yard with Becca. To be a child and be able to forget things so easily.

Tears sprang to my eyes, and I wiped hard at my cheeks. "There are some days everything goes perfectly, and I feel fine, and there are other days I get so overwhelmed and feel like I'm failing her."

"Failing her, how?" my mom asked. "Keeping a roof over Darcie's head, putting money away for her future, making sure she's fed and clothed? Loving her?" My mom pulled me to my feet. "I think you're doing an amazing job," she added quietly.

I watched Darcie across the yard. James laughed, and her face shone with excitement. A smile crept across my face. She was the most perfect thing ever. I blinked away the blurriness. "She's so much like Carly."

"Yes, she is," commented Darlene. She and Bryson had been standing close by. "She has Carly's ability to make everyone feel important and needed. She never meets a stranger."

"That's the truth," agreed Bryson. "You should probably wish she was a little shyer. The guys are going to love her."

I shot him a look I wished lasers would have come out of. "Don't need to hear that."

Bryson chuckled.

My mom wrapped her arm around my waist. "She'll have James to make sure the guys are always respectful."

We laughed as we watched Darcie pull Becca's Frisbee from James's grasp. They had a minor scuffle, and Darcie came out as the clear winner.

"But I don't think she'll have any trouble defending herself," Darlene chuckled.

We left the kids in the backyard, playing with Becca, and went into the house. The unorganized chaos that was my life hit me. Shit was everywhere.

"It's a good thing Darcie thinks I'm amazing. Maybe she won't realize I suck at keeping up with housework." I didn't mean to say that out loud, and the raised brows I got in return didn't make it better. "Look, I know I'm doing the best I can, but I'm just not Carly, and I know I'm not doing all the things right. Hell, I can't even keep up with the laundry."

"Bro," Bryson held his hands up in front of him and made sure he had my attention. "Maybe you should get a sexy nanny. She could clean up your mess, help with Darcie when you're working, and when Darcie starts kindergarten, she can help you with anything else you may need." He wiggled his brows and nodded his head.

I didn't have a chance to respond before Darlene whacked him hard and square in his gut. He doubled over and gasped for breath.

"Serves you right." Darlene turned toward me. "I'm sorry your brother's a pig. I'm sure that's not something you want to think of today, of all days."

Bryson grimaced. "I don't know why you've got your panties . . ."

"Don't you dare finish that statement, Bryson Allan McKendry."

"The whole name. You're up shit's creek, bro." I chuckled.

"Boys, enough." Mom held up her hands. "I agree with Bryson."

"Good choice, Mom." Bryson crossed his arms. "You think Jamison needs a hot nanny, too?"

"Mom?" Where was she going with this? I wasn't sure I could deal with her usual sarcasm.

"No, Bryson, he doesn't need a hot nanny, not yet anyway, though a little nookie every now and then wouldn't be such a bad thing."

I glared at her, which didn't bother her at all, and she waved off my irritation. "But a little extra help wouldn't be so bad either." She leaned on the counter and pointed her finger at me. "You need help around here, and I've been thinking. I want to help you, but I can't do much more than one day a week. *Have* you ever thought of hiring someone to come in and clean?"

Bryson wiggled his eyebrows and dodged another swipe from Darlene.

"I'm being serious," my mother continued. "There are plenty of businesses that clean and do your laundry, even if it's only one day a week. They could come on Tuesdays when you aren't home."

She really wants me to get a maid? Let a stranger poke around in my belongings? "Umm, I don't know if that's for me. I don't want a stranger folding my underwear."

She chuckled and turned back to loading the dishwasher. "Remember, I'm heading down to Florida soon with the girls, and I'll probably be staying longer with my brother. I would like to know that when I leave, someone will be here to help you out."

Bryson leaned against the counter, his arms crossed, with a shit-eating grin on his face.

I walked away from him. I needed more caffeine. Dealing with this family was a bit much. "Fine, Mom. Maybe I'll look into it." I turned and took a sip of my coffee.

"Thank you, baby. That's all I ask." She again patted my cheek and kissed it. "And Bryson, we don't need any more unnecessary suggestions from you," she added as she turned back to the dishes.

Bryson didn't waste any time. He wiggled his brows, made an obscene gesture with his fist next to his cheek, and earned another smack from Darlene.

I loved my sister-in-law.

"Tonya, have you talked to Kaye today?" Darlene asked as she got comfortable on a stool at the counter.

"Not yet. Why?"

"I heard from Kora that Rose is picking up Lilly from the airport today. She's coming home."

My Mom turned toward Darlene; her eyes huge.

"Lilly hasn't been home since Dad's funeral, has she?" The shock in Bryson's voice reflected the shock on Mom's face.

"No, she hasn't," my mom said with a head shake. "Wonder what brings her back now?"

"Lance told me her divorce was finalized months ago," I said. "But she was going to try to make a go of it in New York." Lilly was the daughter of Kaye, one of my mom's closest friends. We all grew up together. Her brother, Lance, is my best friend.

I leaned heavily against the counter. Lilly was coming home. I couldn't ignore the gallop of my pulse as blood coursed through my system. Memories of over a decade ago—before Carly—filled my mind.

"Alright, everyone, I've gotta go. I have a meeting with the book club." My mom interrupted my thoughts as she gave me a hard hug.

"You mean the gossip channel," Bryson replied as he hugged her.

"Whatever," Mom said, brushing away his comment.

"Thanks for everything, Mom, and don't forget I'm going out tonight," I said.

"You mean your weekly meeting with the guys for drinks at the pub while talking about the upcoming football season?" she asked as she squeezed me tight.

"Yep, that's exactly what I meant."

"It's Friday night. Of course, I know that." She hugged Bryson and Darlene. "And if you two want to bring James to my house, too, I'll have a sleepover, and y'all can get the night off."

"That sounds wonderful, Tonya. I think we'll take you up on the offer," Darlene said.

"Good." Tonya grinned. "Drop my grandbabies by the salon this afternoon. We'll play with the goats and chickens at Kora's before we eat pizza at my house.

"Thanks, Mama. You're the best," Bryson said as he squeezed her.

"Tonya, don't say anything to Kaye about Lilly. It might be a surprise." Darlene cocked her head. We all knew keeping a secret was not my mother's talent.

"I promise I won't." She swiped her hand through the air. "Now, you three drop these kiddos at the salon today and take the rest of the night off. Go out and have fun."

CHAPTER 2

LILLY

Between the flight from New York to Tennessee and the current car ride, I had been sitting for close to three hours, and my ass was numb. I needed to get out and get some exercise, but right now, I was a passenger in my best friend Rose's car.

Rose picked up my daughter, Madeline, and me from the Nashville airport, and we were heading home to Orlinda Valley. The quiet between us filled the cab with more debilitating stress than a lack of oxygen. Okay, maybe not that bad, but still, when you didn't like quiet, the least bit made you think the worst. The only sound was from the hum of the road and Madeline's soft breathing in the back seat. She was out cold.

Last night, I'd called Rose, my best friend since birth, and told her Madeline and I were coming home. Our flight got into Nashville at one-thirty in the afternoon, and I needed someone to pick us up at the airport.

And here she was.

"So." I had to break the silence. If I waited on Rose to ask questions, I would be waiting for eons. She was never one to pry and always said when I was ready to talk I would, and she was always right. "Thank you for picking us up."

"Lilly, of course, I would pick you up without question. I told you years ago, when you were ready to get out of there, just call." She glanced quickly at me with a small, understanding smile. "You finally did, and here I am." She gestured with her head to the back seat. "She is so much more precious in person. Those brown eyes are . . . wow."

"Thank you," I answered as I leaned my head on the cool glass of the window and watched the somewhat familiar Tennessee landscape fly by. The familiarity of the openness and rolling hills calmed my throbbing pulse. "Don't you want to know why we're home now?"

She shook her head and kept her eyes on the road. "You had a shitty marriage and, for some reason, when your divorce was final, you—a small-town girl from Tennessee—thought you'd try to make it on your own in the big city." She shrugged. "I'm guessing the doubt Kristy and I heard in your voice the past four months finally strangled you and made you cry uncle."

I chuckled a little at her answer. Rose was the sweetest friend and didn't believe in telling lies. She had a way of putting you in your place without cursing or putting anyone down. Our friend Kristy and I always said we were lucky because everyone needed a Rose. "I can't say you're wrong. I needed to get some space between Anthony and me. He was toxic even when we weren't married, and still never had time for Madeline."

"Not a surprise," Rose acknowledged. "I'm glad you're home."

I squeezed Rose's hand and leaned my head back against the window as Rose flipped on the turn signal and took the ramp to Orlinda Valley.

"Can you believe I left ten years ago and have only been back once?"

Rose nodded. "I've lived here without you. Trust me, I know how long it's been since Anthony pulled you away from us."

"God, he was a dick." I turned quickly to make sure Madeline was still sleeping in the back seat and didn't hear me trash talk her father. Even though it was the truth, I didn't have to say so to her.

"We'll be pulling into the hair salon soon, so you better spill things. Once your mom sees you, we won't be able to talk. Why did you decide to come home now?"

"Well, lots of reasons. Nothing that will surprise anyone. One," I held up a finger. "New York City is too expensive, and two," I held up another finger. "Since I finally have the chance to raise Madeline wherever I choose, I want to raise her in the country in Tennessee, not the concrete world of the city. Oh, but there's something else."

"What? That all sounds about right and like you said, not a surprise."

"Yeah well, no one knows I'm coming home. Not even Momma." I glanced at the car's clock. It was just after three. "She may not even be at the salon this late." One thing about Momma, when my older brother Lance and I were little, she worked early on Saturdays. She wanted to be home when we woke up.

Rose glanced my way. "What?" Her eyes went wide. "You didn't tell her you were coming home? No way, Lil."

"They added on to the school. It's about time." I looked out the window at Orlinda Valley High School as we passed by.

"Lilly." Rose hissed my name in the way she did when I irritated her. Some people never change. That's why I called her. After all these years, she was the one friend I knew I could count on. "Don't you dare change the subject. Why didn't you tell your mom you were coming home?"

"I don't know." I avoided eye contact. "It was stupid of me, but everything happened so quickly. I had a job at a law firm—a pretty shitty one, but it was a job. Anyway, they had to make some cuts, and last week I was let go. I found myself with a choice to make. Find a new job in the city or use this as a sign it's time to take my daughter home. Anthony never used his visitation. He always had something else more important going on, anyway. So, I asked him to allow me to take her home. He agreed and even bought our tickets. It was like he couldn't wait to get rid of us. I know I should have called Momma, but there was never any love lost between her and Anthony, and I didn't want to hear I told you so, so my friend Gianna helped me pack what we could take on the plane and drove us to the airport."

"Well, God bless Gianna." Rose stopped at a stop light, the only one in the small town, and glanced at me. "Everyone will be so happy to see you, and we're all glad you finally left that dweeb."

I cocked a brow. Dweeb was harsh language for Rose.

"Anyway, I guess I'm taking you to your mom's house. Your mom isn't here."

I glanced out at the square as we passed the small parking lot where the house, which was Shear Perfection Hair Salon, sat along with a short strip mall. My mother and her business partner, Diane, owned the salon and the property adjacent to it. The strip mall housed a small boutique, a walk-in sandwich shop slash coffee shop, and a gym. The coffee shop was new. "Is the coffee good?" I loved fancy coffee. Coffee shops on every corner were one thing I'd miss about New York.

"Yep, pretty good. You want to stop?"

An Irish cream latte with extra whip sounded great, but I was anxious to get home. "No. I think I need to get to my mom's."

Rose shrugged and kept driving.

I watched as the town passed before my eyes. Even though it had changed, it was just enough the same and, surprisingly, still felt like home. *Deep down, some things never change. Hopefully, other people will see that, too.* My mind wandered to a long-ago summer, kisses under the moonlight, and a handsome dark-haired man.

Rose took a left at the elementary school, and just past the Baptist church was my mom's road. She pulled into the asphalt driveway and stopped in front of the garage next to a black Ford F-150.

The house looked the same. Momma and Charles, my stepfather, had rose bushes neatly trimmed which lined the front and the walkway. They were well-shaped, and the mulch looked new. There were pansies hanging in pots on the front porch with two black rockers. The biggest change I noticed was the shutters. They used to be black and falling apart, but now they were stained wood and brand new.

My pulse raced and nerves caused my stomach to churn. I was suddenly afraid I might puke. Why was I so nervous about coming home? I knew my mother would welcome us with open arms, and Charles would be just as happy to see I left my crappy situation.

"You got this, Lilly." Rose leaned over and squeezed my hand.

"Thanks." I smiled and gave her hand a squeeze in return. "You sure you don't want to come in and say hi? I don't think I want to go in there alone."

"I can't. I need to get home. Nolan and I are taking the kids to his parents for the night. We'll be at Jerry's Pub later. Maybe you can come by."

Last time I was home, it was for the funeral of the husband of one of my mom's best friends, and I didn't have a chance to do anything. Before then, Jerry's was a nasty hole-in-the-wall. "Jerry's Pub looked so different when we drove past. I might."

"Yeah, it's come a long way since you were home last. It's a great place to go and enjoy the night. I'd love to hang out with you and be able to have a legal drink together."

"Damn. We've never gone out since we've been legal. I have been away for too long."

"Yeah, well, that doesn't matter anymore. Now go and see your mom. Remember, you aren't alone." She nodded toward the back seat. "You have Madeline. She'll take most the attention off you."

I chuckled. "True." I gave Rose a hard hug. "You really are the best. I can't thank you for this enough." I sniffed back the tears, which were ready to escape.

"Don't you dare start crying. I'm glad you're home. Now our girls can grow up together, and everything can be just like we always wanted." She gave me a reassuring hug with an extra squeeze.

Rose's daughter, Lena, was five years old. Madeline would have a friend, and they'd start kindergarten together in August.

"If you need anything, remember, I'm here for you. I'm expecting you to fill me in on everything. Maybe tonight over a drink or two," she said.

I answered her squeeze with a smile. "I promise, you'll hear all of it. The bad, the really bad, and the extremely ugly. Soon. And I can't wait for our girls to meet each other." I turned around and gently shook Madeline awake. "Hey, squirt. We're at Gramma's."

I climbed out before I lost my nerve and helped a sleepy Madeline out of the back before I grabbed our suitcases. We waved as Rose started to back out of the driveway.

Madeline yanked on my arm.

I crouched next to her as her large brown eyes took in her new surroundings. "So, what do you think?" I asked as I raked my fingers through her shoulder-length straight brown hair. What would a city girl think of the small-town life and the cows hanging out in the pasture next door?

"It smells different." Madeline wrinkled her nose. "What's that smell, Mommy?"

I stood and breathed deeply. Fresh country air filled my lungs. Green grass, trees, and yes, the musty smell of cattle.

My heart fluttered at the memories those scents created. A childhood filled with late nights catching lightning bugs with a yard full of friends. Riding my bike to the elementary school to play on the playground. Or walking the mile to town to meet up at Orlinda Valley Pharmacy for a milkshake. Madeline would now have the same experiences. The stress which had infiltrated my bones and muscles seemed to evaporate instantly. "That's the country, squirt," I answered as I pulled our suitcases to the front door. She followed close behind.

"Well, it smells funny."

I laughed a light, hearty laugh. I couldn't remember the last time a laugh felt that good. This was a little girl who was used to the smells of the city: car exhaust, smog, and pollution. "I guess it does, but you'll get used to it. Now let's go surprise Gramma."

I stood on the front porch and stared at the door for a split second, trying to decide if I should ring the bell or just open it. It had been five long years since I had graced these steps.

But suddenly the choice was made for me as the front door was jerked open.

I was greeted with a loud scream from the house. First out of fear, probably because my mother wasn't expecting anyone to be standing so close to her door, then a scream of recognition hit my ears. "Lilly. Maddy. What the . . ."

"Gramma!" Madeline stepped around me and flew into her grandmother's arms.

"Oh, my," Momma said as she wrapped Madeline in a hug and buried her face in her hair.

I stood there and watched as tears fell down my mother's face. It had been too long, but at least our weekly FaceTime calls ensured Madeline knew her grandmother well and loved her.

My mother pulled away from Madeline and looked at me, her brows raised in question.

She might have been fifty-seven, but she sure didn't look it. Her hair was still a beautiful dirty blonde and cut in a cute cut just above her shoulders. The lines around her eyes from her smiling just made her look even more amazing. I felt the shield I put up on my emotions finally start to crumble, and the tears I had been holding in for years finally spilled down my cheeks. "Momma."

"Baby girl." Kaye held her arms wide.

I stepped through the door, grasped my mother in a desperate hug, buried my face in the familiar scent of her shampoo and Bergamot essential oil, and the sobs came.

My body shook as my shield went from a crumble to all-out disintegration. My mother didn't flinch. She did what she did best.

She held me and made it better.

"What's going on here?" Charles's voice filled the room. "Maddy. Lilly?"

I took some deep breaths, got control of myself, wiped my face with my hands, and sniffled as a laugh escaped me. "Hi, Charles."

Charles yelled over his shoulder. "Guys, you need to come here." Then he turned to me. "Lilly, this is a surprise." He wrapped me in a hug, then picked up Madeline which caused her to giggle.

I looked over, and Lance was there.

"Sis. What the hell?" He squeezed the breath out of me, then held me at arm's length. I had to tip my head up to see him. He was always tall, and even now at thirty-six, he still had his college football build. The typical high school PE teacher and football coach. His dark blond hair was always kept longer on top as a kid and still was, and his brown eyes gleamed with excitement.

I laughed despite the tears which spilled down my face. "We're home."

"Like, for good?" he asked, brows up. I nodded. He let out a whoop of joy and threw Madeline over his shoulder and the house was instantly filled with her laughter.

"Welcome home then," said Charles. "It's about time." He placed his arm over my shoulders and led me into the kitchen behind my mom, Lance, and Madeline.

My heart was full. This was exactly what I should have done. If there was any doubt still lurking anywhere inside me, seeing my family stopped it cold.

"Hey there, Lilly-Pad."

My breath caught in my chest as Jamison appeared out of nowhere. He wore jeans and a T-shirt that hugged tight to his muscular chest. The term of endearment he used—my nickname from decades ago—made me weak in the knees. Before I could fully wrap my head around him being there, he wrapped his arms around me in a strong hug, and his scent was just as I remembered—clean and fresh, like he had just stepped out of the shower, with a touch of cedarwood. His cologne always had a magnetic effect on me, and I couldn't deny that I still enjoyed it, right down to my core.

"Welcome home." He kissed my cheek. He was almost as tall as Lance at six-two, and with my arms wrapped around his midsection, I could tell he was as well built as I remembered.

I pulled away and gave him a small smile. "Thanks," I answered as my eyes raked over him. His hair was dark brown and cut short and tight around the ears, and his eyes were a soft blue. Damn, he was handsome. I don't know why that surprised me. He was always the best-looking guy in Orlinda Valley. And when he smiled, butterflies took over my stomach.

After all these years, I still had it bad for Jamison McKendry.

What the hell?

Chapter 3

Lilly

"You're just in time." My mother gestured to the stools at the counter and the chocolate chip cookies sitting on a cooling rack, fresh from the oven. If the greeting we just received didn't make me glad to be home, Momma's baking sure did.

Lance placed Madeline on one of the stools by the counter while my mother poured her a glass of milk. "Have a few cookies, sweet girl. They're Gramma's secret recipe."

Jamison made eye contact with me and gestured with the coffee pot toward a mug.

I gave a nod, and as soon as he turned away, my eyes wandered from his broad shoulders, down his wide back, to his fine-looking ass in those jeans. My brows popped. Yes, he was as fit as I remembered.

Jamison McKendry was my lifelong crush and the first man to ever break my heart. He and his girlfriend Carly had been dating for a while when he announced their engagement, and I shouldn't have been surprised. I never had a chance to tell him my feelings. As far as I could tell, he only saw me as his best friend's little sister—a real relationship between us was impossible. I was only Lilly-Pad to him and nothing else—at least once he had met Carly.

The summer before Carly, though, I truly believed I meant something.

He placed my mug in front of me along with half and half, and my mind flew back to the present. Here Jamison was in front of me. He's a single father, and I'm a divorced mother. Anything was possible.

I waved off the sugar. With the cookies I planned to eat, I wouldn't need the extra sweetness. "Thank you." His eyes were the same blue that made my heart stutter years ago, and yes, it stuttered again. I switched my attention to the pile of cookies in front of me, and my daughter next to me. "I better grab a couple before you eat every last one, squirt."

Madeline smiled with her mouth full. I gave her a peck on her nose, then ate my cookie and drank my coffee.

Jamison grabbed a handful. "I gotta go and make sure Mom didn't forget anything. Darcie and James are having a slumber party with her." He picked up his travel coffee mug. "Lilly, I know you just got in, but maybe you should tag along tonight. Come to the pub with us."

"Sure, sis. It'll be fun. We haven't hung out for a damn—" Lance cleared his throat when Madeline giggled. "A long time."

I honestly don't remember ever hanging out with Lance and Jamison at the same time. I was under twenty-one when they were going to bars, and by the time I was finally old enough to drink legally, I was with Anthony in New York. I shrugged. Going out might be fun, but I was exhausted. "I don't know, y'all. It's been a long day, and we just got in."

"Think about it. It's still early," Jamison said as he brushed his hand against my shoulder.

I knew he didn't mean it as anything but a friendly gesture, but no one told my heart. It fluttered and flipped madly in my chest. *Get a grip. You haven't even been home an hour yet and you're already swooning. And he's Jamison.*

I focused on my coffee to get my brain off the warmth of his touch, which still lingered on my shoulder and sent my mind to the past.

"Think about it, sis. It would be fun. Let me know if you change your mind. I'll stop back by and pick you up." Lance kissed my cheek and messed up Madeline's hair as he followed Jamison out the door.

My mom started cleaning the kitchen, and I finished my coffee.

"I'll tell you what." She leaned against the counter and brushed a lock of thick hair from Madeline's face. "Charles and I will keep this little princess here for the next couple hours, pamper her, get to know her, and you go out."

My mom was the best. She was always willing to offer a shoulder to cry on, and the space needed to figure your shit out. And God knows I had a lot of shit to figure out. "Thanks, Mom. Rose asked me to go out also. Maybe I will once I get settled and cleaned up a bit." Adult time with no worry of needing to get home before Anthony got angry would be a much-needed change of pace. I lifted Madeline's chin. "Whatcha think, squirt? You good with staying here with Gramma and Grandpa, and I'll go out for a little while with Uncle Lance and Rose?"

"Of course, Mommy. Gramma can do my nails and braid my hair, and we can eat more cookies and see you later." Madeline gave me a smile, slipped off her stool, and walked into the living room. Her curiosity got the best of her.

My heart lifted. My sweet daughter could always make the best of every situation. Thank goodness.

"Why don't you give her a quick tour and get settled? You can either share your room or use Lance's as well. If you feel like talking later tonight, you and I can stay up late, and you can explain to me what brought you home without letting me know you were coming."

"Mom," I began as guilt sliced through my gut. "I'm sorry."

"Nope. Don't be sorry," she said, holding up her hand, which forced me to stop the onslaught of apologies I planned to spew her way. "I'm just glad you're finally done with that sorry ass, and super glad you're here and finally home where you and our beautiful girl belong."

Leave it to my mother to not beat around the bush. "I love you, Mom."

"I know, now get."

I knew better than to argue, so I left the kitchen to find my curious little four-year-old.

"Look, Mommy. It's us." Madeline was sitting on the couch with a frame in her hands.

I looked over her shoulder. It was the picture I sent Mom and Charles this past Christmas. It was Madeline and me in front of the Rockefeller Christmas tree. Gianna took it.

I'd had to finalize some things with my lawyer that day, and Gianna had watched Madeline for the morning. We met for a late lunch, then walked around the city admiring the lights and the store windows all decorated for the holiday.

My heart lurched. I was going to miss Gianna and the bustle of the city. I needed to make sure to keep in touch with her. She was very important to us and had been my rock when I needed someone to confide in or a shoulder to cry on. When the divorce was final, she took us in and gave us a place to live. I would have been lost without her.

"Yeah, baby. It is us. That was a fun day." I placed a kiss on her head and pulled out my phone. "Why don't we take a selfie and send it to Gianna, so she knows we made it okay."

"Good idea, Mommy."

Madeline touched her head to mine, and I took the picture and sent it with a quick note saying we made it. "There. Now she won't be worried." I pocketed my phone as I stood. "Let's take our suitcases to my bedroom and get cleaned up."

"Your room?" Madeline asked. Her voice went up in tone, and her eyes became huge.

"Yep. The very one I lived in until I left home." I led her up the stairs.

"Yay." Her voice filled with joy as she bounded up the steps. "Let me try to find your room, Mommy. Don't tell me."

I stopped at the top of the steps and watched as she skipped down the hall, opened each door, and gaped into each room. She was almost five and had never been inside my childhood home. That was so wrong. I shook my head and sighed deeply. My ten-year marriage to a man who I now know never loved me, just loved being in charge of a small-town girl, had kept me from my family and a life I loved.

"This is your room, Mommy. I know it." Madeline ran into the last room on the left, and yes, she was right. I stepped in behind her and was immediately thrown back to my perfect life before marriage. Before Anthony.

Yes, my mother had changed my room since I left, taken out all my belongings and high school and college decorations. It was more adult-looking and more adult-me, but there were still some touches of growing up. A picture of a river with Lily of the Valley growing alongside—the flower I was named for. There was a painting, painted by Rose. She was an artist and painted all of us a picture of a bouquet in a vase. A rose, a lily, a chrysanthemum, and a daisy. One representing my four best friends. Me, Rose, Kristy, and Kimber—the flower sisters.

My eyes swam with tears. It had been so long since we had all been together. Kimber was married, and her husband was in the Army. Kristy was still here, in town, and like me, she was divorced. Her marriage didn't last long at all, and now she dated and stomped all over the male hearts of Orlinda Valley.

I opened the drawer of my desk and pulled out my photo album from days long gone. Pictures of high school and college years. "Here, squirt. Why don't you look at this and see if you can pick out pictures of Mommy, Uncle Lance, and Gramma while I unpack and get us settled."

Madeline eagerly jumped on the bed and sat cross-legged as she flipped the pages of the album. Her giggles and laughter filled the room and again helped me relax.

It didn't take long to unpack our suitcases. I would have to do some shopping, and soon. I jumped in the shower adjacent to the bedroom while Madeline played on my phone, then I got her washed up as well.

"I feel better already. How about you?" I asked as I brushed her hair.

She nodded. "Yep, and I'm ready to have Grandma braid my hair."

We headed downstairs and to the kitchen with Madeline leading the way. She had a bounce to her step, which I hadn't noticed in a while and a smile filled my face. *Thank God, I brought her home.*

The smell of cooking meat permeated the air, and my stomach grumbled. Ham steaks, homemade macaroni and cheese, and broccoli greeted us for dinner.

"Yum, my favorites," Madeline exclaimed as she climbed into a seat at the table.

"Mine too." I agreed. "It smells delicious, Mom." I filled Madeline's plate, then did the same with mine. I took a large bite of the macaroni and cheese. This was my favorite side dish growing up. My mom made the best macaroni and cheese. Just enough cheese, perfectly gooey, and so delicious. As I chewed, the flavors exploded over my tongue. "This is still the best macaroni and cheese, Mom."

"Thank you."

Charles joined us at the table. "It is so good having you two at our table." He said as he filled his plate.

"I love your house, Grandpa. And this is so yummy," Madeline said between bites. She didn't wait for any of us to comment as she continued to shovel forkfuls of food into her mouth.

"Lilly, have you not fed her all day?" Charles asked with laughter in his voice.

I shrugged, too into my meal to stop chewing and use words. I watched Madeline take in the room around her as she ate. Her eyes darted to every corner and every space. The kitchen was roomy, and the table sat in a little breakfast nook. Madeline and I sat by the wall, and she could see the entire kitchen from there.

There was a desk in the corner with a picture frame on it. The picture was filled with a large group of people. "Who are they?" Madeline asked.

This was one of my favorite pictures. It was taken the last time I was home, five years ago. It was a quick overnight visit. "Those are Gramma's and Grandpa's friends and their families. They're our extended family."

Madeline wrinkled her brow.

"Extended family are people who Uncle Lance and I grew up with and are as close to us as real family." I picked up the photo and pointed at each person. "There's Gramma and Grandpa, and there's Tonya, Ruth, and Diane. Gramma's oldest friends."

"These are all their children and husbands. You know Gramma, Grandpa, and Uncle Lance." I pointed out. "This is Rose, who picked us up at the airport, and her husband, Nolan, and their oldest son. You'll meet him soon. And this is Bryson and his wife, Darlene."

Madeline squinted as she studied the picture harder. Her face lit up, and she pointed. "And this is Jamison. I met him today."

Jamison was standing behind me, next to Carly. Carly was a beauty, and even though I never wanted to like her, you couldn't help but love her, and she did make him happy. You could see it in the way his eyes shone, and he stood with his arm protectively around her. When my mom told me about her death two years ago, my heart broke for him. "Yep, you did, little one."

"He's really handsome. Don't you think so, Mommy?"

I wanted to say, *Oh, hell yeah, honey. That's exactly what Mommy thinks and always has.* But that would probably not be a good choice of words. Instead, I said, "Yep, he is. He's Uncle Lance's best friend and like a big brother to me."

A big brother I spent my entire high school and college years fantasizing about, and it seemed like my body was still reacting to him.

CHAPTER 4

JAMISON

I entered Jerry's Pub, the best place for food, beer, and friends in Orlinda Valley. It helped when most of the regulars were people you grew up with and had known forever. The pub was decorated with a cool variety of small-town high school life and firefighter paraphernalia since it was now owned by a group of local firemen. I went out through the opened garage door, which led to the patio, and found Lance at a table with Bryson and Kai, my cousin Kora's fiancé.

I sat on the bench next to Lance and graciously took the beer he offered. "Where's the woman?" I asked. I was positive Lance would be able to talk Lilly into getting out for the night, and Kai was hardly ever seen without Kora.

"Kora's doing some wedding planning with Darlene and Summer," Kai said. "So y'all got me instead."

Talk went briefly to Kai and Kora's wedding, but Kai couldn't give us many details. He knew the date and did what Kora told him. He was a smart man. My cousin was the most organized woman

I knew, so she probably had her wedding planned down to the smallest detail.

"Rose and Kristy grabbed Lilly for some much-needed girl time and catching up," Lance said. "They might stop by later." Lance shook his head. "I wish I could get my hands on that piece of shit Lilly was married to."

"Was it really that bad?" Kai asked.

Lance shrugged. "All I know is he kept her from her family for too many years. My mom and Charles went to New York to visit a couple of times, but . . ." He shook his head. "What kind of guy would keep a woman from her family?"

"She's home now," Kai answered. "It won't take long for her to get right back to how things used to be. That's something I learned quickly about Orlinda Valley. Everyone's always welcome, and no one's a stranger."

That's so true. Most of us were born and raised here, and those who were new to town, like Kai, were welcomed with open arms. I had no doubt the same would be said for Lilly once word got out she was back.

Conversation changed to the upcoming football season—high school and college—and a local country band started warming up. It would end up being the usual night of dancing, pool, darts, cornhole, and drinking at Jerry's.

"Looks like the girls made it." Bryson gestured toward a table inside.

Lilly, Rose. and Kristy sat at one of the high-top tables with drinks. Lilly waved across at Lance, who tipped his beer toward her. "She looks more relaxed than she did earlier," Lance said.

"You better be careful," I said. "She didn't like you hovering over her when she was in high school. I'm sure she'll really hate it now that she's an adult."

Lance grunted. "Yeah, well, if I would have stayed focused on her all those years ago, she wouldn't have gotten involved with that dick. I got a bad vibe from him early on."

Bryson nodded. "I remember. When she brought him to the house for the weekly barbecue, you were anything but cordial."

"If everyone would have listened to me, maybe we could have kept her from moving to New York with him," Lance said.

"Like that would have worked. She was twenty and wanted to leave." I slid another beer toward him. "You need to let it go."

"I agree with Jamison," Kai said. "She's divorced now. No one can live in the past—trust me, I know better than anyone. Be glad she's home."

Lance huffed and became quiet. I sipped my beer and casually watched the girls across the patio. I guess I need to stop seeing them as girls. They were women. Lilly was a woman. It's amazing what ten years could do to a person. She wore her hair on top of her head in one of those messy buns, and with her best friends Rose and Kristy flanking her, she looked much happier and more relaxed than she had earlier. Her smile was genuine as she participated in their conversation, and it almost met her eyes as it showed off her perfect teeth. She always had a pretty smile; now, it lit up her face.

She gestured toward us and stood from the table. Rose and Kristy followed.

"Hey, guys," she said as she tapped Lance on the shoulder.

"Hey, sis," Lance greeted her.

Bryson stood and wrapped her in a hug. "Glad you're finally home, Lilly."

"Thanks, Bryson."

"Have you met Kai, Kora's fiancé?" Bryson asked her.

"I haven't," she said as she gave him a hug. "Congratulations."

"Thank you," Kai said with a smile.

"I love Kora like a sister," Lilly said. "If it wasn't for her, Rose and I would have been ignored by all the guys. She ensured we were always included, even though we were the youngest. It was the guys versus us."

"Truth," Rose added.

"She's told me lots of stories, and it's good to meet you, too. I know she'll be glad to see you," Kai said.

"I sent her a text earlier," Lilly said. "She mentioned they were going to try and stop by tonight."

"Anything's possible with those three," Bryson said as he took a swig from his beer.

"It looks like they left me." Lilly glanced around. Kristy and Rose had taken seats at a table next to us. "I'll talk to y'all later. Good to meet you, Kai."

"You too, Lilly," Kai answered.

I watched her as she sat at the table with Kristy and Rose. They leaned their heads close together to talk, and I couldn't take my eyes off her. She seemed to be enjoying herself, yet at times, she fidgeted with her glass or the ring on her right hand—a nervous habit. I didn't remember her ever having a nervous habit before.

"Hey." Lance whacked me on my back, and I jerked my attention to him.

"What the hell, man?" I said with more irritation than I felt.

"You were zoning. Just checking on you. You good?" Lance's brows raised.

"Yeah, I'm good. I was just thinking when the last time was I saw Lilly outside of my dad's funeral. It was our graduation party and the day I announced to everyone Carly and I were getting married."

Lance's face got serious. "I remember. I never knew a man could glow, but you did." Lance got quiet, then said, "You and Carly were perfect together."

I couldn't talk due to a sudden lump in my throat, so I nodded instead. Bryson placed his arm over my shoulder.

Kai broke the silence. "Kora has a group picture of all y'all on one of her tables. It was taken before all the kids. She told me about Carly. That sucks, man. I'm sorry."

Again, I couldn't talk. I just pinched my lips together and nodded.

"Today is the second anniversary of her death," Bryson said.

Lance raised his beer. "To Carly. The most beautiful soul I ever had the pleasure of knowing, who loved my best friend huge and would want him to be happy."

Kai and Bryson touched their beers to Lance's, and I followed suit. She would want me to be happy. I glanced over at Lilly, and our eyes met. She gave me a tight smile, which I returned.

I puffed out a breath. "I agree with all of you. Carly sure wouldn't want me moping around. Don't forget. I tried dating. It was a disaster."

"That was what, six months ago?" asked Bryson.

"And I wouldn't call it a complete disaster. It could have been much worse," said Lance.

"True," agreed Bryson. "It could have been beer and margaritas you spilled all over her, not just water."

"Yeah, well, beer and margaritas might just be the key to having a woman fall in love with you. It worked for me," Kai said with his arms wide.

I chuckled. Kai was right. Spilling alcohol all over Kora was part of their story. "Yeah, well, bathing a girl in anything doesn't usually work. I decided right after that that if a relationship was meant to be, I wouldn't have to try. It will just happen. My main concern right now is Darcie and making sure she's happy."

The band started playing, and the vibe around the table picked up a bit. "Let's not talk about this anymore tonight and just have a good time." I motioned for the server and gestured toward our empty pitcher of beer.

"Look at her," Lance said as he filled our cups.

I glanced over to where Lilly sat. Rose and her husband, Nolan, went off to dance. Kristy leaned in to say something to Lilly when a guy came to the table. Lilly nodded and Kristy followed the guy on the dance floor as well.

I didn't know Kristy well, but I did know she was divorced. She had always been pretty. Blonde hair, blue eyes, thin, and since her divorce, she took advantage of men whenever she could. In a small town, you knew these things.

My gaze fell on Lilly, who was now alone. She kept spinning her glass around and had hardly taken a sip.

"You should ask her to dance."

I jerked my eyes toward Lance. "Me? Why?" I ignored the sudden uptick of my heart in my chest.

"It'll relax her. She always looked up to you, and it would be weird if I did it."

He had a point. Just then, some dweeb walked to the table and leaned toward her. She shook her head, but he didn't leave.

Heat warmed my face. "Fine." I sauntered the few steps to the table. "Hey, Lilly. Is everything good?"

A quick flash of something went across her face, but I couldn't make out what it was.

"I was just going to dance with this beautiful lady." The guy who had been talking to Lilly was a beanpole at least six feet five as he stood taller than me, but not an ounce of muscle lived on those bones. I didn't know the guy but had seen him around town. "Karl, isn't it?"

"Sure is man." He gave me a ridiculously large, toothy smile.

I nodded and turned to Lilly. "What do you say Lilly-Pad, want to dance with me?"

Lilly smiled a small half-smile. "Sorry, Karl." She shrugged and grabbed my hand, and I pulled her to the dance floor.

"Poor Karl. He seemed a little hurt," I said as I wrapped one arm around her waist and held her right hand in mine. I kept a safe distance between us. I didn't want her to feel uncomfortable.

She gave a small laugh, which made her face light up. "I'm sure he'll get over it."

"You should laugh more often. It always looked good on you, and it still does."

Her face filled with a smile, and she rolled her eyes.

"That does, too," I said and smiled back. "Is everything okay?" I led her around the fake dance floor, which was placed over the grass on Friday and Saturday nights.

"Yeah. I'm just so glad to be home and am a little tired. It's been a long day."

I waited for her to say more, but she didn't. It shouldn't surprise me. There was no reason for her to open up to me. I'm just her brother's best friend. There was one time—a split second—where things might have changed, but . . . I shook my head to clear the memories, which had no room here and enjoyed her company instead. We danced in silence for a bit more.

I enjoyed the feeling of her body near mine and held her close. Suddenly, the couple next to us stumbled and fell into us.

My grip on Lilly tightened to keep us both from tumbling to the ground. Her laughter rang out, and the light caught her eyes. My hands grabbed her waist. I wish I could say I touched her shirt, but she wore a short crop top, and my fingers touched the soft skin of her back as I righted her.

The man held up his hand in apology.

"It's all good," I assured him, then placed my attention back on Lilly.

She held my gaze with her eyes, which were still filled with laughter. Mine went wide as my entire body froze.

I swear electricity shot from my hands where they touched her soft skin, straight into my veins, and caused my blood to flow to all parts of my body. Including parts that had no right to be affected by my best friend's little sister.

Her grip loosened, but neither of us moved. I caught a whiff of coconut again and wanted to brush my hand through her soft hair. *It's Lilly. Enough already.* "You okay?" My voice sounded like a frog took up residence deep in my throat.

She nodded. "I'm good. Let's finish the dance." She wrapped one arm around my neck, grasped my hand in hers, and pressed her face to my chest.

I held her gently and laid my cheek against her head. I willed my eyes to stay open and focused on my breathing. My gaze wandered around the room. *Get your thoughts on mindless shit.* I watched others dancing. Two teams played cornhole across the lawn, and Lance and Kai were laughing about something at the table. Lance's gaze caught mine, and he lifted his beer in my direction. What was that for? Was he okay with me dancing so close with Lilly?

Finally, the song ended, and we pulled away from each other.

"Thanks, Jamison. But I need a drink."

Thank God, because I needed some space. "Let's go." I led her back to the table with my hand on the middle of her back until she was safely back with the girls.

"Thanks for the dance, and saving me," Lilly said.

"Anytime you need a dance or saving, you know you can give me a call." I gave her hand a squeeze and went back to join the guys.

Lance placed a cold beer in my hand. "That couple was trashed and would have taken Lilly out if you weren't there to catch her."

That's what his look was for. I sighed quietly, relieved. "You know me. Always willing to go to bat for Lilly."

"I know, man," Lance said. "It's good that if I can't keep her safe, she'll always have you looking out for her."

Yeah. That's what I was good for—looking out for Lilly. Now, just to get my body to realize she was off limits.

CHAPTER 5

LILLY

I tried my best to ignore the heat that lingered on my lower back from Jamison's hand on my skin. I had been home for less than ten hours and my feelings for the amazing Jamison McKendry were back and stronger than ever. So much for my promise to Gianna just last week that I was off the market until further notice.

I downed my now lukewarm margarita and shivered as the sour drink burned my throat. I wasn't one to drink much. Anthony didn't like when I did, so I was used to one or two glasses of wine—wine was the proper choice for women, according to my ex.

I'd almost ordered wine tonight but quickly changed it to have margaritas with the girls. But now I was second-guessing that decision. Tequila was not my thing.

"Well, that looked hot," Kristy said as she sat next to me. The man she danced with walked away with a shrug.

I giggled. "I think he was expecting a little more time with you."

Kristy swiped her hand through the air. "Whatever. It was just a dance." She wiggled closer to the table and leaned in. "What was it like when Jamison grabbed you to keep you from falling and pulled you tightly against his strong, muscular chest?" she asked in a seductive voice.

My eyes went wide, though I tried to act like his touch hadn't caused my insides to heat up in a way they hadn't in . . . well . . . a long time. I failed miserably.

I tried a different approach. "I don't know what you're talking about." To avoid her glare, I concentrated on filling my glass. Even though the alcohol was far from what I wanted, it gave me something to focus my attention on. "Need a refill?" I asked as Nolan and Rose joined us again at the table.

Kristy placed her hand over Rose's glass and lowered her eyes to mine. "Don't ignore me. I asked you a question."

Rose's brows perked up. "What did we miss?"

"I asked Lilly how it felt to be held close by Jamison."

I met Kristy's gaze and shot her a go-to-hell look, but of course, she didn't get the hint. She hadn't changed at all.

"Come on, Kristy," Nolan cut in. "Give Lilly a break. She just got home, is fresh out of a shitty marriage, and doesn't need you to try to get her all worked up over her high school crush."

I cocked my head toward Nolan. He was our year in school, and because he and Rose started dating junior year, he'd been around a while and was part of the group. But I couldn't decide if I should thank him for siding with me or tell him to shut the fuck up.

"Nolie," Rose cooed. I cringed at the pet name Rose has called Nolan since . . . well, forever. "That's sweet of you to support Lilly, but we shouldn't talk negatively about her marriage."

"Are you fucking shitting me?" Kristy blurted out. "Pointing out the obvious can't be avoided. Her shitty marriage kept her from us for how long? Let's not forget she had to hide our weekly FaceTime call."

Rose sighed, "I know, but still . . ."

The two of them would go on all night talking about me like I didn't exist, just like all the FaceTime calls that went the same way. I know they cared, but enough was enough.

"Y'all." They didn't hear me and kept going back and forth about how shitty my marriage was and how much of a dick my ex is. As if I needed the reminder.

"Y'all." I raised my voice. "Dammit." I slammed my hand on the table, and our drinks sloshed everywhere, and of course, just then, the band stopped playing, and my voice echoed over the now quiet outdoors of the pub.

A few eyes turned toward us, and even Lance and Jamison cocked their eyebrows. Luckily, my friends also got the message and shut their mouths.

"Damn. Y'all." I seethed after the moment had passed, and the music started again. "I don't need any reminders about my ex or my failed marriage. I live it every day, but y'all have to remember I left him in December and had been out of my marriage emotionally way before then, and the divorce was finalized in March. Just because I just got home doesn't mean it all happened yesterday." My blood was boiling, and I could feel the heat rising on my cheeks. I didn't want people to think I was upset and having a hard time with this. My marriage was over a long time ago, and I was ready to move on. I needed to move on.

I held up my hand to stop Kristy from continuing her ridiculous onslaught of Jamison inquiries. "And I agree with Nolan. There's nothing between Jamison and me. We danced, and he kept me from falling on my ass. As always, he's watching out for me. I'm still his best friend's little sister." I held Kristy's gaze and hoped she would drop it. "I just got home. I need to spend my time figuring out what I'm going to do next. I need a job, but I have very few skills and no desire to get another desk job."

"You have your associate's degree. Your major was nursing. Have you thought about that anymore?" Rose asked.

I sloshed what little ice was left in my drink around in my glass and shook my head. "No. I'd have to finish my degree, and right now, that's not something I want to spend time on." I stared in my glass and watched the ice. I hadn't thought about nursing in forever. I shrugged. "I didn't work my entire marriage. I became little Susie homemaker, then when I had Maddy, I was the perfect mother. All I can do is cook, clean, wash laundry, and organize a house." I looked up and made eye contact with each of them in turn. "With my limited office experience, I can add answering phones and taking messages to my skillset. It's not the best credentials, but it's better than nothing."

Everyone avoided eye contact with me for a bit. We sat in silence. Then Rose finally broke through the quiet. "Do you enjoy organizing and cleaning?"

I glanced at her. She was serious. I chewed on my bottom lip. Did I enjoy it? I'd never thought about it. I just did what was expected of me and what came naturally.

Rose continued, "I remember back in high school when we shared our lockers, you always made sure our books were separated. 'Easy in, easy out,' you always said."

"God, and your room." Kristy scooted to the edge of the stool. "Everything had a place. It was so overly organized. Well, except for the clothes you always threw on the floor, but your closet and drawers were annoyingly organized. I'd move something around just to irritate you."

I laughed. "Yeah, I remember that. It *was* irritating. But why does it matter?"

"You can clean and organize people's houses," Rose said.

"You could." Kristy shrugged. "I pay good money for someone to come in and clean up after me once a week." She took a quick drink. "If you like it, why not?"

I listened as they both, again, went back and forth about me starting a cleaning business. I was only half listening.

I could do that. It wouldn't be difficult, and helping others organize their lives might give me something to be proud of while also giving me something to do and put money in my pocket. "You're both right. Things being organized and clean makes me feel better and in control. I guess I could get the word out that I'm available and see if anyone would like some help."

"I'm sure if you say something to your mothers, they will get word of mouth going at Shear Perfection," Nolan added. "They know everyone and everything that goes on in this town."

That's the truth. The book club gossip group are the women who know all there is to know about the town and the people in it.

I entered my mom and Charles's house around midnight. I don't remember the last time I was out so late and had so much fun. I tiptoed into the kitchen and about lost my last margarita when I turned on the light, and my mother was there. I jumped back and placed my hand on my racing heart. "Mom, you scared me. What are you doing sitting in the dark?"

She chuckled and got up from her stool. "It's not dark when you've been sitting here as long as I have. The light over the stove is just enough." She got out a mug. "Let me get you a cup of tea."

Hot tea. My mother's medicine for everything. The flu, a sore throat, a broken heart, or just needing to talk in the middle of the night. I took the mug and sat on the stool next to the one she just vacated.

"How was Maddy?" I asked as I took a sip of the hot liquid.

"She was an angel." My mom's face lit up. "I took her to Tonya's to meet Darcie and James. They hit it off and became fast friends. They got along so well, she asked to spend the night. I hope it's okay; I said yes."

That was great news. I hoped Maddy would make friends. She didn't have many in New York. Yet another issue with having a controlling father. "I think it's awesome she wanted to stay. Thank you for letting her."

"Oh, of course. It was so wonderful seeing her play and laugh with the grandkids." She blinked rapidly.

"Mom, come on," I placed my hand over hers and squeezed. "Don't cry."

She patted my hand and wiped her eyes. "Oh, honey. This is how it should have been all along. It's too bad these babies needed to wait almost five years to become friends."

"I know, Mom. I know." My heart clenched. My mother couldn't realize how true her words were. It was time to explain.

"Mom, things with me and Anthony were pretty crappy from the beginning." She started to say something, but I stopped her. "Please let me finish. I need to explain." I placed my hands around my mug. The warmth of the liquid gave me courage.

"The first year in New York was fun. We went to all these parties and had an amazing life. I didn't have to work and went to lunch at the club and the spa with the women. Anthony and I had fancy dinners at home or in expensive restaurants. I thought I was living this amazing life." I took a deep breath. "Then he started traveling more and more for business. When he came home, he would question me about what I did and explain what the expectations were for me as his wife when he was gone, as if I didn't already know. The second year, I became pregnant, and it was instantly an issue. He had no time for children or for 'his wife getting fat.'" I enunciated those words. "Luckily . . . God, that sounds awful . . . the pregnancy didn't last long before I had a miscarriage."

Mom's eyes went wide.

I glanced at her with tears clouding my vision. I'd never told anyone about that except Gianna. She knew because she was the one who took me to the doctor. "I'm sorry I didn't tell you, Mom. But it wasn't something I ever talked about. During the few months of my pregnancy, things with Anthony became really rough. He started yelling a lot. I thought if I wasn't pregnant, things would become better. Then I had the miscarriage, and a part of me was glad and thought he'd be happy again. But things never changed, and I realized then he didn't love me."

"Honey. I wish you had said something."

I shrugged and shook my head. I didn't have anything to say that could change anything. I took a sip of my tea.

"Lilly, please answer one thing. And be truthful." My mom held my hand tightly. "Did he ever hit you?"

I chuckled. "No, Mom. He was never physical with me. That was always my fallback when Gianna would mention his behavior. In my mind, everything was fine because he didn't hit me; now I know he had control over me mentally." I paused, took a sip of my tea, then continued quietly and thoughtfully, "Until he started cheating. I should have left him then, and I wanted to. When I came home for the funeral, I wanted to stay. I didn't want to go back, but I had to, or at least I thought I did. The day before I left New York, I found out I was pregnant and decided I needed to give our marriage one more shot, for the baby." My mom squeezed my hand. I smiled and wrapped her hand in mine. "It didn't go well, as you know, and once Maddy was born, he became so much stricter and more stressed. He hated her crying and hollered at me for being a bad mother and not knowing how to keep her happy."

Tears started falling down my cheeks. I wiped them away. "Gianna was there for me, and gave me the name of a divorce lawyer, so I started to plan how to ask for a divorce when Maddy was one. It just took a long time for me to work up the courage."

"Wait, you were pregnant when you came home?" Tears streamed down my mom's face. Shoot. I didn't want to upset her.

I nodded.

"Baby girl."

"Mom, I'm sorry. I wanted to tell you, but I didn't know how. I was scared and knew I needed to tell him first. Gianna was with me when I told him. She was my rock, Mom."

"I know she was. When Charles and I visited, I could tell she was a good friend. She was such a sweet person."

My mom sat up straight and jutted out her chin. "Baby, all that is just water under the bridge. You're home now. You and our sweet girl. Now, you get to live the life you deserve and surround yourself with people who love and care about you. About both of you."

"Mom, thank you so much." I gave her a hard hug. We held on to each other for what seemed like forever, and when we let each other go, everything was better. I sat up taller. My confidence had returned. "Now I need to find a job, and the girls helped me think of something I can do."

I filled her in on my discussion with Rose and Kristy about starting a cleaning service. She thought it was a great idea and asked me to come by the hair salon on Monday. They could get me started and put the word out.

Home was a wonderful place to be.

CHAPTER 6

LILLY

"Mommy."

The sweetest voice in the world filled my ears, and Madeline jumped into my arms. I was on the pool deck in my mom and Charles's backyard with Rose. It was a perfect morning, and the cup of coffee in my hand had never tasted better. It was almost ten, yet here I sat in shorts and a tank top, enjoying the realization I had nothing to do and no one harping on me to do something. Sitting here chatting with my childhood best friend was rather refreshing.

I hugged Maddy. "How did you get home? You didn't drive, did you?"

Maddy giggled. "No, silly. Gramma brought us home. She's inside." She stepped away and grabbed the hand of the little girl standing next to her. "Mommy, this is Darcie. Jamison is her daddy."

Darcie was the spitting image of Carly. Her red hair and green eyes were absolutely stunning. "Hi, Darcie. I'm Lilly, Maddy's mom." I stuck my hand out. I didn't know if she was shy, and I didn't want to scare her with a hug, but she had other ideas.

"Hi, Lilly." She wrapped her tiny arms around me. I was stunned for a split second, then gave her a squeeze. "I like your name," she said, "because I like lilies. Did you know they were my mommy's favorite flower?"

Her comment stopped my heart. She looked at me with the sweetest, most innocent look on her face, and my heart felt like someone was squeezing it. I shook my head. "No, I didn't know. They're one of my favorites as well."

"Mine too," she said, her green eyes going wide. "They are the prettiest flower. Me and my daddy plant one every year under our weeping willow tree to remind us of my mommy."

"That's so sweet." I swallowed the lump which was beginning to form in my throat.

Thankfully, Madeline interrupted. "Can we swim?"

Okay, that was a random question—which was quickly met with squeals of joy and begging. "Did you bring a swimsuit?" I asked Darcie.

"We don't need one," Madeline replied. "We can swim in our clothes."

"Yeah." Darcie squealed, and they jumped up and down.

Rose met my eyes and shrugged. "It's warm enough, and they're both in shorts and t-shirts," she said. "Why not."

I laughed. "Sure. Why not."

"Yay." They squealed and jumped in the pool and floated on noodles. I watched them for a bit. Madeline was happy, and they were smiling and enjoying each other.

"Looks like they got along well last night," Rose said. "Darcie and Lena hang out at gymnastics and our weekly get-togethers. It will be great having Madeline in the mix. I think they'll all be fast friends."

My grin filled my face. "We haven't been here twenty-four hours, yet I feel like we've been here forever, like we finally found a home."

Rose reached out and squeezed my hand. "That's because you are home. I'm so glad you're here."

My vision became blurry, and I raised my eyes toward the sky to blink away the tears. "Thanks, Rose. I shouldn't have waited so long."

"Nonsense. You're here now, and in a week, it will feel like you have always been here. Just wait and see."

God, I hoped so. I wanted things to be simple for Maddy so she wouldn't miss New York and the few friends she had. "I want us both to be happy here. I'll feel better once I know I did the right thing."

Rose raised an eyebrow in question.

I lifted my hands to hold back her concern. "That came out wrong. I know I did the right thing. I should have done it earlier, but once I know Maddy has settled in, I'll feel much better."

"Don't think of what you should have done. We always have to look forward and know we can only control what we do from now on, and right now, you're on the right path."

"Look at you, the philosopher." I laughed. "It must be nice to have always known what you wanted. You always wanted to marry Nolan and have kids, quick, and that's what you did."

"I know," she agreed. "But there was a time after you left, and I was pregnant with JR, I wished I had gone on to finish my degree. I wasn't ready to be a stay-at-home mom, and it was hard."

"What?" I asked, and had to pick my jaw up from the floor. "You never told me this before. Of course, I was on the East Coast, but still."

It was her turn to wave off my concern. "It's not a big deal any-more. Six months after JR was born, Nolan made me get out of the house and find something I wanted to do. I worked until Lena was born; now, I'm quite happy being a stay-at-home mom. With two, it makes things so much easier." She shrugged and turned back to the girls in the pool. "So, have you thought any more about starting a cleaning business?"

"I talked with my mom last night when I got home. She thinks it's a great idea. She's going to have me do some cleaning at the salon for a while and help spread the word so I can fill my calendar with clients."

"Good." Rose beamed. "You have a plan."

"There she is." Our discussion was interrupted when my mom, Tonya, Diane, Ruth, and Lena came out the back door.

"Well, there's my girl," said Rose.

"Hi." Lena had a sweet little voice and hugged Rose tight.

"Lena, this is Lilly. You've talked to her on the phone, but she and her daughter Madeline"— Rose pointed toward the pool— "are the ones I told you just moved back home."

"Hi, Lena." She was a perfect combination of her parents. She had Nolan's dirty blond hair and Rose's brown eyes.

"Hi." She smiled at me and turned to her mom. "Can I jump in the pool with the girls?"

And that was that. She jumped right in. I watched as Darcie introduced Lena and Madeline, and they were instantly lost in their world of whatever four and five-year-old pre-kindergarteners talk about.

"Don't leave us hanging here waiting for our greeting." Tonya stood with her arms wide.

I smiled. "Hi, Tonya." I stood and wrapped her in a hug.

"Welcome home." Tonya, the loudest and most fun of the bunch and my favorite person, hugged me tightly.

"Thank you." I gave her a hard squeeze. "It's great to be home."

"Well, I want to tell you those girlies had so much fun last night. Poor James, though, needs some boys to help him out. That poor guy is going to have his hands full with the three of them."

"Don't forget when Leila and Adler are around, he also has to contend with Skylar," Diane said. Diane was my mom's business partner. She and her husband, Tom, never had children of their own, But Tom's daughter, Leila, came to live with them five years ago when she found out she was pregnant. "You'll love Leila," Diane told me after she greeted me with a hug. "Her daughter, Skylar, is also four. They're all starting kindergarten this year."

"Yeah, but she won't be going to school with our kiddos," Tonya said.

"True, but still. She's a part of this family even if she lives in the next town over. They'll be rivals," Diane said.

"Wow," Rose said. "Can y'all slow it down? They haven't even started kindergarten yet. Let's not start the rivalry thing."

"Rivalry about what?"

"Daddy!" Darcie squealed as Jamison walked onto the deck. His dark hair was wet like he just got out of the shower, and with a tight gray T-shirt over his chest and the black basketball shorts he wore, he looked good enough to eat. I sucked in my bottom lip as butterflies took up residence in my gut.

Darcie climbed out of the pool and threw herself in his arms, dripping wet . His muscular, manly body hugged his little girl tight, and I didn't think it was possible for him to look more delicious, but damn, was I wrong.

Rose cleared her throat, and I tore my eyes from him as the book club ladies wandered back inside.

She bit her lips to hide a smile, and I swatted her arm before I sat back in my chair.

Jamison put Darcie down. "So, I guess you girls needed to swim."

"Yes, we did, Uncle J," said Lena.

"Uncle J?" Madeline asked.

"James calls him Uncle J, so I just call him the same thing," Lena said.

Maddy tilted her head and brought her finger to her lips. "Should I call you Uncle J, too?"

Jamison squatted in front of her and shrugged. "Uncle J, Uncle Jamison, or just Jamison. It doesn't matter."

Madeline chewed on her bottom lip, which was what she did when she was deep in thought. "I'll think about it," she decided.

Jamison chuckled and tapped her nose. "You do that. You know what?" He asked her.

"What?"

"Your mommy used to chew on her bottom lip just like you whenever she was deep in thought."

Madeline smiled wide. "Our friend Gianna always told me the same thing."

He turned to me, and the smile he gave me made my mouth go dry before he turned toward Darcie. "Anyway, princess. What do you say we get you home? I think you girls have spent more than enough time together, and we have our usual Sunday chores to get done before we go to Uncle Bryson's for dinner."

"Do we have to, Daddy?" Darcie puckered her bottom lip out. "I want to stay with the girls."

Rose stood. "It's okay, Darce. We're leaving as well. And no complaining." She pointed at Lena, cutting off the protest before it ever left her lips. "Daddy and JR are at home waiting for us."

Lena turned to Darcie and whispered something. They both agreed and started jumping up and down. Then they turned to me.

"We think Maddy should come to gymnastics with us," Darcie said.

Maddy's eyes got wide. "Oh, Mommy. Please? It sounds like so much fun." They all started squealing and jumping in a circle, holding hands.

We all laughed and plugged our ears at the earsplitting octave the three of them hit.

"It's Monday night at six at Five Stars Gymnastics," Rose said. "I bet she'd have fun."

"And since they'll be on the kindergarten squad, they'll cheer at the football games once or twice a season. It's adorable," Jamison said.

"At the football games? Aren't they a little young?" I asked.

"Nah. It's always a highlight of halftime. The town loves it." Rose hugged me as she was getting ready to leave. "Think about it. Your first time is free. You could bring her tomorrow and see what she thinks."

It sounded good. "Why not. If you want to," I said to Madeline.

I was greeted with a wet hug and another loud squeal from the trio.

Rose and Lena left, and Jamison and I headed into the kitchen with the girls.

"Why don't I take these two youngsters to get some dry clothes on?" my mom offered. "I'm sure I can find some extra." She took Darcie and Madeline to change.

Tonya slapped the counter, and I jumped. "I've got an idea," she said.

"It better be a good one, T," Diane answered. "You scared me so bad I think I added another gray hair or two."

"Trust me, Diane, you have no gray hairs. You've colored them all," Tonya said. "Jamison. You need someone to keep your house clean, and Lilly here is interested in starting a cleaning business." She held her hands out and bopped her head back and forth between us. "It's perfect."

I stared at the counter. Was she serious? She was Tonya. You never could tell. I glanced at Jamison. His face didn't hold any of the uncertainty I was sure mine had. Being around him and his things. Cleaning for him. Seeing his house. Being close. Could I do that effectively? Would I be able to keep my crushing feelings at bay long enough to clean his house well?

"I guess." Jamison sounded unsure. "If you think I need one, *Mother*."

I laughed. Couldn't help it. He enunciated "mother" so forcefully.

"If you're really interested, you could have Lilly over and see what she thinks," said Tonya.

"Yeah. I'm sure she'd agree." Jamison stood back, his hands up.

"She'd agree about what?" Mom asked as she and the girls returned, now in dry outfits.

Tonya placed her arm around Jamison. "I found Lilly's first house to clean, and Lord knows this one needs all the help he can get. And it will free up my Friday mornings."

"What, you don't want to feed me and your granddaughter breakfast anymore?" he asked. "That's rude."

"No. I love taking care of you two, but I have important things I need to be doing."

Jamison and Tonya kept talking like I wasn't involved in the conversation, which was fine with me. A part of me wanted to say no, it's not a good idea, but I didn't have a reason.

My mom chuckled. "Oh, whatever, T. You have nothing pressing for importance on Friday mornings, and I think it's a great start. Shear Perfection gets a deep cleaning on Mondays, and Jamison gets some help on what day?"

All eyes turned to me. It looked like it was already decided. I shrugged. "Tuesday?" I asked him.

"Tuesday it is. Come over Tuesday morning. I'll show you around, and you can give me a quote." He held out his hand. "It's a deal, Lilly-Pad."

I placed my hand in his, and damn, the warmth that filled my body again. What was it about Jamison McKendry that always affected me?

CHAPTER 7

JAMISON

"Okay, Daddy, how's this?"

I took the rolled-up socks from Darcie and inspected her sock-folding ability. For a five-year-old, it wasn't bad. It would do for the sock drawer. "It's perfect, princess. Thank you."

I tossed them in the growing pile of socks. *When was the last time I did laundry?* It didn't matter. We were finally finished. I filled her basket with clothes, and she followed me into her room where she excitedly put the clothes in the dresser while I hung up what she couldn't reach in her closet.

"Daddy, Madeline is really nice. Me, her, and Lena, are already best friends. I hope she goes to gymnastics; then we will be even better friends and be able to do everything together."

I laughed at her excitement. She had been like this ever since we got home. I think I knew every little detail of their entire night, morning, and swimming session. I doubt she left any bit out. "I'm glad you girls got along so well. It's always good to make friends, and with Madeline being new, she'll need you and Lena to introduce her around."

"Yep. And we will." She closed her drawer. "Can we go now? I need to see Aunt Darlene and Aunt Kora. We have things to discuss."

My eyes went wide. "What do you have to discuss?" I closed her closet and looked at my little girl. Sometimes, I forget she just turned five. The things that came out of her mouth made me a little fearful of what she would be like when she became a teenager.

"Girl stuff, Dad." She rolled her eyes. "Come on. We gotta go." She pulled my hand and led me from her room. I barely had time to grab my keys before she pulled me into the garage and climbed into the car.

"Alright, princess. You buckled in?" I glanced in the rearview mirror, saw she was, and backed out. She stared out the window and was quieter than she had been all morning. "What's got you thinking?"

A soft sigh came from her.

What did my daughter have to sigh about? "Darcie?" I asked. "What's wrong?"

"I'm just sad for Madeline. I asked her if she missed her Daddy, and she said she didn't know. He wasn't ever around much, anyway. Then she said her mom never seemed happy until today. It makes me sad thinking what it would be like if you were never around."

Wow. Those words were like a punch to the gut. "Well, thankfully, you won't have to worry about that at all, princess. I'm not going anywhere, and there's no one I'd rather be with than you."

"I feel the same way, Daddy. But maybe we can help Lilly be happy."

Help her be happy? "What do you mean?" I had no idea where my dear, sweet baby girl was going with this. But I would be lying if I said I wasn't totally interested.

"Well, Daddy. Sometimes I see you're sad and miss Mommy. And Lilly is sad because she's lonely. Maybe you two can spend time together and help each other not be sad, and then I can spend lots of time with Maddy."

"Umm." What the hell do I say to that?

I concentrated on the road. Lilly hadn't been far from my mind ever since we hugged when she entered Kaye's. Her smile still lit up the room, even when it was slightly shrouded, like it had been Friday when she got in. And then her body. It felt perfect in my arms. *Get your head back to the present and out of your pants. Neither of you are looking for anything.* "I'll see what I can do." That's all I was willing to promise, for now at least.

"Good. I'm glad."

Her voice was its typical chipper tone once again, and she smiled and hummed to herself as she looked out the window. That was more like her. Again, it amazed me how she could jump from one feeling to the next so quickly. I wish it were that easy for me.

Lilly's face floated in my mind. Thankfully we pulled in front of Bryson and Darlene's, and I could ignore whatever the hell was going on inside my mind.

"It's so good to see Lilly and Maddy. Kaye and Charles are excited to have them home," Mom said. "I know Kaye was going all out for dinner tonight. It's been ages since she's cooked for Lilly, and she's never had that little angel at her table." She lifted her coffee and took a sip. "I couldn't imagine." She tsk tsked and shook her head.

We had just finished dinner, and James and Darcie were headed to James's room to play.

My mom wasn't wrong. It had been ages since Lilly had been home, and her family was treating it like a holiday. "I know Lance is glad she's home," I said as my stomach curled again at the thought of what kind of husband she'd had. How could a man treat a woman with such disrespect?

"Seems like the kids are glad she's here. The two of them couldn't stop talking about Madeline during dinner," Bryson added.

I chuckled. "Darcie and Lena talked Lilly into letting Maddy try out gymnastics tomorrow night. You should have seen them cheer."

"Better yet, hear them," said Mom. "The squeal they let out was so high pitched, I'm sure all the dogs in the neighborhood started howling."

"It seems like you might be spending some extra time with Lilly then." Kora sipped her coffee and peered at me over her cup.

"Why would I?" I met her gaze.

She shrugged. "The girls are friends. I just figured."

"It's possible." I took another brownie from the plate on the table to keep myself from looking more interested than I needed to be. And I can't lie—I did seem to be a little interested. Which might be a problem.

Kora said, "Well, it seems like Lilly will be cleaning not only the hair salon but also your house."

I stopped mid-chew. "How the hell did you hear about that?" I turned my gaze toward my mother, who shrugged and looked like a cat who ate the canary. I shook my head. Could she ever keep anything to herself?

"Interesting," Bryson said with a Cheshire grin on his ugly mug. "Wonder what Lance would say about his best friend spending so much time with his little sister."

"They did look comfortable on the dance floor last night," Kai said.

Kora smacked his arm. At least I had the women on my side.

I shot him a glare. "Seriously, Kai. Aren't you still getting used to being a part of this family? It seems you might be getting a little too comfortable."

"Oh, son. Settle down." My mom placed her hand on my arm. "There would be nothing wrong with you and Lilly being interested in each other. You're both single."

"She's barely divorced. It hasn't even been a year," I said. I needed to stop this conversation before it got out of hand. "And I've known her forever. She's basically like my little sister."

"Yeah, but she's not." Bryson waggled his brows.

"You're a dick," I told him.

He laughed deeply. "And you're getting a little defensive, big brother. Wonder why?"

I stuck my middle finger up at him.

"Jamison Carl." My mother scolded me.

"Mom, sorry, but he's being a . . . not a nice person."

Snickers came from around the table. I rolled my eyes and looked at my phone. Thank God. It was eight o'clock. A good time to get my daughter home and get her ready for bed. I stood. "Gotta go. Darcie has Mother's Day Out in the morning, and I have to work."

CHAPTER 8

JAMISON

I'd worked later than usual, and my mom picked Darcie up from Mother's Day Out and brought her home. I threw a quick and simple dinner together—turkey sandwiches, a perfect dinner before gymnastics.

"Darce, let's go. We'll be late." What the hell was taking her so long? I only sent her to her room to get her clothes. They were sitting on her bed. It shouldn't take her that long, but I'd finished cleaning the kitchen when she finally appeared.

I cocked my head.

She was in her black leggings with stars all over them, and I'd laid out the red gymnastics tee—what she usually liked to wear to class—but instead she had on a yellow T-shirt with daisies. She looked adorable, but it wasn't like her to go through her drawers and find something else.

"What was wrong with the shirt I had out for you?" I asked her.

"Lena, Madeline, and me all decided to wear a shirt with flowers on it so we could be like their mommas and be flower sisters too." She plopped down on the floor and put on her sneakers.

I forgot Lilly and her friends had called themselves that in high school. Cute. "Okay." I grabbed my to-go cup of coffee. "Ready?"

Like most things in Orlinda Valley, it didn't take us long to get to Five Stars Gymnastics, but the small parking lot was almost filled when I pulled in.

Darcie hopped out and ran toward the door. Her excitement was contagious. As usual, I was one of the few dads in attendance. The class was about fifteen girls, and mostly mothers brought them, but I did wave at the other lone father. Gary White. Gary was a year ahead of Lance and me in school. His wife was a nurse, so he was often the one who brought their daughter, Clara, to class.

"There they are, Daddy." Darcie skipped away to meet up with Lena and Madeline.

I smiled as I caught up, and the girls went onto the mats together. "Those three seem happy to be together again," I said as I sat on the bleachers next to Lilly and caught a scent of coconut in the air.

"This has been all Maddy's talked about all day," Lilly said.

"Lena as well. She's been exhausting," Rose added.

"Are you both ready for kindergarten registration?" I asked. I had been dreading it, but it was this Wednesday and Thursday. I couldn't avoid it much longer.

Lilly shrugged. "Honestly, I didn't know when it was and hadn't thought about it, but I guess I should have. It's always in July."

"Yep," said Rose. "We can take the girls together. I was planning on going Wednesday around one to beat the crowd."

"Sounds good," Lilly agreed. "When are you going?" she asked me, and I got lost for a minute in her eyes. Those brown eyes, so big and always bright and shining.

I cleared my throat. "I'll have to wait until after work. I'll probably go Wednesday and be a part of the after-dinner chaos. Hopefully, because of it being a church night, it won't be crowded."

Class started, and our conversation focused on the girls. Madeline caught on quickly and was soon tumbling and running with the others. Rose, Lilly, and I laughed a lot. How could you not? A bunch of four and five-year-olds doing the tumbling and cheering they were doing. I loved watching it.

I was paying attention to Darcie and not listening to Lilly and Rose. I didn't usually talk much when I was there, so this wasn't anything new.

"Jamison," Rose said, "Could you take Lilly and Maddy home? They came with me, but I need to pick up JR and some of his friends from practice. Nolan just got an emergency call."

"I hope nothing serious is happening," I said. Nolan was Orlinda Valley's fire chief.

"I really have no clue. But what do you say?"

"Sure. Not a problem," I said. "If it's okay with Lilly."

"I'm not going to walk, so I guess you'll do," she said with a damn sexy smile on her face.

To say the girls were excited when they found out they would be riding together was an understatement. Lena, on the other hand, started to pout. It wasn't fair that they rode together while she had to ride with a bunch of "stinky, gross boys."

Lilly squatted in front of Lena. "You know, I wouldn't be happy about hanging with gross boys either, but your mom can't help it. What do you say we promise to all go out for ice cream next time?"

Lena gave a small smile and shrugged.

"She'll be fine. Come on, kiddo," Rose said as we walked to the parking lot. She and Lena turned to their car, and I followed closely behind Lilly and the girls, and my gaze fell on Lilly's ass. What can say? I'm a guy, and she's sexy.

As soon as we were all in my truck, my senses were filled with the scent of coconut and something else I couldn't make out but liked all the same. I turned to Lilly, and her brown eyes met mine. I was caught off guard as my stomach did a somersault, and I suddenly became nervous. I wiped my hands on my pants quickly to dry them before I pulled out of the parking lot.

Thankfully, I didn't have to come up with any conversation because the girls talked nonstop about class and what they learned. We talked and laughed. It was a good time for such a short trip, and by the time I turned into the driveway, my nerves had vanished.

"Can Darcie come in really quick?" Madeline asked. "I have to show her something in my room. Please?"

Lilly glanced at me, and I shrugged. I had no clue what could be so important, but what could it hurt?

"Sure," Lilly said. Then she turned to me. "I guess you're coming in even if you don't want to."

I'd had a lot of fun tonight and wasn't ready to go home, anyway, so I followed behind the girls. Well, two girls and one woman. One very sweet and sexy woman whose ass I was staring at again.

Lilly unlocked the door, and the girls took off through the house and up the stairs. "I don't know if they can walk anywhere," I said.

"I was thinking the same thing," Lilly said as she closed the door, and we went into the kitchen.

The house was quiet. "Where's your mom and Charles?"

"Don't have a clue." She flipped on the kitchen light. "Want a drink or anything?"

"Just a water."

She got two water bottles from the refrigerator, handed me one, and then leaned on the counter. I leaned on the counter, too, and took a look around. I had even been in this kitchen with Lilly so many times. My wandering gaze fell on her, and my heart skipped a beat.

Her shoulder-length brown hair reflected the lights from above, and her eyes were bright. "Your eyes are still so pretty," I whispered. I didn't even mean to say it.

"Thanks." She smiled a small, crooked smile, and her cheeks got a little color in them. She was beautiful, but when she blushed, she became even more radiant. Her eyes met mine, and we stood there, and time stood still.

Part of me wanted to ignore the thumping of my heart, and I knew I should look away, get Darcie, and go. But another part of me refused to move. Refused to take my eyes from hers.

I moved like I was in a dream. I placed my water bottle on the counter next to her and touched her hair. It was soft, like I remembered. I tucked it behind her ear and drug my fingers lightly down her neck and across her collarbone. She shivered so softly that if I hadn't been touching her, I wouldn't have noticed.

We were close, and again, I could smell the scent of coconut and something else. "What perfume do you wear?"

"Perfume?" Her voice was almost a whisper.

"You smell amazing." My heart started palpitating like I had just run a marathon, and every nerve ending was at attention.

"It's probably my shampoo. Coconut and rose?"

I nodded. My eyes dropped to her lips, and I noticed how plump and desirable they looked. She must have sensed me staring at them because she sucked in her bottom one and ran her tongue across it. That little movement I could never ignore.

My heart sped up even more, and my blood pooled in areas I wished it wouldn't. This was crazy. I was one hundred percent attracted to Lilly, and I wanted to taste those lips and feel her porcelain skin. I reached out and dragged my thumb across her chin to her jawline until it rested on her cheek.

Our eyes locked. She sucked in a quick breath, and before I knew what I was doing, I touched my lips to hers. Her lips were cold from the water, yet sweet and tantalizing. I took the kiss a little deeper, our tongues touched, and I laced my fingers in her hair, holding her tight.

Suddenly, the patter of footsteps carried across the house and got closer. I stepped away. Lilly's eyes fluttered open, and I leaned back on the opposite counter as the girls entered the kitchen. I sucked in my lips and glanced at the ceiling, concentrating on my breathing.

My lips tingled with the sensation of the kiss, of Lilly's lips. My palms were still warm from the feel of her soft skin under them, and my crotch throbbed with need. What the hell did I just do, and how the hell would I keep from doing it again when every nerve ending in my body just woke up in a way they hadn't been for years?

CHAPTER 9

LILLY

"I'll talk to you later," Jamison said. He gave me a smile, which set my girlie parts to tingling, and followed Darcie down the front walk.

I shut the door behind them and leaned heavily against it. My nerves were still on edge. That kiss. His lips. I closed my eyes. I had this need to ingrain the feeling of his lips on mine in my brain. You would think that after all these years, I'd be able to move on, find someone else to obsess over, to want.

"Mommy, can you read me a story before I go to bed?" Madeline asked.

I sighed and opened my eyes, coming back to the present. "Of course, squirt. Go get ready for bed, pick out a book, and I'll be right there."

Madeline ran off, and I stared after her. I touched my fingers to my mouth. I swear I could still feel Jamison's warm lips on mine.

Jamison's lips on mine—What? This was crazy. I felt a pull between us, even at the gym tonight. It was like he was hanging on my every word. Rose kept giving me a look, but I ignored her.

God, she would die if I told her what happened. Hell, I don't even know what just happened. Did Jamison really kiss me? I lifted my fingers and brushed them against my lips again and fell back against the door. Jamison kissed me!

It was a perfect, soft, sweet, and sensual kiss wrapped up in a perfect Jamison package. Yes, it was brief because the girls interrupted us, but that made it so much better.

I froze. "I was just kissed by Jamison," I told the empty house. My pulse raced. God, it *was* real. My hands came to my face, and I squealed into them.

Damn, woman, you're acting like a high school girl kissed by the captain of the football team whom you had been crushing on for years.

Oh, well, it's because you were just kissed by the captain of the football team whom you've been crushing on for years.

I grabbed my purse from the chair I'd placed it on and took the stairs two at a time to read my daughter a book and get her to bed.

To say I wasn't into *Goodnight, Farm Animals,* the book we've read since we've been here, is an understatement. Madeline called me out on my lackluster animal sounds multiple times until she decided it was better to go ahead and just go to sleep.

I kissed her good night and went into my room and dialed Rose. I hoped it wasn't too late, but I thought I would explode if I didn't share what happened.

"Holy shit, Rose. I've got to talk to you. Do you have a minute?" I gushed as soon as she said hello.

"Of course. Hold on," she spoke in a hushed voice.

I heard her close a door. "I just put Lena down." Her voice was at a normal level. "What's up? Is everything okay? You sound a little flustered."

"Flustered?" I paced back and forth across my bedroom floor. "Girl, I'm more than flustered. Holy shit. You'll never believe what the hell just happened to me."

"I hope nothing bad. You don't usually curse unless you're mad or upset."

"I'm not upset. I'm just . . ." I huffed out a breath. I had to calm my pulse and heart rate. "Give me a minute." I closed my eyes and did some deep-meditation breathing to relax. I used to do that when Anthony upset me, but now it has another use.

"You're scaring me," Rose said.

"Okay, sorry. I'm just going to tell you. God, I feel like a college girl again."

"And you're acting like one. What the heck? Did you and Jamison give in to the hot sexual tension that hung between you two tonight and make out in the laundry room or something?"

This was why she was my best friend. It was like she could sense everything that happened to me. It may not have been the first time I'd kissed Jamison, but of course, she didn't know our history. I'd never told her about it before—I never told anyone.

"Good gosh, Lilly. Did you?" Her voice went up an octave. "Oh, my God. You did. Tell me everything."

I sat back against my pillows before I spoke. "Maddy wanted to show Darcie something in her room, so Jamison came in, and I offered him a water. I was leaning against the counter; he was leaning against the bar. Our eyes locked, and he touched my hair, then brushed his thumb against my cheek, then he kissed me." I relived the whole thing again. The feel of his lips against mine. The warmth of them. How my heart fluttered madly when our lips touched then felt empty when it ended.

I continued, "It was amazing and quick and sweet and surprising and . . ." I stopped to breathe and thought over my words. "Rose, I don't know why. I don't know how."

"Kristy and I knew there was something between you two at the pub, and tonight at gymnastics, I could feel the electricity bounce between you."

"Oh, that's not good. What if others did also?"

Rose laughed. "I'm sure they did. You two were hard to miss. But, so what? You're both adults and both single. You're free to do what you want and like whomever you wish."

She was right. But it was Jamison. "What was he thinking? What was I thinking? I'm so confused." My mind needed to calm down. It was going a mile a minute.

"Relax. Hold on." Rose must have put her hand over her phone. I could hear a muffled conversation and Nolan's voice asking what was wrong. Rose said nothing, but of course, he knew it wasn't true. "Sorry about that," she said. "Nolan wanted to know what all the excitement was."

"Don't you dare say a word." I hissed. "This is going to be awkward enough without the entire town hearing about it." News in Orlinda Valley spread faster than a forest fire over dry grass in the summer.

"Well, he kissed you. He must feel something. I guess you'll find out tomorrow when you go to his house."

My eyes popped. "Shit. I'm going to his house tomorrow." My heart, which had just calmed down, skipped right back into an off rhythm.

Rose giggled. "You are. What time do you need to be there?"

"Ten."

"I'd say I'd fix us lunch when you're finished, but who knows how long you'll be." She laughed again. "Let's grab coffee after we drop off the girls at Mother's Day Out tomorrow and talk before you have to go."

"That sounds good. I might need some encouragement."

"Well, then you'll have it."

"Great. See you tomorrow," I said, but I don't know if she heard because the line died. I fell back onto my bed. What the hell was I going to do? How would I act when I saw him?

My mind was going over every possible scenario. I doubted I'd ever get to sleep.

CHAPTER 10

LILLY

Rose and I had dropped the girls off at Mother's Day Out before coming here for some quiet one-on-one time. I was grateful they found an opening for Madeline. Yet another great thing about being from a small town and having a mother who had all the right connections.

I ordered a sugar-free caramel latte and a blueberry muffin and grabbed a table in the back corner of Café Mocha. It was my first time in this coffee shop, and I could see what all the fuss was about. The atmosphere was relaxed, yet it had a very big-town coffee shop feel. It seemed like something I'd find in the city, not in Orlinda Valley next to Shear Perfection.

"Okay. Now, tell me all." Rose sat across from me, her eyes were wide and glimmered with anticipation.

I promised myself last night—or early this morning as sleep eluded me for quite a while—that I would not allow my teenage fantasies about Jamison to interfere with my current state of singleness. Well, there was more to it. They weren't just teenage fantasies anymore.

Hopefully, I could convince Rose it wasn't a big deal. I took a large bite of my muffin. "Damn, this is amazing." It truly was. Soft, moist, and the blueberries burst with sweetness. There was no doubt they were real, and this was homemade.

"Yeah, whatever. Don't stall or change the subject. You were kissed last night by the one guy you fantasized about all during high school. I still think you only ran off to New York with Anthony because Jamison broke your heart when he proposed to Carly."

Well, she's not totally wrong.

Rose kept her gaze on me as she sipped from her cardboard coffee cup. I stared right back. The girl was sweet and quiet, but she was also determined and had an uncanny ability to get what she wanted out of you. I felt sorry for JR and Lena. They would have difficulty as teenagers trying to pull one over on their mother.

I couldn't hold her gaze any longer and let out a sigh. Rose was my best friend. There was only one thing I'd kept from her over the years, and it looked like it was time to come clean. "I didn't quite tell you everything last night."

Her eyes bulged so wide I was scared they might pop out.

"Oh, my gosh. What else is there to tell?" She sat on the edge of her seat and placed her coffee cup on the table.

"Rose," I chuckled. "It's not what you're thinking."

Her body deflated like a balloon with a slow leak.

I chewed on my bottom lip for a bit. "Well, you weren't quite wrong about why I ran off to New York with Anthony."

She waved her hands in the air and bounced in her seat. "Come on already. Come out with it."

Here goes nothing. "The summer before Jamison started dating Carly, we were sort of together."

"Holy . . . Wow. What?" Rose's mouth fell open.

I thought back to that summer, our amazing summer of secrets. "He came over one day, and no one was home yet. I was on the deck in a bikini, lying out, reading a book. He sat down, and we started talking. I don't even remember what about, but it was the first time we really *talked.* He asked if I wanted to go kayaking, and I said yes. We ended up kayaking down the Red River. When we banked, and I tried to get out of the kayak, I lost my balance and fell into the water. We started splashing and messing around, and then his arms were around me, and we kissed—and kissed some more." My stomach fluttered at the memory.

"Why didn't you ever tell me?" Rose's voice was a whisper as she hung on my every word.

I shrugged. "If you remember I sort of went missing a lot that summer."

"I remember." She sat up tall and smacked the table. "Kristy and I thought you got abducted. You were never available to hang out with us. You were with Jamison the entire time?"

I nodded slowly, trying to keep an unscrupulous grin from my face. "We thought it was best to keep it between us. He was worried Lance would be upset if he knew. Hell, I was worried Lance would go ballistic." I played with my muffin wrapper. "Like I said, it only lasted the summer. Just two months, and damn, they were amazing."

"Like amazing, amazing? Sexual amazing?" she asked.

My shoulders met my ears, and I tried to be sly.

"Girl, and you kept it quiet all these years. What happened?"

I shook my head. "He had to get back to school. He no longer played football because of his knee, but he helped out with the team."

"And? He ended up with Carly soon after he got back to school, and by graduation, they were engaged," she finished.

"Yep." I nodded. "We left things open. We knew we had to get back to college and didn't know what to tell everyone, so we just ended things—sort of. Then at Thanksgiving, he told me he was seeing Carly."

"You were so quiet. I remember." She reached for my hand. "Lilly-blossom, you should have said something."

"I handled it the best I could, and got over him, until the graduation party."

"And that's why you attached yourself to Anthony." Rose sat back and sipped her coffee.

"And now we kissed again. Neither of us has anyone else tying us down, and I need to go to his house and act like nothing weird happened and hope to God I never have to face my brother again."

"What does Lance have to do with anything?"

I lifted a brow and held up my hands. "Come on, Rose. He's Jamison's best friend." How could she not see the issue?

"And Lance isn't in high school. Jamison isn't in high school, and you aren't in high school. It's not like Jamison is trying to deflower Lance's baby sister."

I laughed hard. Again, she sat up straight, and her eyes were huge. Unfortunately, I had to disappoint her. "No. No deflowering of any type took place—remember the first guy I met at college?"

Rose nodded. "I do. I told you not to do anything stupid, but . . ."

"Yeah, whatever. It was a long time ago. Anyway, let's say that my experience made our summer even more amazing."

She shook her head, and her gaze held mine.

"What?" I asked her.

"I can't believe you had a summer of hot sex with Jamison—your dream guy—and kept it from me, your best friend." She pinched her lips together. "Anyway, I'm over it. Now, you're a beautiful, sexy woman—a divorced woman with a child. Jamison is hot and single—and has been for two years. You have chemistry; no one can deny it. Lance has no reason to be weird about any of this."

If only it were that easy. I dropped my gaze and focused on my blueberry muffin and latte. I couldn't bring myself to tell her what was gnawing at me—the fear that even after all this time, I might never be good enough for Jamison.

Finally, I spoke. "I know you're right. Even if Lance has an issue, he has no right to. But I can't help but think our latest kiss was a mistake. A fluke of nature because we were both so drawn into the excitement of the girls." I shrugged.

Rose reached across the table and squeezed my hand. Her voice was soft when she spoke. "Lill, that could be part of it. You're both one hundred percent into your daughters, as you should be. But I know there's more between you."

I knew she was right but refused to meet her gaze. I stared off across the coffee shop and read the menu.

"Hey," she squeezed my hand which was still in her grip. "Look at me."

I slowly met her gaze, and she continued. "Please realize you deserve a man who loves you deeply and knows how amazing you are. You deserve someone who makes you happy, and I want you to go out there and find happiness, no matter who you find it with."

I swallowed against the lump lodged in my throat and blinked quickly to clear my vision. Rose always knew what to say. I smiled. "Thank you," I whispered.

"You're welcome. Now get out of here and show Jamison that cocky, outgoing, woman everyone loved—including him. I know she's still in there somewhere, and he was interested once upon a time."

"Love you, Rosie." I jumped up and hugged her. I felt much better and was ready to go show Jamison why he needed me as his cleaning person—and possibly why he needed me in general.

That old confidence, which carried me through high school and college, rushed through me as I drove the short distance across town to Jamison's house. I pulled into his driveway and jumped out of the car with a sureness I hadn't felt in a long time. Then I came to an abrupt halt at his front door and thought I was going to hyperventilate. Fear and insecurity gripped my gut, squeezing all that confidence I'd felt just seconds before from my being like a boa constrictor.

The door opened, and I jumped. Startled.

"Hey. I thought I heard something. Come on in." Jamison looked as handsome as ever in khaki pants and an unbuttoned polo. I stepped inside, and a beige dog stood there, tail wagging in anticipation of meeting someone new.

"Well, hello." I stuck my hand out and was greeted with a sloppy kiss. I laughed and petted the dog's stringy fur. "And who is this beauty?"

"That's Becca. A big baby who's never met a stranger."

Becca turned circles as Jamison closed the door, and I laughed again. She was precious.

"Come on. Let me show you around the house so you can see what you'll be getting yourself into."

Jamison's house was a spacious, two-story home. Upstairs were Jamison and Darcie's bedroom, and each had a private bath, while a cozy third room served as Jamison's office. Downstairs featured a large master suite with a luxurious bathroom and a deep jacuzzi bathtub. The inviting living room flowed into a modest dining area, and the kitchen boasted a charming breakfast nook by the window overlooking the backyard.

"It's not much, but there are times everything gets out of control, and I think there's an entire football team living here. I try my best to keep up but struggle, big time."

"I don't know, Jamison." I said as I looked around the tidy kitchen. "Everything looks clean and in its place for the most part."

"Yeah. For the most part, but only because my mother was here on Friday, and we haven't had a chance to mess anything up yet."

"The downstairs master bedroom seems to be immaculate. Does anyone ever use it?" I asked as I thought through how much time it might take for me to clean the entire house.

He shook his head. "Honestly, no. That was Carly's and my room, but after she . . ." He paused, and his eyes took on a faraway look. My heart went out to him. ". . . passed away, I moved upstairs to be closer to Darcie. I thought it would be just temporary, but two years later, I'm still there. It's just easier."

I smiled a tight-lipped smile. "Makes sense. My old house in New York was huge. The master was on the top floor. There were three floors, but I never liked to sleep one floor above Madeline. Whenever Anthony was out of town, which during the past five years was a lot, I slept in Madeline's room with her. The bed was big enough, and

I enjoyed her room more, anyway. It was comfortable and inviting." I met his eyes, and the loneliness I saw in them a second ago was a feeling I knew well. But the look that was there now was no longer sadness but something else. Something I couldn't quite put my finger on. Was it interest? Or God, forbid . . . desire? I hoped not. I sure wasn't ready for that.

Was I?

Chapter 11

Jamison

"Wow, Daddy. The house looks so nice," Darcie exclaimed as we entered the kitchen from the garage. After I picked her up from school, we went grocery shopping so I could fix us something to eat besides chicken nuggets and mac & cheese.

Earlier, after I'd finished showing Lilly around, I left for my forty-five-minute commute to Nashville as Tuesday was the one day a week I had to go into the office. One of the many awesome things about working for my tech company was that I didn't have to make the commute daily. Fighting the traffic every day would drive me crazy.

Choosing Tuesday for Lilly to clean was probably a good thing. I don't know if I would have been able to concentrate on work with her in such close proximity all morning. I was still trying to decide what to do about that kiss.

I placed the grocery bags on the counter and looked around the kitchen. Darcie was right. The countertops gleamed, and the appliances shone. I brushed my fingers across the counter. It was smooth as silk. I was almost too afraid to cook for fear of messing things up.

Darcie dropped her daycare bag on the floor and ran through the house as I unloaded the groceries and set out to fix our food. I placed the rotisserie chicken on a pan and into the oven to warm, a thing of boil-in-the-bag rice in a pan of water on the stove and made a quick salad with ranch dressing. At least I could feel like I wouldn't win worst dad of the year.

As the food cooked and warmed, I focused on setting the table. My heart stopped when I opened the cabinet. Everything was organized by size. I opened the cabinets with the glasses and cups, and the same organization greeted me. I didn't even know I could have cabinets look this nice. Even the silverware drawer had new organizers and was neat and straightened.

I wandered through the house and noticed Lilly didn't just put her touch on the kitchen. She'd cleaned, organized, and straightened up everything. All drawers and cabinets. Everything looked amazing and accessible.

That wasn't in the plan. My gut suddenly felt heavy. The last thing I wanted was for her to do this much for me. Vacuuming, dusting, and wiping things down was all I expected. This was too much. I sent her a text as Darcie came back to the kitchen.

"Hey, you. Why don't you take out any pictures you did at school today and put them on your board? Let's keep things clean."

"Yeah, Daddy. Everything looks so good. I've never seen our house look this nice before. Did Mommy clean like this?"

My mind rewound itself to when Carly was alive. Everything had a place; the house was clean and happy and filled with love and laughter. "Yes, princess. Your mommy kept the house looking like this."

"Well, then she'd be happy that Ms. Lilly is helping you out, Daddy." She held up a crayon drawing of a sun and a rainbow. "Here, I colored this for you. It's outside on a bright sunny day after it rains, and God puts a rainbow in the sky. We learned the rainbow was a promise that God is always there for us and loves us no matter what." She hung her picture on the refrigerator. "I'm putting this here, Daddy. I want to remember that promise. Don't you? I think Mommy is in the sky watching us and wanting us to be happy. When I see a rainbow, it will always remind me of God's promise and that Mommy is up in heaven watching over us."

Carly and I took Darcie to church when she was a baby. Bryson, Darlene, and our mother go just about every Sunday.

I stopped after Carly died.

I studied the picture. It was of a man, I guess me, holding a little red-haired girl's hand, Darcie. They were under a rainbow, and my heart stuttered. A person who looked so much like the little girl, red hair and all, was above the rainbow with a big smile on her face. My eyes watered and I blinked hard.

Did I believe God is always there for us? I didn't know. I didn't know what to believe anymore. All I knew was I'd lost the woman I planned on growing old with and having a lot more babies with. My light was taken away from me, and to be honest, I believed God left me that day as well. But I couldn't tell my daughter that.

I met her innocent, wide green eyes. *How do I tell her I don't know what I believe anymore? Sometimes I feel like God moved on and forgot about me, but I can't say that.* I took a deep breath and said the only thing I could. "Yep, princess. Now help me set the table."

I got Darcie to bed after a decent dinner for once, and I walked around looking for laundry to fold or something to clean. There was nothing. "Oh, well. Come on Becca." I went outside and sat on the front steps as Becca ran around the front yard sniffing. She barked excitedly when Lance pulled into the driveway.

It wasn't unusual for him to stop by this late—well, it was only eight thirty; it wasn't really late. His apartment complex wasn't far away.

"Hey, Becca." He petted the dog's head and threw the stick she brought to him. "Hey, man. What's up?"

I shook my head and gestured to the dog. "Just brought her out here instead of the back to run around a bit."

"Is the little princess asleep?"

"Yep." I stood and opened the door for him. "I'm going to have a coffee. Want anything?"

"Just water. I can't believe you can drink coffee at this hour."

I chuckled a bit. He always said that, but I could honestly drink coffee at any time and hop right into bed. Caffeine didn't have an effect on me.

We got our drinks, went into the living room, and got comfortable. Lance let out a low whistle. "I heard Lilly came by today. She really did a job on your place. I haven't seen it this clean and organized in years."

"I know," I agreed. "I feel bad. All I expected her to do was the basic cleaning, but she went all out. Everything's organized. Even Darcie's closet."

"My mom said she also did amazing things at the salon. I can tell you she had this talent hidden all growing up. Her room was always immaculate, but helping around the house was not something she ever did."

I laughed as a memory came back to me. Lilly and Rose sitting on her bed with the door open. Lance and I asked if they wanted to go to the Creamery, the local ice cream shop at the time. She said she couldn't until she vacuumed, and she had no desire to do the simplest chore. "Yep. She only kept her room clean. Not even ice cream could get her to push a vacuum."

I'd be lying if I said I hadn't noticed Lilly then, but being my best friend's sister, someone I had known all my life—created an invisible barrier between us. She was someone who I couldn't approach.

My mind drifted back to the summer before I graduated, and the fling Lilly and I had. So much for that invisible barrier. I couldn't deny I had some sort of feelings for her, but I didn't think much about them because I met Carly soon after returning to school, and my heart was hers from the start.

My heart beat rapidly, and I had a sick feeling in my stomach. Was kissing her again a bad idea?

"Hey. Everything good? You're zoning out again," Lance said.

I nodded and pushed those thoughts to the back of my mind. "Yeah. I'm just grateful for your sister. Darcie was so excited about how clean everything was. She actually asked me if Carly kept the house this clean." I got quiet, and the sick feeling in my stomach churned a bit. "It kills me she has no memories of her mother. None at all." I lifted my gaze from the carpet and looked at him. "I'm also starting to forget her. Little things. Her laugh. How she felt. And it scares me."

Lance moved to the edge of his seat. "I don't know what it's like to lose someone as perfect as Carly, but I see her so much in Darcie. Darcie looks just like her and has her bubbliness and love of life. Her tenderness. You have a mini-Carly right up there." He pointed to the ceiling. "And Carly loved you so much. I know she'd want you to find someone and be happy. Not alone all the time. I just had the same discussion with my sister."

My pulse picked up. "Why? Did something happen?" I couldn't hide my concern.

"Not really. We were just talking. She told me Anthony didn't care about her for most of their marriage, and she wasn't his only woman. He had them everywhere, and there was nothing she could do about it because if she left, he would cut her and Madeline off. It took every ounce of courage for her to go to the lawyer and file for divorce. Thankfully, her friend Gianna was there to encourage her."

He scrubbed his hands over his face and looked hard at me. "I told her I needed to meet Gianna. Anyway, she admitted she was over him. He just had a way of getting under her skin. She knows she and Maddy deserve to have a man who wants to treat them special." Lance sat up straight. "Both of you deserve to be happy. You're my favorite people."

I glanced at him, then back to the carpet. Should I tell him about the kiss? Would he understand? I raked my fingers through my hair. Not now. Not yet. "I know, man. I was thinking the same thing earlier."

Our conversation changed to the upcoming college football season. Yeah, it was summer, but in our world, there were two seasons—football season and almost football season.

CHAPTER 12

JAMISON

I had gone through every drawer and cabinet in the house, and their contents were strewn everywhere, but I still couldn't find Darcie's vaccination record or birth certificate anywhere. "Where the hell could they be?" I said under my breath as I threw shit out of my way so I could get deeper into the hall closet. I finally found the file boxes I was looking for.

Thank God.

I crouched down and started rifling through the papers and documents. "They've got to be here. I've looked everywhere else."

Nope. No luck. "Fuck."

"Good Lord, did a tornado come through your house, Jamison?"

I stuck my head out of the closet as my mom, and Darcie came into the hall entry. "Shit, is it lunch already?"

"Daddy, you owe me money. Money. Money." Darcie sang as she skipped in a circle.

My shoulders drooped, and I stood. "Okay, princess. I do." I pulled my wallet out of my pocket and gave her the dollar all cuss words cost. You'd think I would have learned by now.

"I bet she almost has her first year of college paid for, and she hasn't even started kindergarten." My mother let out her loud cackle laugh as she went into the kitchen.

I didn't need her humor right now. "Yeah, whatever, Mom." My words were clipped with irritation.

"What's wrong with you?" she asked.

"Oh, nothing serious," I said as I took two glasses and a plastic princess cup for Darcie from the cabinet. It was her favorite and the only thing she liked to drink out of at this current moment. Last month, it was a cowboy cup she took from Bryson and Darlene's. Who knew what it would be next week. "I just can't find Darcie's birth certificate or vaccination record. I know I got it from the pediatrician when we went for her kindergarten appointment, but I have no clue where I put it, and we have to have it to register her." I placed the princess cup on the counter with enough force the contents spilled on the table.

"Bless your heart, baby. What am I going to do with you?" My mom tsk tsked her tongue and grabbed a paper towel to clean up the mess.

"Don't know, Mom, but I'm sure you have no choice but to keep me around for a little longer."

"That's right, Jamison. I wouldn't know what to do without you. She patted me on the cheek, reached into her oversized bag, and pulled out a yellow envelope.

My brows raised. Now I remembered. I couldn't find it because she'd gone with me, and I'd asked her to take the papers with her. I was scared I'd misplace them before kindergarten registration. I wasn't the organized one in the family. That was Carly's specialty. I was more of an out of sight out of mind kind of person, and every drawer in the house had demonstrated that issue perfectly. They were all filled to the rim with absolute junk—well, until recently.

"Thanks. I guess you have a purpose, Mom." I gave her a tight hug. "I know for a fact I'd be lost without you."

She hugged me tightly. "I'm always here for the two of you, but I have no doubt someone will steal your heart again one day, and then I won't be needed as much."

A rock seemed to wedge itself beside my heart, which was already taken and filled to the brim with love for Carly and Darcie. Lilly crept into my thoughts at that very moment, but I shook it away. I wasn't ready to go there. Not yet, anyway. "Don't expect it too soon."

"I'll never rush you, honey. Do you want me to go to the school with you tonight?"

I shook my head. "No, thank you. I'm finished with work for the day, so I'm going to go with Bryson and Darlene. Darlene wants to get a picture of Darcie and James together on registration day." I put the envelope by my keys so I'd remember to take it. "But if you want to go, you know we would love to have you."

"Nope, it's alright. I'm going to the salon and get my nails done and talk with the girls."

Just then, Darcie came skipping into the kitchen, dressed in her favorite green sundress. I loved her in that dress. It brought out the green in her eyes.

"Good timing, baby girl. Gramma's leaving." My mom gave Darcie a hug and kisses. "Have fun today. I know you're going to be turning all the little boys' heads looking as pretty as you are."

Darcie scrunched up her face. "Ew. Boys are gross."

"You don't think James is gross," my mom said.

"He's not a boy. He's my cousin. Totally different."

I chuckled as she hopped onto the barstool, and I slid a plate with her peanut butter and jelly sandwich and her cup of milk in front of her.

My mom gave her a kiss on the head and patted my arm. "Have fun, you two, and send me pictures."

I assured her we would and settled down on the stool next to Darcie to eat my sandwich as well.

Soon enough, I pulled up beside Bryson's truck at Orlinda Valley Elementary. "You ready, princess?" I got out and went around to open Darcie's door. She wasn't even out of her seatbelt yet and was picking at her fingernails, a nervous habit of hers that I had recently noticed had gotten worse. I crouched down so I could see her better. "What's up, princess? I can tell something's bothering you."

Her eyes glistened with tears when she turned toward me. My heart fell. I brushed away a lone tear as it fell silently down her cheek. "Talk to me, Darce."

"I'm scared, Daddy," she said, her voice soft. "What if I don't have any friends, and what if my teacher doesn't like me?"

My heart ached for her, "Darce, this is just registration." I brushed hair off her forehead. "We are going to fill out some forms and go see the kindergarten classrooms. You aren't staying today," I lifted her chin so her eyes met mine. "I know school can be scary, but you already know so many kids and have so many friends. And Kora and Aunt Darlene are teachers here, so if you ever need anything, you know you can go to them."

I tugged lightly on her arm until she was out of her booster seat and standing at the door. She was small enough to be able to stand and lean out of it, and I held her around the waist as she wiped at her face. "You're smart, and kind, and polite, and funny. I have no doubt you will love school. I know you're ready."

Her green eyes met mine, and sadness reflected back at me. "But, Daddy"—Her voice was soft and shaky— "I'll miss you. What if you get sad because Mommy's not around, and I'm not around? Who will take care of you?"

There it was. She was thinking about me. I felt a vice grip my heart. I picked her up and squeezed her tight. "I'll be fine. I'll miss you like crazy, but you need to grow up. And as a daddy, I've had to prepare to let you go a little. I'll be here to pick you up or wait for you at home every day. And we'll eat dinner and tell each other about every second." I gave her what I hoped was a proud smile, though my insides were clenching and tearing apart. I thought I'd have the hardest time with my baby growing up, but it looked like we were both struggling to let each other go.

"Darcie," a tiny voice called from across the lot, and a smile filled Darcie's face.

Madeline skipped her way to us, and Darcie wiggled out of my arms. They were attracted to each other like magnets, and the sadness was wiped immediately from Darcie's face.

My gaze fell on Lilly. Her dark hair was pulled back from her face, and she wore a blue and white flowered sun dress which fell just below her knees. It hugged her waist slightly, and I couldn't miss how amazing she looked. My eyes dropped briefly to her soft lips. "Hey." I breathed out the word as they approached.

Her face was lit up with a smile which met her eyes. "Hey, back. These two are excited." She laughed.

"It seems like it." I held up a finger to get them to wait while I got the envelope from the front seat and locked the truck. "Come on, girls."

They walked hand in hand ahead of us. "You look nice." Nice? Was that the best word I could use to describe Lilly? She was better than nice. I sighed heavily and hoped we wouldn't be uncomfortable with each other because of the kiss, or whatever this pull was between us.

"Thank you. Is everything okay?"

"Believe it or not, Darcie was upset right before y'all appeared. She doesn't want to leave me. She's scared I'll be lonely." I glanced quickly at Lilly.

"That's sweet," she said, as she touched my arm lightly. "She'll be fine, and so will you."

The warmth of her fingers went straight to my vice-gripped heart, and it calmed noticeably. "I know. I just didn't expect to do all this alone."

"You're not alone, Jamison. I'm here for you." Lilly pulled open the door, and Bryson, Darlene, and James were waiting inside. "And so are they." Lilly smiled, as I reached around her for the door. My arm brushed against her shoulders, and a sense of calm fell over me.

Chapter 13

Lilly

"It's been a week." I let out a heavy breath as I pulled into Mom's driveway Friday night. Tonya did exactly what she had promised, and my cleaning schedule was now full, but exhaustion seeped into every muscle in my body.

I turned off the car and breathed deeply.

Rose's car was in the driveway. She and Nolan wanted me to meet them at the pub tonight, but I asked if we could stay home instead, so Rose brought Lena to the house, and we were going to have a nice quiet girls' night in. Or that's what I'd thought, but there were many other cars here as well.

I let out a sigh as I pulled myself from the car. So much for a quiet evening.

As soon as I opened the front door, Madeline ran into my arms. "Mommy! We're having a party tonight. Everyone's here."

"I see." I laughed at her excitement. "Hello, Lena," I said as Lena and another little girl I didn't know joined Madeline. The other girl was pretty, with long blonde hair. I crouched to be more on her eye level. "And who might you be?"

"I'm Skylar," she said excitedly.

"Mrs. Diane is her grandma," Madeline said as she pulled the other girls toward the kitchen. "We gotta go play, Mommy. Bye."

I waved to the three girls as they ran into the kitchen, and I heard the sliding door open and close.

"Hey. I thought I heard someone." Rose wrapped me in a hug.

"So glad to see you. I was greeted by the girls and met Skylar. She's adorable," I said.

"Yes, she is. And she's just as sweet."

I followed Rose through the kitchen and into the backyard. The ladies were sitting on the patio having a glass of wine. I hugged Tonya, Diane, Ruth, and my mother. "I guess it's ladies' night at Kaye's," I said.

"It is," Diane said. "And I thought this would be the perfect night for you to meet my bonus daughter, Leila. Leila, Lilly." Leila was about my height with thick brown hair and hazel eyes that gleamed.

I put my arms out. "Hope you don't mind. I'm a hugger."

Leila smiled. "Of course not."

I gave her a hug. "It's great to meet you," I said to her. "I just met Skylar. She's beautiful. With those blue eyes and blond hair, you're going to have your hands full keeping the boys away."

Leila laughed. "No kidding. Her father's already having issues, and she hasn't even started kindergarten yet. He's threatening to send her to an all-girls boarding school."

I laughed and watched the girls play in the back corner of the yard. "Well, it looks like they've been friends forever. I'm so glad. Madeline didn't have many friends in New York."

"Skylar loves playing with all the other grandkids, so Diane brings her to Orlinda Valley when she keeps her and gives me and Adler a child-free weekend."

"Child-free weekends are wonderful sometimes," Rose agreed.

We joined the women and gladly took the wine Diane offered.

"I wouldn't know much about child-free weekends," I said. "The only child-free night I've had in recent memory was last weekend."

"Well then, we'll have to fix that," Tonya said. "Every mom needs time to herself. Maybe a girls' weekend should be in the works."

A girls' weekend. Something I wasn't used to. "Maybe soon, but I'm not sure."

"Oh, nonsense. We could have a big camp out with the grand-kids," Ruth said. "It would be fun.

"And slightly chaotic," Diane agreed.

"That's why the grandfathers would need to be here to help out," Mom answered. "It's not like it would be the first time. Remember last year when it was Skylar, Lena, Darcie, and James?"

"Oh Lord, yes." Tonya laughed. "Poor James. He was so out-numbered." Tonya turned to me. "The girls wanted to play princess and dragon. Tom and Charles made them a clubhouse, and they dressed up in princess outfits but James, of course, refused to be a princess, so they made him the prince. The grandfathers were the dragons, and they ran around being chased by the 'dragons.' James was supposed to rescue the girls from the dragons' castle when they were caught, but he refused."

"Lena and Darcie were so mad he wasn't playing by the rules," Diane said with a chuckle.

Ruth laughed. "But he was playing by *his* rules. He said it was much quieter with the girls locked in the castle."

"He came in the house and ate a bunch of cookies before we realized they were waiting on him," Mom said.

"My grandson sure does have a way with the women," Tonya added and shook her head. "The girls finally stomped into the house with their arms crossed, but James didn't care at all."

"Poor James," Kaye said. "He needs another boy or two in the group. Those girls will drive him crazy."

Rose, Leila, and I sipped our wine and laughed at the stories the women told about the grandkids over the years.

"What did we miss?" Lance asked as he, Jamison, and Darcie entered the backyard.

"Darcie," the girls all squealed as they surrounded her, and she jumped right into whatever they were playing.

My heart jumped too, and heat crawled up my neck.

Rose glanced at me with a smirk, which she hid quickly with her wine glass.

I sucked in my bottom lip to keep a grin from my face as Lance and Jamison joined us.

Lance sat in the only chair open, leaving Jamison to sit next to me on the love seat. I moved over so he could sit, and he gave me a small smile.

I fixated on those lips. Their softness. Their feel against mine. I lost track of the discussion as I couldn't help but focus on the close proximity of his body and the sexy manliness of his cologne.

"Well, now that everyone is here, ladies, let's go get dinner ready." Mom stood. "Y'all, we have salad and sandwiches for dinner. It's not fancy, but we expect you to stay and eat."

Jamison leaned back, placed his left ankle on his right knee, and laid his arm over the back of the seat. His arm was close enough I could feel the presence of it near my shoulders.

"I think we know better than to argue with the book club," he said.

"That's the truth," agreed Rose.

"I wouldn't argue, anyway. I will never say no to free food," Lance said.

"So true." Mom laughed, and she gave me a smile as she passed and squeezed my hand. "I'm so glad to have both my kids here, and my beautiful granddaughter."

"Thanks, Mom." My voice was soft with gratitude. "Can we help with anything?"

"Nope." She waved me off. "Just sit and talk. We have everything under control."

I watched them walk into the kitchen. "I feel bad, them waiting on me."

"Sis, relax. Mom and the ladies planned this. Mom's so glad you're home. She wanted to do something special," Lance said.

"You and Madeline are all they've been talking about," Jamison agreed.

I felt the light pull of a strand of my hair and the soft pressure of his hand on my neck. A tingle of electricity ran down my spine, and I had to hide a shiver.

He continued, "My mom called me this morning and told me when to be here with Darcie. So, sit still, Lilly-Pad, and let the moms do what they do best—take care of us and their grandkids."

Jamison stopped playing with my hair, and his hand rested against my neck. I glanced at him. My pulse raced with his closeness, but when he touched me and called me the familiar endearment, "Lil-ly-Pad," my heart skipped a bunch of beats.

He gave me a smile, and there went another missed beat. "Fine. I won't help." Staying right here seemed like a much better option anyway.

Rose refilled my wine, and Lance handed Jamison a beer. I watched Lance to see if he thought anything between Jamison and me was off, but he didn't seem to notice. Rose, on the other hand, had a ridiculous smirk glued to her face. I widened my eyes and tilted my head. "Rose, do you have an issue you need to discuss?"

She shrugged. "Not one I think needs to be brought up at this moment." Her smirk grew wider. "So, Lance, what's this buzz I hear about you and Jayla?"

Lance pursed his lips. "Don't know what you're talking about."

"Oh, no?" she continued, "You and the English teacher having something going on is pretty big news in this little town."

"Time to eat," Tonya said, her arms filled with food, and everyone followed her.

"You're saved, Lance," Jamison said as we went to the table.

"Lance is saved from what?" Mom asked as we settled around the table. Lance, Jamison, me, and Rose on one side, Leila on the end, and the book club on the other. The girls sat on a blanket in the grass. They were excited to have a real picnic even with a straw picnic basket. They ate and continued their childlike discussion while we ate, and I was finally able to relax with Jamison beside me.

"The latest woman who has grabbed his attention," Jamison said.

"Oh, Jayla," Tonya said. "From what I heard, Jayla has it bad for you, Lance."

"How did you hear that?" he asked before taking a bite of his sandwich. My brother was a ladies' man, always going from woman to woman and refusing to settle down.

"I know everything that happens in this town. There are no secrets."

"No truer words have ever been spoken," Diane said. "I heard a little rumor today when I was cutting Gertrude's hair."

"Mrs. Gertrude, the librarian?" I asked, my eyes wide.

Diane nodded.

"She's still around?" I asked.

"Damn, Lilly," Jamison said with a chuckle. "She's not old."

"Come on. She has to be," I said. "She was the librarian when I was a senior in high school."

"Maybe," Jamison replied. "but she was just a couple years ahead of me in college when she got the job."

"You know a lot about her," Rose said.

Jamison shrugged and got quiet.

"My boy had a short stint in the hay with Gertrude, if I remember correctly," Tonya said.

"Mom, seriously?"

"Totally serious, baby," she said to Jamison and leaned on the table.

I didn't miss the eye roll Jamison gave her.

"Anyway, I went out to the barn to take care of the goats we had at the time and walked right in on Jamison and Gertrude having some fun on the hay."

"Oh, my gosh," said Ruth, her eyes wide. "Jamison."

Leila stood as she recovered from laughing. "On that note, I think I've got to go."

Rose gave her a hug. "Why are you leaving?"

Leila hugged her back. "I have an appointment I need to get to, and Adler's meeting me." Then she hugged me. "It was great to finally meet you, Lilly."

"I'll bring Skylar home later. Let her stay and play longer," Diane said.

Leila agreed and saw herself out after saying goodbye to Skylar.

"I think we should play a game," Jamison said.

"Are you trying to change the subject?" asked Lance.

"Yep. I'm over talking about me."

"When was the last time y'all played Spoons?" I asked.

Jamison and Lance glanced at each other, then at Rose. Rose's shoulders rose as she thought. "Probably Christmas?" she asked the guys.

"That's right. We introduced Kai to the game. He had never played," said Jamison.

"It got pretty intense," recalled Lance.

"Yeah, because Jamison and Bryson kept cheating," said Rose.

Jamison's mouth dropped. "No one ever proved it."

"My boys are always being accused of cheating." Tonya said as she and Ruth returned from the kitchen.

"Yeah, Mom. Can you believe it?"

Tonya laughed. "Don't make me answer that, son."

"Wow," I said, laughing. "I don't know what that says about you when your mother won't stick up for you. Guess I've got to watch you closely."

Jamison pushed his shoulder against mine. "I don't know, Lilly-Pad. If I remember correctly, you were quite the cheater back in the day. You and Kora needed to be watched all the time."

I shrugged. "That was so long ago; you wouldn't be able to prove anything."

"Well . . ." Rose started.

I elbowed her.

"Hey." She rubbed her side. "Innocent people don't need to resort to physical abuse."

I hugged her. "Sorry, Rosie. But I need you to back me up."

"Okay, okay," Diane interjected. "Let's get started."

Chapter 14

Jamison

As usual, that was the wildest game of Spoons probably ever. At one point, Lance got his matches and pulled a spoon, and by the time Lilly and I noticed there weren't many left, we both went for the same one. The electricity that passed between us as we battled for the last spoon was intense. I finally let go because we had gained an audience, and I didn't want the book club to get any ideas. The entire afternoon was already suspect as it was, and the raised brow from Lance after our little battle was questionable.

"Well, this has been fun and all, but I've got to get out of here," Lance said.

"And Lena and I have a family to get home to. I had fun." Rose stood and said her goodbyes.

Lance gave me a man-hug pat on the back. "It was fun, bro. You goin or stayin?"

I glanced quickly at Lilly, then at the girls sitting in a circle on the grass. "I think I'm going to hang out a bit more. I don't think Darcie's ready to go quite yet."

Lance shook his head. "Okay, have fun." He turned to Lilly and gave her a hug. "Bye, sis. I love having you home."

Lilly smiled wide. "I agree." She kissed him on his cheek.

"Ladies, I think we should go clean the kitchen," Kaye said.

"Yep, then Skylar and I will need to be heading home also," Diane said.

Suddenly, it was just me and Lilly on the patio with the three girls playing in the yard.

We were quiet for a while as we watched them play. The space between us filled with a little tension. Why did I have to kiss her? Everything seemed awkward now. Then earlier—her hair was so soft. I didn't even realize I was playing with it, but I needed the contact with her.

I glanced at Lilly. Her gaze was far away, but the corners of her mouth turned up. Even after all these years, she was beautiful.

I wonder if she ever thinks about that summer. God, I was going to start my senior year. If I hadn't started dating Carly, what would have happened between us?

Lilly turned toward me. "So, has Darcie said anything about registration? Maddy has been talking about the school nonstop. She's so excited. Honestly, I'm surprised she's not more anxious. She's usually quiet and reserved in new places—well, she used to be—but since we've been here, she's been a totally different little girl." She looked out across the yard again. "I told her Anthony was moving to London and is getting married. She was surprisingly happy for him and said maybe I should find a new husband."

Her eyes met mine for a second, and my stomach lurched hard. I pulled my gaze from hers.

Lilly chuckled uneasily. "I told her I wasn't ready for that yet, but it was very grown up of her to be happy for him." She scrunched her eyes, cocked her head, and laid her hand on my thigh. "What's up? You seem far away."

That small gesture sent my pulse racing. Should I mention the kiss—ask her out—or just ignore this pull between us? She just told me about Anthony. I shook my head. "Nothing." I stood. "I think Darcie and I should go as well. We're going to see Carly's parents tomorrow, and she's staying the week. We have to get some things packed."

"It was a fun afternoon. I'm glad you came over and brought Darcie." Lilly's eyes were shrouded, and her voice was soft.

"Me too." I smiled, and my eyes held hers for a second. I wanted to kiss her again. God, I wanted to. But it wasn't right. She wasn't ready; I wasn't ready. *Not gonna happen.* "What time will you be by on Tuesday?"

She glanced at the sky. "I don't think we ever chose a time. You go to the office, so I guess after you leave would be good."

I nodded and stood. She didn't realize how good being gone before she got there would be. "It would. I'll get you the code to the garage, and you can get in that way."

"A secret code to your home. What if I'm an ax murderer?"

I chuckled. "I've known you since you were born. I think I'd know if you were an ax murderer."

Her shoulders met her ears. "People change a lot in a decade. Who knows what I got into in the big city." She rose from the seat.

She stood right in front of me. In short jean shorts, frayed at the ends, a tight pale-yellow shirt that hugged her perky, and if my memory recalled correctly, soft breasts, and the sunlight caught the highlights of her hair perfectly. I took a strand which fell over her shoulders in my fingers, again. It was soft—like silk. Our eyes locked, and time froze. All of my nerve endings were at attention and took her in. Her flowery scent, her clear porcelain skin. I touched my knuckles lightly across her cheek—then the kitchen door opened.

I stepped away.

It was Diane. She called Skylar, and I grabbed the interruption and Darcie and called it a day.

"Daddy, can we stop at the burger stand and get a milkshake? I'm dying for ice cream." Darcie was buckled in the back seat.

I needed to get home, but I could use ice cream. I could still finish the laundry, get her washed up, and have an early night. I planned on being on the road early tomorrow morning—by at least seven. Carly's parents lived two hours away. It's not a long drive, but if we got there early enough, we could grab lunch; I could visit for a bit, then get home in time to relax and prepare for a few virtual meetings I had Monday morning.

"Sounds great, princess." I pulled onto the road and made the short drive to Burgers and More, a drive-in burger stand. "I want to stay in the car, though. We've got to get home."

Well, my perfect plans were short-lived. When we pulled into a spot to order, Lance was there eating with Johnny, a long-time friend of ours.

"Hi, princess," Lance said as he opened Darcie's door. "Want to eat at the table with me and Johnny?"

Darcie's face fell. I could see it through the mirror when I glanced back before taking our order. "I can't. Daddy said we need to get our milkshake and go straight home." She pushed her bottom lip out in a pout.

Great. Lance could never ignore that look on her face. I unbuckled. I knew when I lost.

"Nonsense." Lance leaned across her and undid her seatbelt. "Come on. Your daddy needs to relax a bit. It won't hurt if you stay for a while."

"Fine. We'll go for a bit." I finished our order and met Lance and Darcie at the table with Johnny. "You know we can't stay. We've got to eat and run."

"Whatever," Lance said.

"Yeah, whatever. I want a milkshake," Darcie said. She sat next to Johnny. "Hi, Johnny."

"Well, hello, beautiful. How was your day?" he asked her.

"It was amazing." Her eyes were wide with excitement, and she gave us a rundown on her day and all the fun she and the girls had playing and having a picnic. "The worst thing about our day was all the noise the grownups were making." She splayed her hands out to express herself. "They were playing a loud game and fighting over spoons. We didn't understand it." She shook her head and rolled her eyes.

We all chuckled at her dramatics and the food was placed in front of us. I had a shake only, as I'd just had a sandwich, and Darcie had a milkshake and fries. She loved fries and was quickly occupied with opening multiple ketchup packets.

"So, how's Lilly?" Johnny asked.

"She's doing okay," Lance answered.

Darcie was busy stirring her ketchup together with a fry then popped it in her mouth. "Madeline told me her daddy called and is moving to . . . somewhere far away and getting married." She sipped her shake. "Madeline also says she likes it here better because her mommy doesn't cry as much as she did before, and she seems happier."

I stared at Darcie. It never ceased to amaze me what she understood.

"Well, maybe I should call her and ask her to dinner and a movie," Johnny said. "Would that be okay with you?" He made eye contact with Lance.

Lance looked at him hard for a moment and shrugged. "Not for me to say. She's an adult."

I stopped eating. "Didn't you ask her out in high school, and she totally dumped your ass?"

"Daddy, don't say naughty words. You owe me money." Darcie pointed a French fry at me.

And there went another dollar. "Sorry, princess."

"It's okay," she said as she popped another fry in her mouth. "You can pay me when we get home."

I stared hard at her and she flashed me a toothy grin.

I shook my head. That girl has me so wrapped around her pinky finger, I'm in trouble. I turned back to Johnny. "I think you'll be wasting your time. Lilly isn't ready to get back into a relationship." My voice came out much more irritated than I anticipated.

Lance's brow shot up. "You suddenly know an awful lot about my sister."

I shrugged. "Our daughters are friends. She cleans my house. We've spent some time together." If I was trying to lie low about Lilly, I was failing miserably, but I couldn't help it. The thought of her going out with Johnny . . .yeah, that wasn't going to happen.

Johnny jumped in. "I'm not quite the football dork now, and you never know. She could be ready to go out with someone. It's not like I'm asking her to marry me."

"Yeah, chill, bro. Lilly doesn't need us to protect her anymore. She's a grown woman," Lance said.

My heart pumped hard, and I clenched my teeth. *Slow your roll, dude, and calm your ass down.*

CHAPTER 15

LILLY

I dropped Madeline off at Mother's Day Out. Rose was going to pick the girls up and take them both to her house for a bit this afternoon. I had so much I needed to focus on, and extra time to run some errands, child-free, would be a treat. Well, it would be once I finished the task in front of me—cleaning Jamison's.

My insides were doing all types of calisthenics the closer I got to his house. It was like they were at gymnastics with the girls. *It's just Jamison, and he won't even be home. Get ahold of yourself, Lilly.*

I pulled into his driveway and let myself into the garage, then froze. His car was there.

He shouldn't be home.

Tuesdays were his days to work at the office and out of the house. This was one of the reasons we chose Tuesdays, and with how crazy my thoughts had been lately about him—about us—I had been looking forward to his empty house and not seeing him.

Stop this childish swooning and focus on your job, not on irrational possibilities with the one person who has to be off limits.

I entered his kitchen as quietly as possible. It was empty. Good.

I placed my cleaning supply bucket on the counter and heard the pitter-patter of paws on wood—okay, it was more like a clump-clump of paws on wood—and was greeted by Becca dancing and prancing in a circle, her tongue hanging from her mouth. "Hey there, Becca." I gave her the anticipated rubs and pets, and of course, the desired dog biscuit from the container on the counter, then let her out into the backyard. She gratefully bounded through the door and out to the grass.

I laughed out loud as I walked into the living room. I liked to do a once over to see how much needed to be done before I jumped right in. "Hello, Jamison?" I called. I didn't want him to think I was an intruder. "It's me, Lilly."

Footsteps thumped quickly down the stairs. "Hey, Lilly-Pad." His smile met his eyes, those gorgeous blue eyes and his hair was perfectly styled.

He wore khakis and a light blue polo shirt with his company's logo, which made his eyes pop even more. That and the fact that his polo and pants hugged all his muscles perfectly caused my insides to flop around like a pile of fish lying on the bank. I forgot what I came in the living room to do.

I forced a cough. I didn't want him to know the spell he had on me. "Hey," I said. "I didn't expect you home today."

"I know, but I've been swamped with a client and don't have the time to drive into Nashville. That's almost two hours round trip wasted, and I just got off a much more constructive virtual meeting."

"Okay, I'll work quietly so I don't bother you. Maybe I'll skip your office."

He shrugged and walked to the kitchen. "Fine. Do whatever you want."

I followed and checked out his ass. *Do whatever I want? What I want to do is see if you are still as good in bed as you were in your twenties.* I choked on the thought.

Jamison turned. "You okay?"

I couldn't talk yet, just nodded and grabbed a quick sip of water. Since I was there, I got to work to get my mind off Jamison and how much I wanted to throw him on the couch and have my way with him.

I filled the dishwasher with the few dishes in the sink and counter. My entire body was totally aware of him nearby. I was so glad he couldn't read my thoughts.

As I sprayed and wiped the counter, I couldn't shake the feeling of his eyes on me. Following me. I pulled my shoulders back and turned carefully. *Stay cool and keep your eyes on his.* I leaned my hands on the counter behind me. "What?"

He drank from a bottle of water, and damn—he looked hot as hell. When he lowered the bottle, his blue eyes sparkled. "How long do you think it will take for you to clean my house?"

"Last week I think it was about four hours, but it shouldn't take as long this week." I paused and got caught in his gaze.

I'd seen that look before. The glitter of mischief in those eyes. The sly grin frozen on his face. Yeah—I'd seen it before—it was the same look that appeared on his face when we were hiding our relationship. The adrenaline of possibly getting caught caused that gleam. "Why?" I asked with reservation.

He shook his head, and the left side of his lips ticked up a fraction. "No reason." He put his water bottle on the counter. "I've got a call to be on. Don't leave without saying bye." He winked and strutted away.

Shit. I Breathed out a long heavy breath. *What am I getting myself into? Just get to work. Cleaning will take your mind off him.* I put my AirPods in my ears and turned the music on.

Cleaning relaxed me. It was the only thing I could control in my marriage. Having a clean and organized house gave me pride, and Anthony never hesitated to brag about it to his friends. Well, sort of brag. He often said things like, "One thing my wife does well is keep the house. She may not have done well at college, but she sure knows where she belongs."

Yeah, he was a dick.

I stopped steam mopping the floor. Usually thinking about him gave me a queasy feeling in my gut. I searched and searched, waited and waited, but . . . nothing. "Good."

I shrugged and got back to cleaning. I'd only been home a couple weeks, but Anthony no longer had a hold on me. It's about time. Out of sight, out of mind was so true.

I cleaned with a new pride. My own cleaning business was what I chose to do. I was my own boss and didn't have to worry about a company letting me go. I was in charge of my future for the first time in a decade.

My favorite song came on, and I sang and finished the kitchen and moved on to the dining room and living room. I got lost in cleaning and didn't realize how quickly I was going.

Up in Darcie's room, I sang along to a Taylor Swift song at the top of my lungs. I shook my hips and waved my hands in the air. It was a dance Maddy and I always did together—yes, my daughter was a Swifty—I spun in a circle and froze.

Jamison was there in the doorway, smiling wide.

"Shit." My hands flew to my chest to try to calm my frantic heart. I turned off the music and took the AirPods from my ears. "You scared the hell out of me."

"Well, you were entertaining the hell out of me," he said with a chuckle. "What kind of dance were you doing, and what song were you dancing to?"

I rolled my eyes. "Just a dance Maddy made up to our favorite song." I gathered the cleaning supplies from the bathroom and walked to the door. Since I wasn't going to clean his office, all I had to do was dry mop the hallway and the steps on my way down and I'd be finished for the day.

But he didn't move.

He remained against the door jamb, blocking my way.

I glared at his neck as it was directly at eye level, and I refused to glance up any further. His neck was tanned and muscular. I swallowed hard.

My eyes drifted up to his chin, covered in a day or two's growth of whiskers. I passed over his lips quickly. I couldn't allow myself to spend time staring at those soft bits of deliciousness.

My eyes found his, and a smile ticked up the corners of those luscious lips I definitely was *not* thinking about.

"You still know how to move those hips, Lilly-Pad." His voice was deep and husky.

I was frozen and lost in his gaze. My stomach warmed and the space between my thighs started to tingle. *Damn, I'm swooning again.*

Without any warning, he hooked a hand behind my neck and smashed his lips to mine.

I whimpered in surprise as his arm wrapped around my waist and pulled me tightly against him. I dropped the bucket and Swiffer, letting them clatter to the floor, but the noise didn't matter.

His tongue pushed its way to mine, and my insides melted. I wrapped my arms around his neck. I needed to hold on to something because I could feel myself drowning once again in all things Jamison.

His kiss was as sweet and tender as before, but there was something else. Desire? Maybe...experience?

Experience which came with age and maturity. Knowing what he wanted.

The scent of him—a mixture of the outdoors and spice—filled my senses. Heat grew inside me, and I whimpered again as the hand cupping my neck tangled itself in my hair and held me tight.

I was hungry for him—starving for him—and it seemed like he felt the same way. I took a breath when his lips finally left mine, but he wasn't finished. He brushed his lips against my chin and, dragged his tongue along the line of my jaw, nipping at my earlobe before trailing kisses down my neck.

Good Lord. He remembered that sensitive area behind my ear, returning his lips to kiss and nibble there again. I wriggled against him, but he wasn't letting go. His hand left my hair and came around to fondle my breast. My shirt was thin, and it wasn't hard for him to find my nipple, pushed tight against my shirt. He brushed against it and circled his finger around it.

It was so sensitive, and my body was on fire. "Jamison," I breathed.

Somehow, I got out into the hallway. He pushed me against the wall and held my arms above my head. His kisses trailed down my neck and to my cleavage. Fire erupted across my skin from his touch. Finally, he broke away and brushed my hair from my face. We were both breathing hard.

"God, Lilly, I want you so much." His blue eyes softened.

It was the look I remembered from long ago.

My heart slowed, and skipped a few beats. "Jamison." I didn't know what to say. I wanted him. I'd always wanted him. I never stopped. But I couldn't figure out what was going on. Where these feelings came from.

I released my hands from his grasp and brushed them across his shoulders and to his chest. "Aren't you supposed to be working?" was all I could think to say. If he had to get back to work, it would be a good reason to stop whatever this was.

But he shook his head and stepped back and put a small bit of space between us. His hands brushed down my arms, and his fingers linked with mine. "No, it's my lunch break. I have at least an hour, maybe more."

He didn't take his eyes off mine but tugged on my hands.

"Please, Lilly?" He gestured with a nod of his head toward his room. "I've thought of you so much since the day you walked back into my life. Feelings woke up inside me when I hugged you, and they haven't gone away. I want to feel you, touch you. It's been too long."

I think my heart stopped. His soft gaze was filled with desire. He tugged again, and I did the only thing I could.

I followed.

CHAPTER 16

JAMISON

When I walked past Darcie's door and saw Lilly dancing and shaking her hips, all the feelings I'd pushed deep down and struggled to keep inside since our kiss in her kitchen rushed to the surface.

I didn't think—I just acted. As soon as my lips locked onto hers, all the blood in my system rushed south. I couldn't think of anything else. Kissing her, feeling her, tasting her, only made me want her—right now.

As soon as we were in my room, I pushed her against the door and let go of her hands. I brushed my fingertips along her hips and up her sides. My heart thudded in my chest, and our gazes held. She giggled and squirmed away from my touch. "Still ticklish." My voice came out in a thick whisper. "Some things never change."

"No, they don't." Her breathless reply was overwhelmingly sexy. And when she licked her bottom lip and sucked it in between her teeth, that was it.

I shucked her shirt over her head and took in her body. "Damn, Lilly, you're more beautiful than I remember."

She shook her head as a shy smile formed on her lips.

"What?" I asked as I closed the gap between us and pressed her warm body against mine.

"It's been a long time since I was told that by a man."

"That's because the person you were married to wasn't a man." I closed my mouth over hers, and kissed her. Her body melted like butter against the door, her hands linking behind my neck.

My cock throbbed with need. "You have the same effect on me today as you did all those years ago," I whispered against her mouth.

"I can tell." She rubbed her thigh against the bulge in my pants. "What are we going to do about it?"

I couldn't hold back any longer. I forced my hands under the elastic of her yoga pants and pushed them to the floor. My hands grasped her soft, warm ass.

She pulled away from my kiss, her gaze was filled with flames of desire and need. She pulled my shirt over my head and leaned in to place a soft kiss on my chest.

I sucked in a breath as she unbuttoned my pants. I helped her slide them down and I stepped out of them, then grasped her around the waist and lifted her up as she wrapped her legs around me. I carried her to my bed and laid her down gently.

The sexiest moan came from her throat as I paused over her to devour the sight of her naked body in my bed. She wasn't twenty any longer. She was a woman, a mother, and every part of her body was a damn sexy turn-on. I stroked the warm velvety skin of her inner thighs. They were soft and warm.

Goosebumps rose on her skin, and she shuddered under my touch.

I felt the wetness between her legs and knew she wanted this every bit as much as I did. I pushed my fingers slowly inside her opening and felt her constrict around me.

She whimpered.

"God, that sound is so sexy." I'd forgotten about the sounds she made until now, her whimpers and moans, which always did me in. I focused on her expression as I withdrew my fingers from inside her, then gently slid them in again. Her eyes squeezed shut, and another whimper of elation escaped her lips. I kissed those lips softly, then trailed my kisses down her neck to her collarbone and finally to her breasts.

She gasped.

I lingered there, enjoying the taste of her nipple, tracing the outline with my tongue.

With a moan, she wrapped her legs around my waist, grasped my cock, and rubbed her thumb over the tip. I pulled in a breath and didn't think I'd be able to last much longer.

"Jamison." She leaned up and kissed me, and my heart raced as the need that was building throughout my body threatened to engulf me. She guided me to her opening, and I entered. We found a rhythm, slow and relaxed.

I opened my eyes and watched as she leaned her head back, arched her hips, and took me deeper inside her. Her face, filled with pleasure, was breathtaking.

I kissed her lips and pushed all the way into her. She wrapped her arms around my neck, making that small whimpering sound that undoes me every time, and my moan followed. God, she felt good.

I brushed hair from her face as I thrust into her, and she tightened her legs around my waist, looking up at me. We finished together, gazing into each other's eyes.

I was breathless, and my heart thumped madly against my chest as I leaned in and kissed her sweet, warm lips.

Everything about this felt right and perfect.

Like I was finally home.

CHAPTER 17

JAMISON

Lilly's head lay on my chest and our legs laced together like a puzzle. We fit together perfectly. I held her close and kissed the top of her head.

Then it hit me.

I just had sex with my best friend's sister . . . *again*.

But lying here with Lilly after sex felt both comfortable and familiar. We were both older now, and—hopefully—wiser after what we'd been through in our marriages, and both having to navigate single parenthood.

"Hey," Lilly said. "You good?" She leaned up on an elbow, her hand tracing circles on my chest, just like she used to. It was as if years had never passed and we'd picked up right where we'd left off.

I kissed her and lingered on her lips. There was nothing I wanted more than to stay cuddled with her for the rest of the day, but I was pretty sure my lunch hour was over. "I have to find my phone and check the time," I said quietly.

She placed a kiss on my chest, and I pushed off the bed.

I found my phone in the pocket of my jeans, where I stepped out of them and checked the time. Yep, as I figured, lunch was over.

"I gotta get back to work." I turned, and my breath caught in my chest. Lilly looked like a goddess lying under my sheets, the tops of her breasts exposed and her arm draped above her head on the pillow. "You are beautiful. Thank you."

Her smile lit up her face. "For what?" she asked as she sat up, the sheet held close to her body.

"For giving me the best lunch break ever." I leaned over and cupped her face in my hands. "I can't explain what's going on here." I kissed her gently, softly. I needed her to understand that even though this was crazy and unexpected, I didn't regret any of it. "But I loved every second of it." I searched her brown eyes for any traces of doubt.

But they glittered and matched the smile on her face. "I did, too," she said as she kissed me back. My heart stuttered, then relaxed. I brushed my hand through her hair and enjoyed the kiss, savoring her taste. When she pulled away, everything seemed different, complete.

"Lilly, I can't tell you how glad I am that you came home. This was so unexpected. Thank you."

"You already thanked me, and I don't understand what else you can be thanking me for."

My gaze held hers. "For still wanting me after all these years." I didn't realize until this moment how true those words were. I was so glad she still wanted me. After over a decade apart, we fit together like we were meant to be.

"Oh, Jamison..." she whispered.

I gave her a quick kiss cutting off her words. "I've got to get back to work." I said as I reluctantly stood and got dressed. "But you just made this day so much better."

"I'm glad," she said with a seductive smile as she pulled on her panties and hooked her bra.

I was completely captivated by her and watched as she finished getting dressed.

When she turned around, her teasing, sexy smile was back. "Like what you see?" She raised her brow, and teased me. "Maybe you'll think of me during your boring meetings." She wrapped her arms around my neck, stood on her toes, and gave me a hard kiss I wouldn't soon forget. "I'll talk to you later," she whispered as she left the room.

I listened for her light footsteps on the stairs, then walked back into my office. I sat at my desk and set about getting my mind back on work so I could get this day over with.

I froze as a thought slammed into my brain.

I had sex with Lilly. And I didn't use a condom. "Shit."

I leaned heavily against my desk. I wasn't worried about diseases. I hadn't had sex in two years—two long and horribly lonely years—so I knew I was clean. Surely she was too. No, I knew she was clean.

But still. If this was going to be something that happened again, I had to be prepared. Hell, I hadn't bought condoms in forever. Who knew I'd be thirty-six and needing to worry about having safe sex? So much for one marriage to last a lifetime.

My phone vibrated on my desk—a text from Lance.

LANCE: HEY. WHAT DO YOU SAY WE GET TO-GETHER TONIGHT? MEET ME AT JERRY'S

Fuck. How could I be around him and act like I didn't have sex with his little sister? Yes, decades ago I did it plenty, but I was different then.

I leaned into my hands and rubbed them hard into my eyes. I wasn't in the mood to deal with Lance and his lectures about needing to get with a woman. It was his typical rant. Maybe I could get out of it.

DUDE, I'M TIRED. I DON'T FEEL LIKE GOING OUT.

LANCE: BULLSHIT. YOU STAY IN TOO MUCH. YOU NEED TO TAKE ADVANTAGE OF BEING CHILD-FREE.

YEAH, I'M CHILD-FREE. THAT'S ALSO WHY I WANT TO STAY HOME AND ENJOY MY QUIET, CLEAN HOUSE AND WATCH SOMETHING ADULT-LIKE ON TELEVISION. NO PRINCESSES NECESSARY.

LANCE: THAT'S FUCKING LAME.

SO I SHOULD START TAKING ADVICE FROM A SINGLE GUY?

LANCE: DON'T FORGET, YOU'RE SINGLE, TOO, AND YOU'LL NEVER MEET ANYONE IF YOU DON'T GET OUT OF YOUR HOUSE. ANYWAY, WE'RE NOT GOING OUT TILL SEVEN, SO YOU HAVE PLENTY OF TIME TO RELAX IN YOUR QUIET AND CLEAN HOUSE.

Touché. Single I was, though highly interested in someone—someone I couldn't let him know about. But the "we" bothered me.

YOU SAID WE. WHO'S WE?

LANCE: DOESN'T MATTER. JUST DON'T BE LATE.

"Fuck." I had a choice. I could either do what he asked or find a new best friend.

I really contemplated the latter. But at a little past seven that night, I was there, parking next to Lance at Jerry's Pub. I wasn't even technically late. I figured I could give him a couple hours, leave by nine, and still get into bed by a decent time.

Lance was at a table for six with Robert Macintosh, a guy we've known forever, and Robert's fiancée, Melissa. Two other women sat with them whom I'd seen around town but didn't know. Lance had his arm around one of them.

Yep, it looked like I was stuck in a blind date, totally set up. *I really need to find a new best friend.* I puffed out a breath. *He has your best interests at heart. Relax a little.*

I slapped Lance on the back a little harder than necessary when I got to the table, but he didn't seem to notice.

"Jamison, buddy. You made it." He stood and patted my back in a man hug. "I ordered you a beer, and some appetizers are coming."

Sitting back down, Lance put his arm around the brunette again. "Jamison, this is Jayla, and her friend is Ella Raye. They both teach English at the high school."

I nodded as I greeted the women, then shook Robert's hand. All three girls sat next to each other around one side of the circular table, so thankfully, the only empty seat was between Lance and Robert. I took it and found myself directly across from Ella Raye.

As we ate and drank, it quickly became obvious Lance and Jayla were interested in each other. This was strange to me. Before the dinner at Kaye's, I'd had no clue he was interested in anyone. Now, here he was, all up into Jayla, and she was hanging all over him. They were acting like college kids, and it made me realize I was over the basic dating rituals.

"Have y'all noticed the state banner at the school?" Lance asked the women as he threw his arm over my shoulder. "Jamison here threw for a state record that year. It still holds today. Between his amazing arm and my receiving skills, we were an unstoppable combo."

"You do realize that was almost twenty years ago, right?" I asked him.

"Yeah, well, if you would've avoided injury in college, I might be able to brag on your professional career."

"You have to excuse Lance," I said to the girls. "High school was the pinnacle of his success. That's why he's back there teaching. He's trying to relive his youth."

The conversation went on like this, Lance and I ragging on each other like always. Finally, all three women went to the restroom together.

"So," Lance said. "What do you think?"

"About?" I tried to act like I had no clue he was trying to fix me up and took a sip of my beer.

"Bullshit, bro. You know about what. Ella Raye is perfect for you. She's fun, pretty, intelligent, and can hold her own when talking about football." Lance held his hand out, palm up. "Well?"

I held his gaze but didn't give him the satisfaction of an answer.

"Lance, don't you see he's not interested?" Robert said.

"Bullshit. He's been into the conversation, right?" He turned to me.

"Yeah, I've been into the conversation. She's fun." I couldn't lie. She was.

"See," Lance said to Robert. "Told you he'd like her." He had a goofy grin on his face.

"Whoa. Slow down. Yes, she's nice, but *like* her? I don't *know* her."

"You're overthinking things," Lance said. "I thought we could go out after the jamboree. Not a big deal. It will give you a chance to get to know her better. What do you say?" Lance sat up tall. "Jamison, you haven't gone out with anyone in . . ." He looked off in the distance. "Fuck, a long time. You need to get back out there." He narrowed his eyes. "Or do you have someone you're interested in? If you do, and you're keeping her a secret, fess up, and I'll lay off. That is, of course, if I approve."

When I didn't answer right away, his eyes widened, and he made a pouty face.

Damn, I hated it when he did that. Since we were kids, he had a way of making me give in. Whenever he wanted us to do something we weren't supposed to, or that one time he wanted me to go on a double date so the girl he liked would go out with him, I couldn't say no. But I sure as hell was going to try this time.

My gaze met his. "Yeah, there's someone I'm interested in."

"What?" His brows went up. "Who?"

I shook my head. "Too early to share. But trust me, she's amazing."

"Why don't I know about this?"

I shrugged and sipped my beer.

"Is it serious? Are you an item?"

I did what I had to do—told the truth. "No. We aren't an item. Yet."

He slapped his hand on the table as I caught a glimpse of the women coming back. "Good," he answered quietly. "Then you have no reason to not give Ella Raye at least a try."

I smiled as the girls joined us. I guess he was right. I didn't have a good reason to not go out with Ella Raye. Well, I did have a good reason. Hell, who was I kidding? I had a perfect reason to not go out with her. But if I pushed it more, he would question me.

I was grateful when the discussion change to Saturday's jamboree. I could always talk football, and since I was a volunteer coach for the offense, I had plenty to add.

"We could all go together, you know," Ella Raye said, her words rushing out. She smiled at me across the table.

"What a great idea," Jayla agreed. "I don't know much about football, but I enjoy watching." She glanced at Lance.

"Jamison and I will be there with the team, but we can get together after."

"You know we'll be there," Melissa said, her hand resting on Robert's atop the table.

All eyes turned to me.

Unless I wanted to spew out something like, I'd love to, but I'm sort of interested in your sister—so interested I just had sex with her earlier today, and I hope to again; I had no reason to not agree.

"I'll see, but I can't make any promises." My smile didn't meet my eyes, but no one noticed.

CHAPTER 18

LILLY

"I totally forgot about this special practice for the jamboree Saturday. I'm glad you called me," I said to Rose. She and I were outside the gymnastics studio Wednesday night, enjoying the surprisingly mild weather for late July in Tennessee.

"I noticed you were out of sorts last night on the phone, and you seem preoccupied now. What's up?" Rose asked.

I sighed. "Between my new feelings for Jamison confusing me, work, and mom duties, I'm more overwhelmed than I have been in a long time, and I didn't get much sleep last night."

"I bet you didn't." Rose chided.

I shook my head. "No, it's not just Jamison, though he's a big part of it. I'm not sure what's going on between us. Is it real, or just residual feelings from our past?" I sighed. "I don't know, but I also don't think I'm ready for a relationship." I continued before she could comment. "I need to focus on me and Maddy. I'm missing her. I haven't been away from her so much before, and now, with all the houses and businesses I'm cleaning, she's been spending so much time with someone else."

"Come on. It's not really someone else. It's her grandmother at the salon, whom she absolutely adores, or the Mother's Day Out program at the church, which has been so good for her."

"You're right." I rubbed my hands over my face. "I know you're right. It doesn't mean it's easy to get used to. I've only been back a couple weeks, and things have changed so much for both of us."

"Well, see it as preparing you for when Madeline starts kindergarten in a couple weeks. These are baby steps to prepare your heart and mind. And I'm not sure what's going on with you and Jamison either, but enjoy it." She looked away for a second and shrugged. "Would it be so bad if you used him to distract you a bit?"

"It wouldn't be too horrible, a diversion in the amazing form of Jamison—yeah, that wouldn't be horrible at all."

Rose smirked. "Well, I hope you're ready for said diversion."

I followed her gaze as a Ford F-150 pulled into the parking lot, and butterflies took flight in my stomach.

When Jamison stepped out of the truck, I swear time stopped. He was still in his work khakis and polo, and damn he looked just as delicious as he was yesterday. I chewed on my lips, hoping I wouldn't drool at the sight of him.

Darcie hopped across the parking lot toward us. "Hi, Lilly and Rose. Gosh, your names are so pretty. Both are my favorite flowers. I wish my name was a flower," Darcie gushed. As soon as she hit the sidewalk in front of the studio, she pulled her hand free from Jamison and asked, "Can I go in and see the girls, Daddy?"

Jamison's laugh was deep and smooth, like a well-barreled whiskey, and his smile was wide. "Of course, princess."

I thought nothing could be hotter than mid-thirties Jamison naked on top of me, but I was so wrong. The sweet smile he gave his daughter, filled with love and admiration—that was so much sexier and hotter that it caused my ovaries to jump into overdrive. I swear I could feel them release a dozen or more eggs. I placed my hand over my stomach. *Calm down, girls.*

"I'll come with you," Rose said, "and make sure the girls are on the floor for class." She wiggled her brows as she left.

Jamison's gaze caught mine, and my palms became sweaty. I looked away and tucked my hands in the back pockets of my jean shorts.

"Are you okay?" he asked. "You look uncomfortable."

God, I have to calm down. It felt like I was going to burst into tears.

"Lilly," he lightly touched my arm. "Seriously, what's wrong?"

"I don't know." I sighed heavily and met his gaze. "What are we doing, Jamison?" I gestured between us. "What is this?"

Parents were entering the gym, and I didn't want this to become Orlinda Valley news, so we walked around to the side of the building, away from prying ears and eyes.

"Lilly." He held my arms, and I froze.

His touch sent a shock through me.

"I don't know what this is," he said. "I. Don't. Know." He turned my face toward him.

My heart pounded in my chest.

His eyes looked confused, and his brow wrinkled with concern.

Feelings churned in my gut like a hurricane in the ocean. I couldn't make sense of anything, but I had to try. "I don't either, Jamison. Being with you is so easy, but I don't know if it's real or just residual feelings from long ago." God, I felt like a college kid again trying to keep my heart from breaking.

"Do you need time?" he asked, "because, honestly, I don't. I know this is what I want, which surprises me. Until you returned, I didn't think I had any room for anyone in my heart but Darcie. Your brother did something the other night that opened my eyes and made me realize how much I feel for you."

"What are you talking about? What does Lance have to do with any of this, with us?"

"Well, we were at Jerry's Pub, and he invited two women he works with, along with Robert and his fiancée. Seems as if we are all getting together after the jamboree Saturday. Not really my plan, but . . ."

My head snapped toward him. "Oh, so it's a date?" My heart constricted in my chest.

"No, it's not a date, and I'd gladly cancel it if I had something else to do after the jamboree." His eyes held mine.

I bit on my lips to keep them from crashing against his. "You do what you want." I shrugged. "I need time to focus on Maddy, anyway. But I could use a friend." *Are you crazy Lilly? Friends with Jamison?* I would've slapped myself if that wouldn't draw attention.

He sighed. "Look, I'm not interested in anyone but you, but I'm not going to pressure you into anything. So, if that's what you want, *friend,* let's get inside and watch our girls."

Yeah, I was going crazy. I'd just gotten a chance to be with Jamison again, and I put us in the friend zone. If he was just a friend, I wouldn't get a tingling feeling between my legs when my *friend* led me through the door with his hand on my lower back. What was I thinking?

As soon as we entered the gym, Rose walked up to us and Jamison took his hand off my back. Good thing, too. If the tingling hadn't stopped, I might have had to pull him out of the gym and have Rose take all the girls home—and so much for the friend zone.

"So, I was just pulled into a very strange conversation," Rose said.

My brows popped, and I turned my attention from Jamison's presence to Rose.

"Stephanie and Nora asked me an interesting question." She glanced between the two of us. "Stephanie asked if there was anything going on between you two. She thought you both looked real cozy outside by yourself, deep in conversation, and Nora agreed. She asked if you were a couple." She paused and searched our faces for clues.

Of course, Stephanie and Nora would ask. Those two have been the nosy busybodies of Orlinda Valley since high school. I might have been gone for a few years, but I'd heard through Kristy and Rose that Stephanie had just gone through her second divorce, and Nora's husband was cheating on her—again. I'd been in her shoes, and should have felt bad for her, but with all the issues she had caused me over the years, it was hard to move on.

Rose continued. "I told her no. You're just friends who grew up together. But then with what I've learned lately . . ." She paused, and I wasn't sure if she was finished or just hoped we would give in and tell her the entire sordid tale.

Well, she wasn't getting either. "Sorry to disappoint. We've got nothing to tell." I stepped away from Jamison and found a seat on the front bench of the stands and forced my attention toward Maddy and the girls on the floor.

Rose sat with me, but I ignored the pang in my chest when Jamison stood by Gary, far from us. "Wow. She's really learned a lot the past two weeks." I said as I watched my daughter on the floor. Yes, I tried to change the subject and get my mind off the distance between Jamison and me—both literally and figuratively—yet it wasn't a lie. I was very impressed with how Maddy had caught on with the tumbling and learned the dance with the rest of them.

I continued to comment on the floor routines the girls were doing and tried my best to ignore Rose. She kept shooting me odd glances.

My time was split between watching Madeline on the floor and Jamison across the room, especially when Nora and Stephanie sauntered up beside him and Gary. The women's laughter traveled across the gym a couple times, and each time, my insides seethed with disgust.

"You know, you could put that show over there to a simple end. Jamison wants you, not either of them," Rose said.

I shot her a look that I hoped would shut her up, but instead, it made her giggle.

The class was finally over, and it couldn't have ended soon enough. I needed to get out of there. Okay, I wanted to get out of there.

"I'll talk to you later, Rose," I said as soon as the girls were off the floor. "Come on. We've got to go," I told Madeline, ignoring her complaints about wanting to get ice cream with everyone. I needed to get out of there before Jamison came over to us. I wasn't running from him, I was just guarding my heart and putting some distance between us until I figured out what it was I wanted.

Chapter 19

LILLY

There was nothing like the feeling of hard work and making money. I cleaned two houses today, a long day that started early—seven o'clock—and it was four-thirty by the time I pulled in to Shear Perfection. I needed a trim, and Madeline had been here with my mom all day.

I'd called a couple times to check on her, and she was having a blast. At lunchtime, she went on and on about all the things which had already filled her day. She took it upon herself to be the "sweeper of hair" for the day and fell in love with the wall vacuum. She now thought every house needed one. It seemed that sweeping hair into a hole in the wall, then pushing a button so the vacuum sucked the hair into a hidden container was the coolest thing ever.

I entered the salon and was greeted with Madeline's sweet laugh over the hum and buzz of all the hair dryers and voices.

I hugged my mom and Diane and found Madeline sitting at a pedicure station as Summer pampered her toes.

"Hi, Mommy."

"Hey, you. Your toes look so pretty." I gave her a kiss on her head and sat in the empty seat next to her. Her nails were a light blue—her favorite color. "Hi, Summer. Is she being good?" I knew Summer through Kora. She was one of her best friends, but I didn't talk to her often.

"She is. Once I'm done with her toes, we're going to do the same color on her fingernails. She'll be the prettiest little cheerleader on the field Saturday."

Maddy gave me a bright smile.

"Well, then I'll let you continue your mani, pedi, and I'll be over with the old ladies." I gave Madeline another kiss on her head.

"Old ladies, huh?" Diane glanced at me as she brushed her customer's hair.

I shrugged. "Y'all are older than me."

My mother laughed. "I hope so, girly. I did give birth to you. It would look strange otherwise."

Dottie Carlise, the pastor's wife at the Orlinda Valley Methodist Church laughed and lifted her hand to her hair as she peered into a mirror. "Looks wonderful, Kaye, as usual." She stood. "Lilly, it's so good to see you home."

I gave her a hug. I had known Mrs. Carlise since high school when her husband came to pastor the church. "Mrs. Carlise, it's great to be home."

"And your daughter is absolutely precious. She was sitting at the front desk when I got here and welcomed me to Shear Perfection and lead me to Kaye's chair." She placed her hand over her heart. "Then she asked me if she could get me a Coke or a water because she wasn't allowed to pour coffee. She is so darn adorable."

I smiled wide. Yes, I was having a proud momma moment. "Thank you, Mrs. Carlise." I grabbed the broom and started to sweep up the floor as Mrs. Carlise left.

"My Lanta, y'all will never believe what I heard today." Tonya hurried through the door of Shear Perfection, followed close behind by Ruth.

I swept the hair into the wall vacuum and turned around.

"Well, looky here. Just who we need to fill us in on all the details they're hiding from us." Tonya crossed her arms and stood with her brows up, staring at me.

What is Tonya talking about now? I leaned on the broom, lifted my brows, cocked my head, and stared right back. I had no idea where this was going, and I wasn't sure I wanted to find out. My mom put her arm around my shoulders, and her forehead creased.

"Well, since you're not spilling anything, Lilly, I will just have to fill everyone in on what *I* heard," Tonya said.

"Like we'd ever expect anything less," Summer interjected from the manicure station. "But be advised, there are some ears that need only G-rated information." She pointed at Madeline.

"Hi, Madeline, sweety," Tonya said as she went over and gave her a kiss on the head.

"Hi, Mrs. Tonya. I'm getting my nails pretty for Saturday." She wiggled her nails toward Tonya's face.

"They are so pretty," she said to Madeline, then turned to Summer. "Don't mess them up. She needs to look perfect."

"Read between the lines, Tonya." Summer held up three fingers.

Tonya waved her off and joined Diane and Kaye again. "Anyway, I was eating lunch at the pharmacy a little bit ago."

"Umm, it's after four, so it's more like an early dinner. Who were you dining with?" Diane asked.

Tonya waved her hand in the air. "Whatever, those details don't matter. But John's brother . . ."

"Mayor John Reynolds?" Kaye asked.

"Yes," Tonya replied, dragging out the *s* and lifting her brow.

"I thought you weren't dating him anymore," Diane added.

"It wasn't a date. It was dinner. Stop getting me off the subject. There are more important people to talk about here." Tonya rolled her eyes. "Anyway, John's brother's wife, Darla, stopped by and told me that she heard from Margie Prant that Phoebe Cross told her that her daughter said that *my* Jamison and *your* darling Lilly were looking really friendly at the gymnastics gym last night."

My eyes went wide. Phoebe Cross, Nora's mother. I huffed out a breath. "Mrs. Cross is as big of a pain in the ass as her daughter."

"Lilly." My mother tilted her head, and her brows lifted.

"Hey, Mommy," Madeline's voice rose from the back of the salon. "Why are you saying those words? Those aren't nice words."

"No, they're not." Tonya said with her hand over her heart. "Maddy, did you know Darcie gets one dollar when her daddy says those words?" She made eye contact with Madeline.

"Tonya," I hissed.

"Ooh, Mommy. Give me a dollar."

And just like that, I'd be broke.

"You do need to show respect for your elders, Lilly. You were taught better." My mother fixed her gaze on me.

Seriously? I hated that look, her don't be rude face. "Mother, I'm a grown woman and can call out the truth when I see it, and Mrs. Cross is as rude and annoying as Nora."

"Well, at least Nora comes by it honestly then, dear," Tonya agreed, "but why would she have told her mother anything about you and my handsome son if it wasn't true?"

"First off, keep your voice down. As we've noticed, my little girl has some good hearing," I said. I also had to slow down and get my thoughts together and my words straight. Until Jamison and I figured out what we were, we sure as hell didn't need our mothers and their friends trying to set us up. "Second, she said it because Jamison and I were talking about the girls outside the gym last night. And we do like each other, as a brother and sister would. As you know, I've known him since birth." I shook my head, stomach churning with irritation. "Anyway, Stephanie—Nora's best friend—has always had a crush on Jamison."

I thought I was doing a good job of convincing them so far, so I continued. "He's never been interested and add to that the fact he and I are close . . . it's called jealousy."

All four women glared at me—hard. Well, at least three of them did. Ruth sat at Diane's station and looked sorry she was in on this.

I gave her a small smile, then focused on the other three. I held my own. I knew these women. They were trying to make me crack. Give up my secrets. I'd been in this situation before, many times.

"She might be telling the truth," Diane said.

"Maybe," said Kaye. "But I'm not sure."

"Mom!" I couldn't believe my own mother didn't trust me. Well, she had a good reason, but still.

"You three need to give her some space. She just got home and went through a divorce."

"Thank you, Ruth." I gave her a hug.

"You're welcome." She pulled me back in and whispered. "Your secret's safe with me."

My eyes went wide, and I backed away.

She gave me a sly wink and walked into the kitchen.

What has Rose been telling her mother? I had no time to contemplate that. I'd have to talk to her later.

"Just because I think they would make the cutest couple, and I know Lilly had a crush on Jamison for years, doesn't mean there's anything there," Tonya said tapping her foot.

"What? Why do you think I ever had a crush on Jamison?"

"Bless your heart, dear, it's okay to not want to admit to something like that. But just know you'd have my blessing if you could ever get Jamison's heart moving forward." Tonya placed her hand on my shoulder, patted it lightly, and looked at me as if someone had died.

"I like Jamison," Madeline said as she skipped up to me, waving her nails in the air. "Mommy, I think we should have him and Darcie over for pizza. I need to show Darcie my nails." She wiggled them high in the air so I could see them better.

"They're very pretty, squirt." I held her hands and admired her light blue nails, then I kissed her knuckles. "Stay here. I'm going to pay Summer." I walked away from the women.

"I wasn't eavesdropping," Summer said when I got to her station. "But Tonya always has her nose in someone's business. Hold your own, and if you and Jamison are having a thing, keep it to yourself."

I handed her my card. "We aren't having a thing. I've known him my entire life, and now our girls are friends. We're hanging out so our girls can spend time together. That's all it is. Nothing else." She handed me back my card, and I put it into my wallet.

Summer nodded slowly. "I've known him forever also—remember I'm friends with Rowan and Kora. I also know he's kept to himself a lot since Carly's death. It's been just him and Darcie. Since you've been home, though, he seems different. So, yeah, keep telling yourself that, Lilly. Maybe one day you'll believe it."

Chapter 20

Jamison

"Hell, yeah. You can stop by anytime," I said aloud after I answered Lilly's text and pocketed my phone.

"Who can stop by, Daddy? And why did you say a bad word?" Darcie asked as she skipped into the kitchen with her hand out.

I really needed to watch my language. It seemed like she was always in listening range. "Lilly asked if it was okay if she and Madeline stopped by with pizza." I pulled a dollar out of my wallet and handed it over.

She grabbed it and jumped up and down, the smile on her face priceless. "Yay, Madeline's coming over."

I chuckled. "Do you get that excited when I come home?"

"Oh, please, Daddy. You're always home. I never get a chance to miss you." She gave me a hug. But I wasn't quite sure if her comment was a good thing or not.

"Well, why don't you run into the living room and straighten up, then check your room. I'm sure you girls will want to play after we eat."

"Yes, sir." She ran, or skipped, I'm not really sure what it was called, toward the living room, and Becca bounded after her, excited and ready for fun as usual.

I loaded the dishwasher, gave the counters a once-over with a paper towel and spray cleaner, and grabbed the small vacuum to get rid of Becca's dog hair. Lilly was just here two days ago. I didn't want her to think I couldn't keep my house clean at all.

Two days ago—Tuesday, and our talk last night.

I dropped my hands on the counter and shook my head. After last night, I wasn't sure what was going on between us or if she really only wanted to be friends, but I'd give her time and space if it's what she wanted. Memories of her soft skin and her body beneath mine filled my mind. I hung my head. *I had sex with Lilly.* My chest tightened in a knot, and it became hard to breathe. *The first person I've slept with since Carly.*

I couldn't decide what bothered me the most. Lilly not being Carly, Lilly needing time, or that she didn't want me as much as I wanted her.

My eyes stung as that last bit sank in—she didn't want me as much as I wanted her. My heart tore from my chest. "God, Carly, I'm sorry," I whispered. "It was supposed to be you and me against the world forever, but . . ." I dug my hands into my eyes to push the tears back. My answer scared the shit out of me, but I couldn't fall apart. Not now. Lilly would be here any minute.

"Shit." Guilt tore through my gut. I never thought I'd have feelings for anyone else. I never thought I'd have reason to.

A FaceTime notification interrupted my thoughts. It was Thursday night, so it would be Rowan. I wanted to ignore it but couldn't.

When he had a chance to call, I needed to take it, and his voice would help.

"Hey, bro." Rowan's face filled my screen, and a smile filled my face. My baby brother and I had always been close.

"Hey." I hoped my smile didn't seem fake and he couldn't see how red I was sure my eyes were. "You look good, little brother." His dark hair was cut in the high and tight style of the infantry, and he looked happy as usual. "It's good to see your face."

He didn't know how true that statement was. I'd told him about Lilly and me years ago. Lilly didn't know I told him, but I had to confide in someone, and he was the one I knew I could trust. He was the only one.

"I'd like to say the same thing about you, but I'm not sure that would be true. Talk to me, bro."

Damn, maybe I shouldn't have taken the call. I should have known I couldn't keep this from him. He knew me too well, but I could sure as hell try. I shook my head. "Nothing to talk about."

"Bullshit. Your eyes are red. You've been upset. You've never been able to hide shit from me."

That was the truth, and I'd never had a reason to. Rowan might have been the baby of the family, but he was always the laid back and focused one, totally opposite of Bryson's need to be loud and busy constantly. Rowan had followed in my footsteps when it came to football, and there was no better therapy than throwing the football and talking in the backyard.

I bit on my lips. *Should I tell him anything, nothing, or everything?* I decided on something, yet I'd keep it G-rated. "I'm just confused. That's all."

"About Lilly?" His eyes didn't move from the screen.

"Fuck," I breathed. "What do you know?" I stared right back.

"Not much, and I wasn't sure if there was anything, but you just confirmed it."

"Shit. Fuck." I looked around the doorframe and listened hard. I could hear Darcie making a little noise upstairs. Good, she didn't hear me. "Who've you been talking with?"

"Summer, of course. She told me she saw Lilly at Shear Perfection today, and Lilly didn't deny something was going on between you two. She didn't confirm it either, so thank you, bro."

I shook my head. Nothing else to do.

"Summer was right. Don't you dare tell her. Keep this between us. Please?" Yes, I begged.

He put his hand up. "Fine. Whatever the hell you want. But what's going on?"

"Look, it's complicated. *We* don't even know what's going on, but I can't deny I feel something for her."

"How does she feel?"

I shrugged. This wasn't the time to go into the conversation last night, and now she was coming over. It was difficult enough for me to comprehend. "It doesn't matter."

I heard Rowan sigh. "Jame, Look at the phone."

I looked at him.

He stared back and shook his head. "You feel guilty, don't you?"

"Damn, Rowan." I plopped my ass in a chair at the table, propped the phone against the small vase sitting in the center, and dropped my face in my hands.

"You don't need to feel guilty." His voice was softer. "Carly's gone, bro, and has been for over two years."

"It was two years, only two weeks ago." I looked into the camera. "It hasn't been long enough."

"Jamison, stop. You and Lilly had feelings for each other all those years ago. It didn't work. You both found other people." He put his palms up. "Maybe you both needed that time to grow up, and now's your time."

"Who are you, and what did you do with my little brother? When did you become a philosopher?"

"Just had time to do the same thing—grow up. Promise me, you'll try to be happy. You deserve it."

"God, now you sound like Bryson."

"Damn, he's not such a dumbass after all."

Those two never got along, and then Bryson started dating Darlene, and we found out the hard way that Rowan had always had a crush on her. That was the last straw in their struggling brother relationship; then all hell broke loose when our father died. "You two have got to get over yourselves. It's not fair to Mom."

"Whatever. It's not like Bryson and I ever got along."

There was a knock on the door, and Darcie came racing down the steps and let out a high-pitched scream.

"What the hell is she so excited about?"

"Her new BFF is here."

"Daddy, look! They're here. Oh, hi, Uncle Rowan. Meet my new friend Madeline." Darcie grabbed my phone from the table and pointed the screen at Madeline, and Lilly squatted next to her. Great. So much for this staying under wraps.

"Hey, Rowan," Lilly said.

"Hey, Lilly. Hey there, Madeline. Nice to meet you." I heard Rowan's voice across the room. I breathed in deep through my nose and took the pizza boxes from Lilly. She smiled at me, but I turned and placed the boxes on the stove. Just the sight of her made my blood race through my veins and heat my body through.

Darcie started to head off through the house with Madeline and my phone, but I grabbed it from her. "Time to eat. Say bye to your uncle, and both of you go sit down."

"Bye, Uncle Rowan." Darcie blew him a kiss, and Madeline waved.

I turned the phone to me. "Okay, bro. I gotta go."

"Yeah, I'm sure you do. Where's Lilly?" She came over next to me, and her presence filled me. Her vanilla and strawberry shampoo caused my boiling blood to pool in my crotch.

"Bye, Rowan," Lilly said as she leaned into me.

"Bye, Lilly." He chuckled. "You two kids be good." And he disconnected the call.

Her face scrunched up. "What did he mean by that?"

I gave a small shrug, made a quick adjustment, placed pizza on plates for the girls, and got bottles of water out of the fridge.

Once the girls were eating, I led Lilly into the dining room. We could eat there.

"You okay? If this was a bad night, all you had to do was say so." Lilly sat and took a bite of pizza.

It seemed as if all of this made sense to her. I wish it were that easy. "Rowan called and asked about us."

Her eyes went wide, and her chin fell to her chest. "How did he find out about *us*?"

"Did Summer say anything to you today?"

"Shoot." She put her pizza on the plate. "I'm sorry. I didn't say anything directly, but I went by the salon to pick up Maddy, and your mother came in and gave me the third degree. When I went to pay Summer, she told me she could tell there was something to all the talk around town."

"What talk around town? And why did my mother give you the third degree? About what?"

Lilly filled me in on the discussion at the salon and how she'd tried her best to keep the women in the dark. Summer, on the other hand, wasn't so easy to convince. "I guess she called Rowan?"

"Of course she did. Those two are worse than girls. They tell each other everything, and I let it slip that there is something."

"What?" She looked at me. "What did he say about it?" Her head tilted to the side.

"It wasn't hard for him to believe. I told him about us before. He knew about us back then."

"Seriously?" Her mouth dropped open.

"When he called, I was upset." I grabbed her hand, and she didn't pull away. "I've been thinking a lot about what you said last night, and you're right. You just got out of a marriage. I'm still getting over Carly, but I can't ignore what's between us."

She squeezed my hand and met my gaze. My heart was a mess of feelings, and I couldn't decide if it was good or not.

She said, "I know I didn't make much sense. I'm over Anthony. We never had a real marriage, and I don't even know if he ever truly loved me. You, on the other hand, had Carly, and you two were so good together." Her voice caught, and she pulled her hand from my grasp and picked at her pizza crust. "I didn't know her well. I just met her a couple times when you brought her home from college and then at your dad's funeral. And those times, I never paid her much attention because I was so jealous of her."

"What? Even all those years later at Dad's funeral?"

She nodded; her lips pursed. "Especially then. My marriage was in the garbage. Anthony and I hardly talked when he was home. I was just an ornament he could have on his arm for company events—when they were in the city." Her gaze went toward the ceiling, and a shadow crossed her eyes.

I tried hard to comprehend this. My father died over five years ago, and she was miserable back then?

Lance knew something was up. She was quiet and left without saying goodbye to everyone—me included.

She breathed out hard, and the shadow was gone, but another look filled her gaze—sadness? She breathed out a heavy breath. "I was with Rose and Kora in your mom's living room when Carly told them she was pregnant. No one else knew. I don't know what I was hoping, what I thought would happen between you and me, but I finally knew then that we were over, and it tore my heart to pieces." She laughed under her breath. "I should have known that way before then, but my marriage was shit, and I . . . It doesn't matter." She sighed.

"Lilly, I know I should have talked to you about my feelings for Carly, but I remember thinking if I ignored it, things would go back to normal with us. Then you met Anthony and seemed happy and in love. I'm sorry. For everything. For how I treated you. For how things ended with us. But I won't be sorry for Carly."

"I know." Her eyes glistened, and she met my gaze. Her voice thick. "I would never expect you to be sorry for your relationship with Carly." She covered her face with her hands, then laced them behind her neck. "We've both been through so much, and that's why I think we need to slow things down. I don't want us to mess things up and lose our friendship. I need to make sure these feelings between us are—I don't know—real? Not remnants from our past. But today I needed to come see you. I'm sorry. This is so confusing. I really need to figure out my shit."

God, I did, too. I wanted to figure this out, but I didn't have a chance to tell her because we got interrupted by two bubbly girls who wanted to watch *Moana*.

"I've got an idea," I said to the girls. "What do you think about having a sleepover and you two watching this movie upstairs in my bed?"

Madeline's eyes were wide. "Can I, Mommy?" And she pressed her hands together like she was praying and pushed out her bottom lip. She turned to Darcie, who mimicked her. There was no way Lilly would be able to resist those faces. Okay, *I* couldn't resist those faces. Lilly—maybe.

Lilly laughed. A sweet, bubbly laugh, which sent my blood roaring. "If Jamison doesn't mind, it's fine with me."

"Let's go get you two settled." I followed the two galloping girls. "Don't go anywhere. I want you here when I get back." I spoke in Lilly's ear and gave her a wink as I passed her. "I won't be long."

CHAPTER 21

LILLY

A rush of both excitement and confusion washed over me, leaving a warm tingling sensation in my stomach. When I thought of coming home, I never considered I'd start a relationship with Jamison. But here we were like we didn't have separate lives for the past decade.

I thought back to Tuesday afternoon. Being with him, in his bed. The feel of his body against mine. The pulse of him inside me. It was so familiar, yet totally new as well—then our discussion Wednesday.

My brother setting him up.

Stephanie still wanting him.

The crushing weight of jealousy caused my stomach to churn.

I sighed heavily. Was I ready for these feelings? For a relationship? I walked to the mantel and looked at the pictures sitting there. He had the same one we all had of our entire extended family at his father, Carl's, funeral. Next to it was a picture of his family: Tonya and Carl, his brothers, and Darlene and Carly. It was obvious by the smiles that filled their faces, everyone was happy. Everyone but Rowan. His smile didn't quite reach his eyes.

I heard Jamison's footsteps as he approached and felt his presence before he placed his hand gently on my back. "When was this picture taken?" I asked and held up the one of his family.

He took it from me and admired it, his face filled with both laughter and sadness. "That was the Christmas before my dad died."

"Rowan doesn't look happy," I said.

"No. He wasn't. He only came home because Mom practically begged him to. He hadn't been home for a Christmas in years." He shook his head. "Bryson and Rowan couldn't be in the same room together when they were kids, but it got so much worse, and I was tired of it. Right before this was taken, I told them both to grow up. It was getting old, how they treated each other, and Rowan had been acting like a big baby. He had so many issues with Bryson that he even chose to miss his wedding."

Jamison continued. "At least he was there for Dad's last Christmas. He'd really have issues if he would have stayed away." He placed the frame back on the mantel. "It doesn't matter. He seems to be in a good head space, finally. Maybe he'll come home for Kora and Kai's wedding. He's actually thinking about it."

"It sucks that they both acted so horribly your dad's last Christmas."

"No kidding. My mom pulled them both to the side the weekend of the funeral and told them that if they couldn't act civil for the weekend, they needed to leave. She wasn't going to deal with their shit."

"I noticed they were both quieter than usual, but I just thought it was because of the situation."

"That was part of it, I'm sure." He rubbed his hands on my arms and moved closer.

The tingle that swept through my body was electric, and my heart skipped when our eyes met.

"Lilly, I know you want us to be friends, and I do, too, but I can't ignore this."

He brushed his thumb across my bottom lip, his eyes fixed there, then slowly pulled his eyes back to mine. "I don't need any more time to know what I want. I want us to be more than friends. I want you."

His gaze held mine, and my heart fluttered wildly. *Jamison wants me, and damn, the feeling is so mutual.* I touched my lips softly to his. I couldn't help it. How he was looking at me and the feelings stirring within my body—I laced my fingers behind his neck and pulled him closer as our tongues met. He brushed my hair away from my shoulder and cupped my face in his strong hands. They made me feel desired and safe.

The kiss was intense, deep, filled with need. I couldn't remember ever being kissed by anyone like this—well, anyone in the past eleven years since the last time his lips were on mine.

He broke the kiss long enough to lead me to the couch. I sat next to him, and we immediately picked up where we had left off. Heat pulsed through my body. I wanted him so badly, but . . . I pulled away slightly. "Jamison. The girls."

His eyes opened, he let out a heavy breath and caressed my cheek. "I know, I know." He placed a kiss there, then traveled to my chin before he pulled away a small smile on his lips.

I couldn't ignore my heart, how it raced, and the tingle that filled my body. The look of desire in his gaze.

The muscle in his jaw ticked. He leaned away, and his hands slid to my thighs. I searched his face and tried to make out his expression, but there was so much there I couldn't understand. "What?" I asked as my heart thumped.

Jamison shook his head. "Bryson and I were talking the other day, and he told me I needed to move on, that Carly would want me to be happy. Lance made it obvious, too, with him trying to fix me up."

"You could have said you weren't ready instead of agreeing to meet them tomorrow night."

Jamison's gaze met mine. "I might have if I knew how you felt."

The seconds ticked by as his gaze bore into mine. My heart practically beat out of my chest.

"How do you feel, Lilly? Because I want them all to know I'm crazy about you. I don't care. They want me happy—us happy—and I'm happy when you're around." His thumb traced my jaw. "Maybe if we tell people, we'll feel better about it. We won't feel guilty."

"Guilt? Do you feel guilty?"

"I don't know. Maybe."

"Why?"

He shrugged. "Because of Carly. Lance. Our mothers. You just out of a marriage."

I kissed him. Not desperate like before, but focused and caring. I lingered on his lips a moment before separating, then stayed millimeters from him. "What do you feel now? This second?"

His eyes grazed over my face. "It feels right. I feel whole. Like I haven't felt in a long, long time." His lips met mine. The kiss was hungrier than before, yet gentle and sweet.

My heart soared, and a smile filled my face. "Me too," I breathed. I brushed my hand across his chin and his five o'clock shadow. "I want us together. I want you."

His smile filled his face, and he let out a breath. "Thank God. You had me worried." He gently rubbed my thighs. And sat up straight. "Let's do it." His face lit up.

I laughed. I couldn't help it. His expression was contagious. "Do what?"

"Tell them." He threw his hands up.

"Tell who, and tell them what?"

"You tell Rose and Kristy. I'll tell Bryson and Kai. We'll start with the easy people. The ones we know will support us without drama."

He looked as excited as a kid on Christmas, and he was just as adorable.

"Tell them what exactly?" I asked and scooted to the edge of the couch.

"Wow. I don't know." Our eyes met. "Shit, Lilly. Let's keep it simple and tell them the truth."

"Lance?" I asked.

"Moms next, then Lance. If we get all of them supporting us, they can bring Lance around."

"How about we come clean tomorrow night at Tonya's barbe-cue?" I suggested.

"That sounds perfect." He said as his lips met mine again.

"Does this mean your date on Saturday is canceled?" I asked.

"Without a doubt."

I was sure a smile was going to be a permanent fixture on my face.

Chapter 22

Jamison

I leaned on my knees as I gasped for air after a long, hard run. My mother came and picked up the girls early this morning, and now I had time to complete some last-minute work before calling it quits for the weekend.

I stomped in the door and grabbed a bottle of water from the refrigerator on my way to the shower. I needed that run. I needed it to clear my head. I didn't sleep well after Lilly left last night. When she was near me, I had zero doubts our feelings were legitimate and right, but as soon as I was alone, doubts crept into my mind like spiders across a counter and spun webs of negativity in their path.

As the heat from the shower beat on my skin, I couldn't help but think of all the reasons why Lilly and I shouldn't be together. If anything were to happen, we would be hurting more than just us. We'd be hurting our mother's and most importantly—our daughters.

My stomach lurched, as if someone had punched me, and my heart pounded against my ribs. With a sigh, I leaned my forehead against the shower wall, the sound of the water cascading down a soothing background. That was it. That was my issue. If Carly was still here, I wouldn't have thoughts of Lilly or even acted on our old feelings.

I stood in the shower and let the scalding water rain down on my skin. The pain from the heat took over for the pain in my heart. What if Lilly's concerns were founded? What if she was just a rebound? What if I didn't have feelings for her like I had for Carly? Could I walk away and keep from breaking hearts in my wake? What about the girls?

I lifted my face to the stream of water and closed my eyes. The drumming of water droplets relaxed me and soothed the stress that filled my chest. I stood in the hot shower allowing the water to wash away my dreariness until the water turned cold.

Once I started my day, work took over my thoughts. I was able to not only complete everything I needed, but one of the customers I had been talking with, finally signed their contract. That was more commission in my paycheck, which was always a good thing.

I signed out of my computer and shut everything down for the weekend just as the garage door closed, and I heard the pitter-patter, or better yet stomp-stomping, of little feet. Becca, who had been lounging in her usual spot in the middle of my office floor, rose to her feet and raced down the steps.

Darcie's laugh filled the house as Becca ran around her. The dog licked at her hands and arms. "Becca," Darcie laughed. "Come on. and I'll give you a snack."

I got to the kitchen as she gave Becca a dog biscuit and a kiss on the head.

"Daddy!" Darcie greeted me when she turned.

I laughed. "Yes, my darling, quiet daughter?"

"Hi, Daddy," she sang as she hugged my legs. "Grammy and I got burgers. I ate mine in the car and drank all my chocolate milkshake. I'm going upstairs. I have to get stuff to take to Grammy's later. The girls and I have stuff to do. Bye." She ran off with Becca following behind as was usual.

My mother put a couple brown bags on the counter. The smell wafting from them caused my stomach to growl. I was starving. "Thanks, Mom." I gave her a hug and kissed her cheek.

"You're welcome. Those girls are exhausting." She fell into a chair at the table.

I sat across from her and divided out our food.

"Just a warning," she said with a lift of her finger. "They are planning their senior trip to Moana's home in Hawaii. Maybe we need to find a Disney movie which takes place closer. Last year, she wanted to go to the beach and swim under the water to meet Ariel."

I laughed out loud. "I think they need to focus on getting ready for kindergarten first. I'm in no rush for them to graduate. But I remember that. We were scared to take her to Uncle Nigel's." Nigel was Kora's father. My mom's older brother. He moved to a small beach town in Florida after he retired.

"Yep, and when we finally did, we had to make sure she understood she absolutely could not go under the water too long. I was scared to death she was going to drown."

"Me too," I agreed as I took a bite of my burger.

A memory hit me like a slug to the gut. I placed my burger back on the wrapper, tipped my head up, and blinked rapidly to drain the tears from my eyes.

"Jamison, what's wrong?" My mom reached across the table and squeezed my hand.

I swallowed down my emotions before I spoke. "Carly's dream was to go to Hawaii for our tenth anniversary. Ten years would have been this year."

I felt Mom pull up a chair, and her arm slid around me. "Jamison Carl McKendry Jr. Listen. To. Me."

I was thirty-six years old, and still, my complete name from my mother forced me to listen. She meant business. My gaze fell on hers.

"You are so lucky; you know that, don't you?"

I had no clue where she was going, but I nodded.

"You and Carly had something special. She was your soulmate, and together, you made a precious angel who lightens up every bit of my day." She grabbed my chin and turned it toward her. "But Carly's gone, son, and you have to move on."

My heart stopped. My mom had been my rock over the past two years. She understood what it was like losing the person you vowed to be with forever, and she'd helped me over so many hurdles.

I shook my head. This might be one thing, though, she was wrong about. "I don't know, Mom. I thought I was ready, but now I don't know." Tears fell down my cheeks. Angrily, I swiped them away.

"Listen, baby. Moving on and finding someone else to love doesn't mean you'll forget Carly. You'll never forget her. Darcie is the spitting image of her mother. You will always have Carly with you." She wiped away another tear as it made its way down my cheek.

"I still miss your father like crazy, but I have him everywhere I look. I see him in your eyes and your work ethic. Bryson has his crazy energy and sense of humor. Rowan is the spitting image of Carl. He's everywhere, and I'll never forget him. Plus, he's always here." She patted her chest over her heart. "But don't let someone else get away because you're afraid to move on and put your heart out there again."

I met my mother's gaze head on. "All this from you. Mom, you've been single for five years."

"Not the same. I was with your dad for thirty years, and I'm not alone. I have Darcie and James to keep me busy. I go out with a man now and then. One day, I'll find someone. But right now, I keep myself busy with my family, and lately I've been concerned about you. I'm scared you're going to let your next love get away. You're too young to be alone, and you have so much to share."

What did she know? My mother was Orlinda Valley's personal blog. She knew everything that went on in this town, and if she didn't, she made it her job to find out. I tilted my head. "What's up, Mom?"

"That's what I should be asking you," she said as she leaned back. "There's been talk around town, and I've heard some things about you and Lilly."

And here we go. "Mom."

"Nope, listen to me. You and Lilly, if there is something there, have all our blessings. The ladies and I thought there was something going on between you two, years ago, but then you met Carly, and she met Anthony. But now here you both are, single and hurting in different ways. Sometimes things happen for a reason. Maybe she's supposed to be here now. I know you've been trying to move on and date. Maybe the couple of women you've gone out with were just opening your heart to the possibility of someone new."

She stood and rubbed my cheek. What was it about a mother's touch that could make a grown man feel like a child again? "It's time, Jami. Open your heart and be willing to let someone else in. It's what

Carly would have wanted." She kissed the top of my head. "I gotta go. Got a lot to do. Oh, I told Darcie to pack. The book club is having a sleepover, and the grandkids are going to camp out." She let out a Tonya cackle. "I feel so sorry for James. He, again, has to spend the night with all the girls. Lena, Madeline, Skylar, and Darcie against poor James. One day, maybe we'll have another boy."

"You could make JR come stay, too," I said, referring to Rose's oldest.

"Yeah, a twelve-year-old does not want to have a sleepover with a bunch of almost kindergarteners." She grabbed her purse. "I gotta roll. Promise me you'll think about what I said?" Her brows went up.

"Yes, Mom. I will, I promise." I gave her a hug as Darcie came bounding into the kitchen, rolling a large suitcase behind her.

"Grammy, can I go with you now?" Darcie asked as she huffed a bit.

"How did you get that downstairs?" I asked, gawking at the size of the suitcase.

"I didn't. I carried all my stuff down in my bag. It took lots of trips. This was in the closet in the downstairs room. Look what I found in the front pocket."

She held up a long black jewelry box. My pulse quickened. I knew that box.

I took it from her, and a smile broke across my face when I saw the contents—a heart locket necklace I gave to Carly. I took it out and opened it. On one side was a picture of me; the other was baby Darcie. I turned it to Darcie; her eyes went wide, and her mouth dropped open.

She let out a gasp. "Is that you and me, Daddy?"

"Yep, princess, it is. I bought this for your mommy when she was pregnant with you. She put my picture in it, then after you were born, she put in yours. I haven't been able to find it. I guess she put it in the suitcase." My heart squeezed tight, and I had to swallow down the lump which formed as I remembered where she took this suitcase last, which was why I didn't find the necklace.

"Why was it in the suitcase pocket if Mommy loved it so much?"

My voice was emotional when I spoke. "The last place she took this suitcase was to her mom and dad's. She must have taken the locket with her." I cleared my voice and crouched next to Darcie. "Here." I clasped the necklace around her neck.

She picked it up in her little hands and opened it. "It's so pretty," she whispered.

I nodded and cleared my throat. "It is. It's yours now."

"Daddy, thank you." She wrapped her little arms around my neck and held on for a bit. I wrapped my arms around her and breathed in the sweet, childlike scent of her.

"Can we get a picture of Mommy to put in it, instead of baby me? Then I'll have my Mommy and Daddy together in my heart forever."

And just like that, tears escaped from my eyes—again. Anyone with a heart of any size wouldn't have been able to hold back tears. I glanced at my mom, and yep. She wiped her face as well.

"Of course, princess." I gave her another hard hug and planted kisses all over her face.

"Okay, Daddy. Grammy and I gotta go." She giggled as she gave me a kiss. "I'll see you later, alligator." She pulled her suitcase behind her.

"You okay with taking her now, Mom?"

"Of course." My mother waved and had an all-knowing smile on her face. "See you soon, baby," she said and helped Darcie out the garage door with her suitcase.

I threw the wrappers from our lunch into the trash and walked into the living room. I picked up the frame on the mantel, the last picture of Carly, Darcie, and me. I held Darcie, who had just turned two. Her hair matched her mother's perfectly, even down to the waviness and the one strand that never stayed behind their shoulders. "I love you, Car. You will always be my first love and will always be in my heart."

I put the picture down and picked up the one next to it, from my father's funeral. Carly was pregnant then, and so was Lilly, but no one knew. We told everyone later that night about our baby.

My gaze bounced between Lilly and Carly. Carly and her red curls and blue eyes, Lilly and her straight light brown hair and brown eyes. Both beautiful. Both important to me.

But only one I was able to talk to, to touch.

Chapter 23

Lilly

I unlocked the door of my mom and Charles's house on Friday night. I was tired from cleaning the two houses I had, but it was so worth the exhaustion. I needed to hop in the shower and change quickly. Rose and Kristy were stopping over for a little girl time before we headed to Tonya's Friday night barbecue. I heard from Anthony today, and I needed to get some frustration off my chest. My best friends were the best way to do it.

I had just finished applying a light coat of mascara when I heard the thump of a car door outside. I froze and stared at my reflection. This was it. After I filled them in on the latest with Anthony, I would let them know about me and Jamison. Yes, Rose already knew some, but I needed their advice, and with this latest news from my ex, it would be so much easier to move forward.

I gave myself one last look in the mirror, dropped my mascara into the drawer, and a smile filled my face. Kristy was going to die. Even though it was common knowledge to—well, everyone, it seemed—that I've had a huge crush on Jamison practically my entire life, Kristy had no clue we had a history.

Now this. *Yeah, she's going to freak.*

"Hey, y'all." I said as they walked up the front steps to the porch. I hugged Kristy first and then Rose.

"Please tell me you have something good to drink," Kristy said as she walked into the house.

"I have white wine chilling in the fridge," I said.

Rose and I followed her into the kitchen where she helped herself to the liquor cabinet. "Wine's fine, but I need something stronger." She grabbed the tequila. "Got a lime?"

I looked through the drawer in the refrigerator and gave her all we had. A lemon.

"That'll work. Got any sugar?"

I lifted my brow, but grabbed the sugar bowel and placed it in front of her. As she cut up her lemon, I poured Rose and me glasses of white wine. I took a sip, and the fruity and nutty flavors exploded over my tongue. I gulped down my first glass—so much for sipping—and poured another.

When I glanced up to take another drink, Rose and Kristy were eyeing me like I was crazy.

"Hard day?" Rose asked.

I took another large sip, set my glass on the counter, and looked at them. "You could say that." I tipped up my glass again.

"So," Kristy waved her hands, "spill it. What's up? You look . . ."

"Happily stressed," Rose finished.

Kristy pointed at her. "Yeah, what she said, even though I really have no clue what exactly it means." Kristy dipped her lemon in sugar, took a shot of tequila, then sucked the lemon.

"Right?" Rose agreed.

"What are you doing?" I asked Kristy.

"Don't knock it. Kora and Darlene call them Lemon Drops." She took another. "They're delicious. You should try one." She held up her hand. "After you let us know what's up."

"Okay." I leaned heavily on the counter. "I heard from Anthony today."

They both raised their brows, and their gazes fell on mine.

Now that I'd had time to digest his words and churn them around for an afternoon, they sat well with me. Yes, I'd have to find a way to let Madeline know, but I'd get to that when it was absolutely necessary. "He wanted to let me know he's moving to London. He got the promotion he's been working on for eons and will be in charge of the London office."

"Wow. That's huge," Kristy said.

"It is, but what about Madeline?" Rose asked. "He's just going to leave and not see his daughter?"

"Well, his mind's in other places, and unfortunately his daughter is far from it, as usual." I fixed my gaze on them. "He's taking his secretary with him. She's knocked up, and they're getting married."

"No shit," Kristy said, her mouth wide open.

"Wow," Rose replied. "How do you feel about that?"

I took another slow sip of wine and focused on my heart and the question. I was somewhat surprised at what I felt. Nothing. Absolutely nothing. I guess this proved I had gotten over him.

"You know, when he first told me this afternoon, I was upset. His secretary is like fifteen years younger than him, and I'm sure he was having an affair with her while we were married." I shrugged. "I divorced him because he didn't love me and didn't want to be a dad." I shook my head. "I found a way to be happy when I left him, and since I've been home, everything's been perfect. Madeline's happy. She has friends, she laughs. It's been a long time since I've really heard her laugh. We've both moved on, and we're better off without Anthony around us."

"Have you told Maddy yet?" Kristy asked.

I shook my head. "Not yet. I will when the time's right."

I took a deep breath and emptied my glass. *No time like the present.* "Enough about my ex. I have something to share with you." I looked at Rose, then Kristy and a goofy smile spread across my face. "I know what I'm getting ready to say may be a shock, but I need your advice." I folded my hands in front of me, sat up straight, and sucked on my bottom lip.

Rose cocked her head and scrunched her brows. "What is it? I'm getting concerned."

"Yeah," Kristy agreed. "And you have a weird look on your face. What did you do?"

I laughed. Leave it to Kristy to always think something's up. Well, in this case, she was right. "Jamison and I are in a relationship." I leaned back and chewed on my lips. I watched, studied their expressions, and waited.

Rose's face lit up, and a smile filled it.

Kristy's expression was the total opposite. Her brows were raised, and her face was scrunched up. "Jamison who?"

My mouth gaped open. Was she serious? "How many Jamison's do we know?"

She still looked shell-shocked. "You and Jamison, Jamison? Like each other? Since when? Are you sure you're not reliving a teenage fantasy?"

Rose chuckled.

I rolled my eyes. "No fantasy. I promise." I drew an X over my chest. "Things have been interesting between us since I've been back."

"That's an understatement," Rose said as she sipped from her glass.

"Shit," Kristy said. "You're serious." She looked at Rose. "What did you mean, and why do you have that silly grin on your face?"

Rose shrugged.

"I'm confused." Kristy looked between us. "What exactly has happened between you two?"

"Last week he kissed me in my kitchen."

"No shit. Did you know?" she asked Rose.

Rose shrugged. "I've known a little, and I think it's so cool that, after all these years, their secret flame has been rekindled." Her hands were over her heart.

Kristy gave Rose a side-eye. "A secret flame? A lifetime crush is not a flame."

Rose clamped her mouth shut, and Kristy glared at me. "What else am I missing out on?"

I grabbed her arms, "I didn't mean to keep any of this from you, but Rose was around when I needed to get stuff off my chest last week. I kept this to myself for years."

Kristy pulled away and crossed her arms.

"Fine. Jamison and I had a thing the summer before he met Carly."

"No shit? A thing as in . . . sex?"

I laughed. "Yes. Sex, and fun. And yeah . . . then he went back to college, met Carly, and the rest is history. Well, that's what Rose meant by rekindled."

"Damn. Who knew about this then?" she asked.

"I didn't tell anyone until last week when I told Rose. Jamison told Rowan back when it happened."

"And now who knows?"

"You two, and Rowan."

"And now you two are doing what exactly?" she asked.

I shrugged. "It's complicated. We've kissed. But I'm confused. What if it's just a rebound for us both and we're trying to pick up where we let off? I'm scared it may not be real, and I told him I wanted to be friends, then last night at his house I kissed him again, and we both acknowledged we have feelings for one another."

"So, let me see if I have this straight," Kristy said with her hands up in front of her. "Teenage dream guy became your sex slave for one summer, and now you're telling us you have the hots for each other, *but,* you're afraid for no apparent reason."

I laughed and nodded. "I guess you could say that."

"Shit," Kristy said with a chuckle. "Lance is going to be pissed. His best friend and his sister have hooked up." She hugged me tightly and laughed. "Damn, girl, this is better than reality TV. I wasn't going to Tonya's tonight. I was going to enjoy a quiet night by myself at home. But now, I wouldn't miss this for the world."

"Umm, I don't really think that's a way to support your best friend," I said.

"You have all the unconditional support and encouragement from Rose. You don't need me for support. You need me for realistic feedback, and this is going to be worth the price of admission."

"It's free," Rose said.

"Yeah, well, it will still be priceless. Can't wait to see all the chaos. Come on." Kristy grabbed her purse and mine, then pulled me out the door, knowing Rose would follow. "Let's get out of here. We have a barbecue to get to."

The relatively short drive to Tonya's was filled with Kristy's play-by-play of how Lance was going to react to my news. Of course, she was looking forward to this. She was an only child raised by a single mother. She loved it anytime she could be a part of family chaos and loved the crazy that was my and Rose's extended non-related family gatherings because something was always bound to happen.

"And look who's here." Kristy parked next to Jamison's truck in the driveway. "Let's get this party started." She wiggled her brows at me with a wicked grin.

As soon as we walked into the yard, my eyes fixed on Jamison. He was standing with Kai, Bryson, and Adler—Leila's husband. Bryson must have said something because Jamison turned slightly and our eyes locked. His mouth ticked up, and my heart swooned.

He left the guys and walked toward me.

"Hi, Jamison," Kristy greeted him in a saccharin sweet voice.

"Kristy," he said. "Hi, Rose. Hey, you." He wrapped his arms around my waist and pulled me to him. Mine went around his shoulders and the hug was tight. He smelled good, and I breathed him in.

He stood next to me and chuckled. "Can I help you?" he asked Kristy.

She passed her eyes from him to me, and a smirk grew on her face. "Nope. Everything looks good here. I'm going to go bother the guys."

"Don't ask," Rose said as we all watched her walk away. "She doesn't like being the last one to find out anything, and she was just filled in on lots of juicy information."

Jamison's blue eyes held mine. "I guess they know?" he asked.

I nodded. "Yep." My stomach did a weird flip, and sweat started beading on my neck, and the temperature was only part of the reason.

"Nolan just got here. I'll talk to you two later." Rose waved. "Be good." She went to meet Nolan, and I was left with Jamison in the middle of the yard.

I glanced around. Bryson, Kai, and Adler were still talking in a group, joined now by Kora, Darlene, Leila, Summer, and Kristy. The kids were running around the yard, and slowly the book club emerged from the house, carrying trays of food. "Looks like we're being watched." I gestured my head toward the kitchen door as Ruth and Diane glanced over to us and whispered with smirks the size of the Grand Canyon on their faces.

His gaze followed my gesture. "I'm sure our mothers are going to hear that we're standing in the middle of the yard alone."

"Maybe we should be a little scandalous and leave the yard and find a private place where no one will find us," I said, only half joking. Standing this close to him made every feminine sense I had leap into high gear. Our eyes locked, and I didn't miss that his dropped for a second to my lips before meeting them again.

CHAPTER 24

JAMISON

She didn't have to tell me twice.

I watched Darcie for a couple seconds. She wasn't paying a bit of attention to us. She was so involved in whatever they were playing on the play set to even notice. "Come on. I have just the place."

I grabbed Lilly's hand and led her down the path between my mom's house and Kora's. This used to be all my parents' property, but after my father passed away, Mom split it between my brothers and me, but when Bryson and Darlene wanted to live closer to town, Mom sold this parcel to Kora. I have the five acres on the opposite side of Mom, but I'm not sure if I'll ever build on it, and Rowan has five acres next to me.

"Are you taking me to the barn?" Lilly asked.

I chuckled as a memory of us hiding out in the old barn years ago surfaced, stealing our time together in private. "Sort of. The property is Kora's now, and she tore down the old barn and built a new one for her goats. It's much cleaner."

"Good to know."

I opened the gate, and the goats came bounding toward us. "Meet Kora's babies. Percy, Jackson, and Baby Goat." Percy and Jackson were white with black and brown patches, and Baby Goat was midnight black.

"They're so friendly," Lilly said as she petted and scratched the goat's heads. When she glanced up at me, her eyes glittered with laughter. "They're adorable. Madeline told me all about them from last weekend when they camped out. I guess they came over here to help Kora."

"Sounds about right. I wouldn't be surprised if the goats follow us back to Mom's. Anyway." I grabbed her hand and pulled her into the barn. The goats got bored and skipped and leaped away, head butting each other as they went.

Inside the barn, the air smelled of hay and straw, with neatly stacked feed containers lining one wall and a shelf filled with tubs and buckets on the other. I led Lilly to the opposite side, and she leaned her shoulder on the wall.

I stood in front of her and took her in. My heart picked up speed. She was beautiful. I reached out and brushed my hand across the side of her face, her smooth skin, and down her arm. I pulled her close, her body warm against mine, and our lips met in a passionate kiss.

This was what I needed. The warmth of her lips and the taste of her tongue. Immediately, heat erupted deep in my gut as our tongues meshed and danced together. All the doubt and confusion from earlier evaporated in that second.

Being here, with Lilly, calmed my nerves and stilled my heart. I curled my fingers into her hair and pulled her deeper into my kiss. She moaned, and it was the sexiest sound my ears had heard in the longest time, well at least since Tuesday, and the heat in my gut settled in my groin causing a tightness in my pants.

A hunger ate at me. I kissed her neck, and my tongue traced a path down her neck and to her cleavage, which was just barely visible at the neckline of her shirt.

I massaged her breasts, and when I felt her nipples tighten against the material, I groaned against her skin.

"Jamison." She whispered my name and pressed her hand against the hardness under my pants.

I was rock hard. "Fuck. Lilly."

She stepped away, her chest rising and lowering with each breath.

"You are so beautiful," I said as my eyes ate her up.

A wicked and sexy smile grew on her face. She pushed me onto a bale of hay and stepped away. She slowly pulled her pants off and dropped them on the ground. She wrapped her arms around my neck, kissed me hard, and straddled my lap.

"Here? Seriously?" I asked.

"Oh, yeah," she answered. "Just like old times." Her voice was raspy, as she pulled my cock from my pants and slid me into her.

"Damn." I sucked in a breath as her warmth wrapped around me. She pulled her shirt over her head, and my hands kneaded her breasts, and I licked her hard nipple.

She rocked and found a rhythm. I opened my eyes and took in her body as she took control. I leaned her back just enough so I could rub her. I wanted to feel her come apart around me.

She picked up her rhythm, and her moans became breathy.

"God, yes." I moaned. With Lilly over me, her face a picture of perfection, it didn't take long before I erupted.

"Jamison." She yelled my name and crushed her lips to mine. Our kiss was desperate at first, then became softer as we both finished together.

Lilly was breathing hard; her eyes were fixed to mine. "Damn," she said breathlessly.

I closed my eyes to take in the ends of the numbness I felt and placed a soft drug-like kiss on her cheek.

Lilly wrapped her arms around my neck and stared into my eyes.

I brushed her hair behind her neck. "That was unexpected, and . . ."

She cut off my words and locked her lips to mine. It wasn't as desperate as before, but soft and gentle.

When the kiss ended, our foreheads touched, and when my eyes finally opened, hers were there staring into my soul. I caressed her cheeks, my breathing finally under control.

"Thank you for bringing me out here," she said as she lifted herself slowly from my lap.

"You are so welcome," I said accepting her hand and pulling myself up. I couldn't take my eyes off her as she stood there partially naked. The light from the setting sun coming through the window, cast a golden glow throughout the barn and made her hair and skin glow. Everything about her was perfect and beautiful.

We slowly dressed, then I wrapped my arms around her waist. I stared into her eyes and ran my fingers through her hair.

"What? What are you thinking about, Jamison?"

I backed away just enough so I could see her better. "You, us, this." I passed my hands between us. "When I'm with you, everything seems to lock into place. Seems right," I breathed out.

She opened her mouth to say something, but I stopped her with my fingers on her lips. "I've been a little overwhelmed with feelings since our talk, but I know without a doubt what I want." I gazed into her eyes. "And I want us together."

Her mouth ticked up in the sweetest smile. She kissed me lightly, and I savored it and breathed in her coconut and rose scent.

"Good, because that's what I want, too," she said.

We said bye to the goats and walked back down the path to my mother's house hand in hand, the smell of grilled pork chops in the air.

I walked with confidence I hadn't felt in a long time. My heart was light, and I wrapped my arm around Lilly's waist. She was mine. I was hers. Everything felt right, like it hadn't been for years. But I stopped before we got into the yard. "Maybe we should wait to make this official," I held up our hands, "until we tell the girls."

Lilly stretched up on her tiptoes and kissed my lips. "I agree," she said. "This might be a lot for them. But remember, you belong to me." A wicked smirk filled her face.

"Trust me woman, I won't forget." The kiss she placed on my lips caused me to adjust my pants before we entered the yard. I winked as we made our way to the line of people at the food table.

"Hey, man," Lance draped his arm over my shoulders. "Where'd you go off to? When I got here, I couldn't find you."

I caught Lilly's gaze, and she bit her bottom lip. Damn if that didn't send blood pooling south—again. This woman was going to be the death of me. I shook my head slightly and hid the smirk which threatened to give me away.

Luckily, I didn't have to come up with something to tell him as he continued on his own. "I talked with Jayla tonight. It seems Ella

Raye is looking forward to seeing you tomorrow at the jamboree. She's really interested." Lance elbowed me in the side as he picked up a plate. "I think you should give it a try."

Lilly gave me the side-eye as she put a pork chop on her plate. I didn't want to talk about this now, or here. I had to try to get out of it. "I don't think it's a good idea."

"Why? You're single, and she's pretty. I think you'd get along well. It's time, bro."

He wasn't wrong, and I knew it was time I moved on, but I sure as hell wasn't interested in moving on with her. I scooped some potato salad on my plate. "Want some?" I asked Lilly.

"Just a little," she answered.

We finished filling our plates and sat at the overly crowded table. I sat on one side of Lilly, and Lance was on the other side of me.

"What do y'all think?" Lance said to everyone at the table. "I'm trying to set Jamison up with Ella Raye. Bryson, you know her."

Bryson raised his brow and made eye contact with me, then flicked his gaze to Lilly. "I know her," Bryson said. "She's sweet, but she's loud and always the center of attention. She might be a bit much for Jamison. He likes the quiet and focused ones." Bryson took a large bite of his sandwich.

"I've gotta agree with Bryson," Kai jumped in. "I think Jamison needs a quiet woman. A single mom might be good. Someone he'd have something in common with."

Okay, this was getting to be a bit much. Was Lance really the only one who didn't know about me and Lilly?

"That would be sweet," my mom said. "A single mom with a daughter about the same age as Darcie would be perfect." My mother leaned across the table and picked something from Lilly's hair.

"You have a piece of hay in your hair Lilly." She studied it before dropping it to the ground. Her brow raised. "Hmm. Curious."

"I wonder how one would get hay in their hair," Diane said, her wine glass almost to her lips.

"Interesting," Kaye answered with a smirk.

Charles and Tom chuckled loudly.

Shit. I glanced toward Lilly. Her eyes were wide, and Rose and Kora snorted with laughter. Damn my mother and the book club.

I could feel my heart thumping and blood pressure rising.

I had to put a stop to this and get everyone's attention off us. "Thanks, everyone, but I think I can decide who's a good match for me on my own. Once I find her, I'm sure y'all will be the first to know."

"I bet we will," Bryson said.

I glared at my brother and wiped my hands on my napkin. The kids were eating and focused only on each other at the picnic table under the tree, thankfully not on this conversation. "Right now, I'm happy with how things are." I put my hand on Lilly's hand, which was on my thigh under the table.

She squeezed it. Good. I wasn't sure if she wanted to bite the bullet and come clean. If we did so right now, I'm sure we would have to start planning our wedding. "Anyway, it sounds like you and Jayla are getting close, Lance. You've talked with her how many times this week? What else have y'all done?"

Bryson and Kai jumped on the new conversation piece, the book club ladies got involved, and the attention was off Lilly and me. I turned to Lilly with a smirk and gave her hand a squeeze.

We sat and talked at the table for a while, enjoyed peach cobbler and apple pie with ice cream, and Lilly and I stole touches and caresses in private under the table when no one was paying attention to us.

"Okay, ladies, it's time for us men to put up the tent for the kiddos. Guys, come help us out," Charles announced as he got up from the table.

"You're being a little sexist, aren't you, Charles?" Kora asked as she stood.

"Now, babe, I'm sure he didn't mean anything by it." Kai wrapped his arms around Kora's waist and pulled her into his lap. "It's just a man's way of getting out of doing the dishes and meal cleanup, which is the worst job ever."

"True." Bryson jumped up. "I'll get the tent. Come on, Kai." Kai kissed Kora before following behind Bryson.

I jumped at the chance to join them and followed them into the garage.

"So, tell us, Jamison. How did hay really get in Lilly's hair?" Bryson asked as he got the tent.

Kai said, "I'm sure they went to play with the goats and Percy knocked her to the ground."

"Yeah," agreed Bryson. "I'm sure that's exactly how it happened."

Lance glanced at us. "I was wondering the same thing. You appeared out of nowhere with Lilly."

Shit. Not exactly what I wanted to talk about right now. "Lilly mentioned Kora's goats. Madeline talked about them, and she wanted to see them, so I took her to the barn."

"I bet you did," Bryson muttered when he came over to me.

I shot him an eat-shit look.

A crash got our attention. We turned, and Lance stepped over cots and stormed out of the garage.

Bryson laid his arm across my shoulders. "Well, I guess he figured out you're fucking his sister."

"Shut up, dick." I punched him in the arm, grabbed the cots Lance threw down, and left the garage.

CHAPTER 25

LILLY

"Hey, y'all, I've got to get going," Kristy said as she stood by the table where Jamison and I were seated. He had just told me about the brief exchange with Lance in the garage.

"This has been fun, but I've got a date with my two favorite men, Ben and Jerry." She tossed her trash in the garbage can. "You want me to drive you home, Lill?"

"Well..." I glanced quickly at Jamison, and he gave me a slight nod. "I think I'm going to stay awhile, get Maddie situated and make sure she's good. I'm sure I can find a ride home."

Kristy immediately made eye contact with Jamison, who gave her a sly smile. "I'm sure someone is very willing to take you home. All right, be careful and wear a condom."

"What?" I gasped.

"Don't act around me. Remember, I know the truth." She gave me a hug. "Love you."

"Love you back," I answered and gave her a tight squeeze.

As soon as she left, Lance sat across from us with a grimace on his face and slammed his beer on the table.

Well, here we go. Lance is acting like a baby. "What's wrong with you?" I asked him.

"Not much. I was getting ready to leave also," Lance said. "Thought I'd do the big brotherly thing and take my little sister home."

Was it my imagination, or did Lance just enunciate "little sister?" I watched him. He never once looked my way; his gaze was fixed on Jamison.

"Thanks," I said as I looked between the two guys. "But I was going to stay a bit. Make sure Maddy's set for the night." No time like the present to bring us up. "Anyway, Jamison said he wouldn't mind taking me home once the girls are situated."

"Oh, I'm sure he wouldn't mind, but I can run you by the house if you want to leave, since Mom and Charles are going to be here for the night with the kiddos. You could have a much-deserved night *by yourself*." He glanced at me quickly then turned his attention back to Jamison.

What the hell? "You know that's really sweet and all," I said, as I felt my pulse elevate, "but I don't want to put you out." This big brotherly, pissed off act was out of hand. If he suspected something, he needed to just come out and discuss it like adults.

Jamison said, "I'm heading home soon, and you know my place is on the way, so I'll just drop her off."

Lance squinted and gave Jamison the side-eye. "You sure, bro? Mom and Charles's house isn't exactly on your way home."

"It's closer to me than to you." Jamison stared back at Lance.

This was ridiculous. "Jamison and I are going to be here for a while more. Our daughters are spending the night, and we want to make sure they're settled. When we're ready to leave, Jamison will take me home."

Finally, Lance looked at me and eyed me hard before he spoke. "As long as he leaves after he drops you off."

I held his gaze. "Seriously Lance? You are such a baby." I was not the little sister he remembered from before. I was a grown woman, divorced, and a mother. I wouldn't allow him to keep Jamison and me from being together if it's what we wanted. He had no right.

This was bullshit. I placed my hand over Jamison's and squeezed. Jamison closed his fingers over mine. "What business is it of yours if he drops me off or stays?"

Lance held my gaze, and the side of his cheek sucked in—his telltale sign he was trying to keep his cool. He glanced at our hands, then at me, then Jamison. The muscle in his jaw clenched and his eyes lowered. "Fine. That's one less thing I've got to worry about. I'll see you guys tomorrow at the jamboree." His eyes traveled between us once more, then he stood and stalked off.

"Well," Jamison turned his hand over and entwined our fingers, "that went smoothly."

"Sorry, but I couldn't stand his accusatory gaze like we were children. He had to know."

"Oh, I totally agree," Jamison said.

"I took the no bullshit attitude and just tore the Band-Aid off." I wiggled my brows and shot him what I hoped was a sexy smile.

"There's the girl I remember." He placed a quick kiss on my cheek, as his thumb glided over my hand and caused my stomach to flutter.

"How the hay got in your hair is becoming more and more clear." Tonya's voice caused us both to freeze.

"Well, might as well finish our bandage tearing," Jamison said under his breath with a grin. He wrapped his arm around my waist and pulled me closer to his side. "Is it, Mom?"

Tonya, Ruth, Diane, and my mother joined us with the stupidest grins stuck on their faces. I felt a blush creep across mine as I met my mother's eyes.

"I'm guessing this was why Lance left like a grown baby," my mother said.

My insides coiled, and I sat up straight. "He was acting like an overprotective brother, and I grabbed Jamison's hand and challenged him to say something. I won't be bullied by Lance. I'm a grown woman and don't need him to protect me anymore, especially from Jamison." My blood was boiling, and I knew my voice was clipped and irritated.

My mom's hands were in the air. "Baby, I'm not here to judge. Trust me. We"—she gestured toward her friends— "thought there was some truth to the talk around town."

"Not the first time we've thought this, I might add," Tonya said.

Rose and Nolan joined us. "Well, it seems the cat is out of the bag, as they say," Rose said.

"No one says that anymore, babe." Nolan wrapped his arms around her waist. "You're so adorable." He kissed her cheek.

"Anyway, we're out of here," Rose finished.

I stood to give her a hug.

"Be good, girlie," she said in my ear.

"Always," I answered. I could feel her shoulders bounce as she laughed.

She pulled away, and we looked at each other for a bit, her face filled with a mischievous smile. "I'll see you tomorrow."

Ruth walked away with Rose and Nolan.

"I'm going to go check on the men. Make sure they have every-thing with the kiddos taken care of." Diane said, leaving us alone to be scrutinized by our mothers.

Jamison's arm tightened around my waist, and we both laughed.

"What?" he asked Tonya,

Tonya's grin was lopsided, and she glanced between the two of us, then to my mother, who lifted her brow.

"Say bye before you leave." They both got up and walked to the tent.

Jamison let out a breath, and I chuckled. "That's one way to let the world know," he said.

"Yep," I agreed. When our eyes met, he pulled me to him and gave me a peck on the lips.

"We haven't told the girls yet," I reminded him.

"We will soon enough. Come on, let's make sure they're situated, get out of here, and see about a round two."

We walked to the tent and shouldn't have been surprised at what we saw. The kids were set up with pillows, blankets, sleeping bags, a table with a small radio so they could listen to music, and a solar lantern on for light. Madeline, Darcie, Lena, Skylar, and James were all on a sleeping bag talking, and Charles and Tom, who were the guardians for the night, were starting a fire. Tonya, my mother, and Diane were sitting in chairs around the fire pit.

"Are you two sure you really want to do this?" I asked the men.

"There's no better place to be than teaching these kiddos all about camping," Charles answered.

"And it's not the first time we've spent the night with them. If we're out here, our wives can talk all night without bothering us," Tom said.

"Yep. At least these kids sleep. Have you ever been camping with the women? They talk a lot. When they have a reason to stay up drinking wine, they get even more talkative, and loud," said Charles.

"That's right," Tonya said. "And if you two aren't careful, we'll start talking about you."

"That wouldn't be the first time," Tom said. The fire was crackling, and he stood and dusted off his pants.

"And it's not gonna be the last," Charles chuckled.

"Yep. It's a good thing they have something new to talk about," continued Tom. "With you two as an item, they'll be up all night discussing what they can do to get into y'all's business."

"Yeah, they will," Charles agreed. "Out here will be a much quieter place to be."

"Y'all two better watch it, or we'll stay out here all night," Diane said.

"Absolutely," my mom added.

"Sorry, ladies. This is for men and grandchildren only," Charles said.

"And we like the grandpas with us," Skylar said. The kids all joined around the fire.

"Yeah," agreed James. "They let us eat tons of s'mores and tell ghost stories."

"And eat popcorn," said Maddy.

"And we can do each other's nails," answered Darcie.

"And braid James's hair," said Lena.

James's eyes bulged wide. "You aren't touching my hair or nails." He waved his hands in front of him like he was waving off evil spirits.

My heart went out to him. The poor guy had his hands full.

"You girls gotta understand," he said. "If I'm gonna be with you, you have to just do some more things than girl stuff all the time, like throw a ball or something."

"Oh, James," Darcie said, "You just need to be good and do as we say. You know this is our last sleepover before we all start school, and we can't do this much anymore. So, if you want me to talk to you at school, you be nice."

"Darce," Jamison picked her up. "Please stop bossing James around. It's okay for him to not want his nails painted." He kissed her nose and cheek. "He is boy."

"Fine, Daddy. But he still needs to listen to us."

Jamison laughed his deep, sexy laugh, which lit up his face. "Okay, princess." He gave her one last kiss. "See you in the morning."

I gave Madeline a hug. "You good?" I asked her.

"Yep, Mommy."

"Good night, then. I'll see you in the morning." I looked at Tom and Charles. "You two have fun tonight. We're going to go and leave you two men in charge of these kiddos." I gave them both a hug. "Maddy, be good, and you listen to Grandpa and Tom. Please don't cause too much trouble and don't bother James."

"Mommy, you know I'll be good. I'm always good." Maddie gave me her cute little smile and looked at me with her big brown eyes.

I gave her another big kiss on her cheek. I couldn't help it. "Yes, honey, you are."

"What about us? What are we in charge of?" asked Tonya as we gave the women hugs.

"Y'all have your hands full taking care of each other," Jamison said as he hugged Tonya. "Be good, ladies," Jamison told them.

"And don't be staying up all night partying too hard," I said. "You know these grandkids will be up at the butt crack of dawn and will be expecting pancakes, bacon, and all the wonderful goodies and donuts they can get."

"But don't sugar them up too much," Jamison said. "They have the jamboree tomorrow."

Tonya gave me a hug. "They're not jumping around that much tomorrow. They have like a five-minute routine and just have to look cute and adorable. They'll be fine. It's y'all two we need to be worried about. You're taking Lilly home to an empty house. How do we know you'll actually leave her there alone?"

The look she gave Jamison caused me to blush.

"You're mother's right. Don't forget you have a game to coach tomorrow, Jamison. Don't be staying up all night doing . . ." Diane stopped mid-sentence.

The book club women all exchanged a look with brows raised and silly grins on their faces.

"Good Lord." I knew I was blushing. It had suddenly gotten very warm by this fire. "Let's get out of here, Jamison."

Chapter 26

Lilly

As soon as we got into his truck, Jamison grabbed my hand. The warmth from the simple gesture made my heart, which I didn't realize was on edge, relax and be still.

"I'm not used to being away from Madeline," I said. "When we were in New York, she never had a sleepover. She was never with friends."

Jamison squeezed my hand. "She has all that now, and once school starts, she'll have more friends than she'll know what to do with,"

I knew he was right. I leaned my head back on the seat and watched as the countryside passed by. I loved the openness of Orlinda Valley. Coming home was the best decision I've made in a long time.

I turned my face toward Jamison, and my gaze traveled over his profile and down his body. *Yes, coming home was the best decision I've made.*

He glanced quickly toward me and winked. My heart fluttered, and I continued. "Maddy always had nightmares or night terrors when we were in New York, so I slept with her almost every night when Anthony was gone."

I gave him a crooked smile. "She never remembered about the nightmares when she woke up and would always ask me why I was in her bed. But you know, since she's been here, she hasn't had one. She's slept through the night every night and has never had a problem."

"Just proves that moving home was good for both of you." He let go of my hand and brushed my cheek with his thumb.

I leaned into his touch and closed my eyes as warmth crept into my gut.

"Have you told her yet about her dad moving to London?"

I took a deep breath and sat up tall as he placed his hand back on the steering wheel. "No. I figured I would do that after the jamboree. I'm not sure how much I'll tell her. I'm going to put my alimony money in her college fund. I don't want it. I don't need it, and she deserves it." My heart clenched a little as I thought of what Madeline had gone through in her short little life.

It's funny how I wasn't upset with how bad my life was and how disturbing my relationship with Anthony had been when we were in New York. I was focused more on Madeline. "Makes me wonder if I didn't have her, would I have stayed in New York and in my nightmare of a marriage longer?"

I stared out the window, and Jamison squeezed my neck. The warmth of his hand sent chills throughout my body.

He stopped at the one light in the middle of downtown. "I'm glad you came back home," he rubbed my neck more.

"Me too," I said as the light turned green.

I don't know if he realized how much I really meant that or how much my heart fluttered when he looked at me like he did. The look he kept giving me now as he drove down the road was the same one that caused my heart to skip all those years ago, and it still had the same effect on me.

All I knew was I still had it bad for Jamison. I don't think I ever stopped loving him. I dragged his hand from behind my neck and held it between my palms and laced our fingers together. I watched him as he drove toward my house. He had small laugh lines around his eyes, but he didn't look much different than he did in college. His face was still strong and chiseled perfectly, his dark hair still cut neatly around his ears. He wasn't as cleanly shaven as he was in college, which made him even sexier.

I dragged my nails through his closely cropped hair at his neck, and he leaned into my touch. This reminded me of our summer. We would drive through town in the dark toward our secret place by the Red River where we could be together. I sat up as, instead of turning left toward my house, he kept going straight.

Could he be going there? When he took the next right, I glanced at him, my brow raised. The grin on his face pumped heat throughout my veins. He remembered.

"It's not quite as private as it used to be. They built a couple houses on the road, but I think we'll be fine." He turned next to a new gravel drive. Someone must have built a house down Johnson's Path Lane. It used to be the perfect spot to park and party, but when it was crowded, we came here. He pulled down the grassy path between trees. We were finally hidden from the road, and he parked with a view of the river.

"There are lights through those trees. Did someone build a house out here?" I asked.

He chuckled. "Yep. That's Kai's place and soon to be Kora's once they're married. This land is also his now, so I know it'll be private."

He unbuckled my seat belt, and I moved toward him. He brushed my hair behind my ear, and my heart skipped a beat. "I wasn't sure you remembered this."

"Why would I forget?" His voice was quiet, yet thick.

"Honestly, I thought you forgot about us as soon as you got back to college. It didn't take long for you and Carly to become an item." I shrugged. This was silly of me, but I was still so jealous of her. "I always figured if I had truly meant anything to you, you wouldn't have forgotten me like you did."

He breathed out heavily, and his face became serious. "I never forgot about you, Lill, but Carly and I, we just meshed, and you and I moved on. I promise you, I always felt guilty. I know I hurt you, and that was the last thing I ever wanted to do."

I swallowed hard, and my insides were mush. My gaze wandered outside to just beyond the tree line to the light in the distance. Kora and Kai were over there. I had been home for four weeks and didn't even know what their plans were after their wedding. Kora used to be like my big sister.

"Hey."

I turned my attention back to Jamison.

His gaze was digging into mine, and my pulse picked up.

"After all these years and all that's happened in our lives, you still look at me and make my pulse race." My voice was a whisper, and I touched the scruff on his face and traced the line of his jaw.

"Is that the only reaction I cause?" He asked as his eyes filled with need and erotic desire. He pulled me to him, and his lips crushed against mine.

He quickly pushed my shirt up, and his mouth found my nipple. He nibbled there, and a tingle traveled straight to my groin. I was turned on instantly. He sucked my breast harder and pinched my other nipple. "God, Jamison." I pulled away from him just enough to straddle him.

He pushed the lever to put more space between us and the steering wheel, but it was difficult to maneuver where I wanted to be. I wiggled, and the horn blasted through the night air.

"Fuck." Jamison chuckled, and I laid my head on his chest.

"This seemed so much easier when we were younger," I said with a laugh.

"I was thinking the same thing." He kissed me again, and the kiss made my toes curl, but the intensity was gone. "I don't think this works."

"No, but my house is empty for now. My mom will be at Tonya's for a while and might even be there the night. She doesn't like spending the night without Charles."

"An empty house and no children. I should have thought about that first, or hell, even mine."

"Mine's closer," I said.

He nodded once, turned the truck around, and pulled on to the road.

Luckily, the drive from where we were to my house wasn't far, and we soon pulled into my driveway. As soon as the truck was turned off, we jumped out, and he pulled me up the sidewalk. I followed willingly. Yes, this was what I wanted—Jamison, in my bed.

At the door, he leaned in for a kiss. It was sweet and gentle. I pushed my tongue in his mouth and fumbled with the doorknob at the same time.

He tucked a lock of hair away from my face and brushed his knuckle down my chin and along my jawline.

A shiver ran down my spine at his touch. Something as simple as a touch caused my entire insides to flare with desire. There was nothing we could do about it here on the front porch. I finally opened the door and pulled him in behind me.

CHAPTER 27

JAMISON

It was early morning when I made it home. I couldn't remember the last time I'd slept so soundly and woke so refreshed. It had been a while, I was certain. Waking with Lilly beside me was something I could get used to.

I grabbed the half and half from the refrigerator and shut the door much harder than necessary. Darcie's picture fluttered to the ground. I picked it up, and my legs became weak. I slid to the floor and leaned on the kitchen bar.

My gaze was fixed on the woman above the rainbow.

Carly. My throat became thick with emotions.

"I miss you so much, Car," I whispered.

Becca, always loving when someone was in her territory, pushed her fuzzy face to mine and gave me a lick. I pushed her away, so she laid on my lap. Nothing like a dog to comfort you.

Her fur was soft, and I thought back to the day Carly and I picked her up at the animal shelter. She was a furry white ball, so tiny. Carly named her and held her all the way home. They were two peas in a pod. "You miss her, too, don't ya, girl?"

Becca's large brown eyes stared up at me, and she let out a little whine. I placed the picture on my lap, scrubbed my hands over my face, and stood.

I paced the kitchen as my insides clenched and tightened.

Carly was gone. I was tired of being alone, and finally, my heart was open to someone again, but it was my best friend's sister and a girl from my past. I glanced at the picture I gripped in my hand. Darcie's words came back to me. Did I believe God's promise that he wanted us happy? *Damn if I know.*

I rested my hands on the kitchen island, leaned on my arms, and hung my head low. "Lord, if you're really watching, and still care about me, why would you have put Carly in my life if I should have been with Lilly from the beginning? We had a good thing so long ago, but I fell in love with someone else and moved on. If you want me to be happy, you could have put anyone else in my life now. Anyone but Lilly." I clenched my hands into fists. "Why her? Why now?"

Rage, hurt, heartache, I don't know what it was, but it welled up and exploded. I punched the wall. My hand went through the drywall, and pain shot through my fist and up my arm. "Fuck," I shouted and shook my hand. Becca came to check on me. "I'm taking a shower, Bec."

I stomped up the steps. I had to get ready for the jamboree.

I pulled into the parking lot by the field house a few hours later. I'd called my mother and asked her if she would get Darcie to the jamboree today.

"You're late," Lance shot at me as soon as I entered the field house.

I rolled my shoulders back and stretched my neck to each side. I didn't miss the irritation in his words. This was not the place to do this. "But I'm here." I pushed past him and met with the other offensive coaches who were talking with the line.

It was time to head to the field. Lance fell in step beside me. "Stay up late last night? You look like shit."

I've known Lance all my life. We've been best friends since preschool, and we've had more arguments than I've ever had with my brothers, and because of how close we were, I didn't miss the edge to his words. But now wasn't the time to discuss it. "Yeah, I did. I was up most of the night. You don't want to hear why though, do you?"

Okay, maybe I shouldn't have said that.

His gaze narrowed, and his nostrils flared a bit. "We'll talk later." He stalked away.

"Hell yeah, we will," I muttered under my breath and trailed behind the coaches and team. One good thing about being a volunteer—they couldn't fire me for not being one hundred percent involved.

"Daddy." My gaze fell on Darcie as we passed the sideline, and my heart lightened a bit.

She was in her blue sweatpants and a gray T-shirt with tigers on it. Her hair was in a ponytail wrapped in a blue, gold, and gray ribbon. She looked like a beautiful, yet miniature, Carly. "You look just like your momma, princess," I told her as I swept her into my arms.

Her tiny hands held the sides of my face. "That's what Grammy said, too." She puckered her little lips, and I placed a kiss on them.

I pulled at her ponytail. "I like your hair and your bow. It's perfect."

"Thank you. Lilly met us at Grammy's and put all our hair in the same ponytails and tied these ribbons around it." She felt the bow. "Me and Lena and Madeline all have the same ribbons." Then she cocked her head. "What's wrong, Daddy? You look mad."

I took a deep breath and tried to relax my face muscles. My issues did not need to upset her. "Nope. Just focused on the game and watching you at halftime."

She squinted her eyes like she did when she was scrutinizing my words. I guess she was okay with what I said because she gave me a kiss and wiggled out of my arms. "Bye, Daddy. Make sure to watch me."

"Of course, princess." She skipped away toward Madeline and Lena, and my eyes met Lilly's. My heart raced. She waved, and I met her at the fence.

The smile she gave me lit her face. "Good morning, again," she said.

I really wanted to kiss her, but this wouldn't have been the right place, and certainly not the right time. "Good morning, again. Thank you for doing Darcie's hair."

"Not a problem." She swiped her hand through the air.

She placed her hand over mine, and when she gave it a squeeze, pain shot through my hand and up my arms. I winced and jerked my hand from her grip.

"Jamison." She grabbed my hand gently, turned it over, and passed her fingers over my red and swollen knuckles. "What happened?"

"Trust me," I said as I pulled my hand from hers and gently flexed my fingers. The pain wasn't as bad as it was earlier. "It's not worth the story."

She gave me the same scrutinizing look as Darcie. "Are you okay?"

I chuckled. "I must look like shit. First Lance said so, then you and Darcie both asked me the same question." I put a strand of hair behind her ear, and the warmth of her skin calmed my racing heart. "Trust me, I'm fine." Our gazes held for a beat, and she brought her hand up and covered mine.

"Good. I'll see you after the game?" she asked.

I didn't miss the question in her tone. I smiled and nodded. "There's nowhere else I'd want to be." Then I walked across the field. It was time to get my mind on the game.

"Good job so far, guys." Lance concluded his after-quarter pep talk. The team had played their first game well. It will be a good year.

"The coaches are heading to Jerry's Pub for pizza and drinks when we're finished here. You're planning on joining us, right?" Robert asked me.

"Well . . ." He caught me off guard. I know we usually go celebrate and talk about the season, but I wanted to be with Lilly. "I don't know. I was planning on taking Darcie for ice cream with Lilly and Madeline."

"Seriously?" Lance entered the office, and his tone was edging on irritated. "You're going to break with tradition to take your daughter for ice cream with my sister?"

"And Madeline. You know, they're best friends." I wanted to focus on the girls, not on Lilly. Well, not totally true. I wanted to focus on Lilly, on everything Lilly, but I didn't think that's what Lance wanted to hear. Especially after how he left last night.

"Can't break tradition. Wouldn't be good juju." Lance slapped my shoulder. "Come with us. You know your mom will take Darcie."

"Yep, the team doesn't need any negative vibes going into the season," Robert agreed. "Hang with us for a bit, then go do what you need to do. With whomever you need to do it with."

"Fine. I'll go for a little bit. Ella Raye better not be there. I'm not a bit interested in her." I made eye contact with Lance. "I'm going to go find Lilly and watch the girls' halftime routine. I'll see if she'll watch Darcie. That way I can see *her* later." I left the office. Two could play this game. If he was going to be childish about me seeing his sister, I'd just have to shove it in his face because Lilly was exactly who I wanted to be with.

We were adults, and he had to grow up.

CHAPTER 28

LILLY

Rose and I were talking by the fence, waiting for the girls to perform, when Stephanie and Nora joined us. I rolled my eyes toward the heavens.

"How's it feel to be back home in small town, Tennessee?" Stephanie asked, her voice the same fake, over-friendly tone I loathed from high school.

My guard went up immediately. Stephanie and Nora had never talked to me without a purpose that served them. I thought of walking away and giving a bitchy retort, but instead, I decided to be more mature and the adult I was, so I smiled. "It feels good. I didn't realize how much I missed Orlinda Valley, or Tennessee for that matter, until I got home."

"Oh?" Nora said. "I'm sure New York City would be so much more exciting than this boring old town."

"No, it's not as exciting as you think. For a city filled with people, you'd be surprised at how lonely it can feel sometimes. I enjoy being able to go into any store and people care about how I am and are happy to see me."

Nora smushed her lips together. "Yeah, I guess that would be okay, but I think I'd like to go somewhere where I could blend in."

Rose and I exchanged a look. Nora's husband had been the talk of the town according to Rose. His extracurricular activities kept him on the gossip channel news—which happened to be led by my mother's bestie—Tonya.

"Is Jamison going to coach full time this year or have time to be in the stands as a spectator?" Stephanie asked, looking directly at me.

Part of me wanted to act like he was mine, and I had all the answers about what he would be doing just to get these two women to stop swooning all over him, but I didn't. "I'm not sure. According to Lance, he helps during occasional practices and will be helping now and then, but Jamison wants to be available for Darcie as much as possible since she's starting kindergarten." Nice conversation. I thought I was doing a good job.

"Oh, that's so sweet. I'm sure it's difficult and lonely being a single father. He works so hard and must do the roles of two parents." Stephanie turned toward the girls on the field, and her expression filled with pity. "It must be so hard for that sweet girl to not have her mother, and Jamison must be so lonely." Her expression was filled with fake concern.

I seriously had to swallow down language that threatened to exit my mouth like a projectile, and then Jamison strutted toward us.

My eyes bulged as I watched Stephanie and Nora. They both thrust out their breasts and jutted their hips. I shook my head in disgust.

"Hi, Jamison," Stephanie cooed. "We were just talking about how sweet Darcie is."

"Thank you."

"It's got to be so hard being a single father and raising a daughter, but you're doing such an amazing job." Stephanie batted her eyelashes. My mouth fell open. I didn't know women still did that.

Rose and I rolled our eyes, and Jamison popped one brow. "Umm, thanks?" It came out as a question. He turned to me. "Would you mind taking Darcie with you for ice cream when they're finished, and I'll meet you later? The coaches are going to the pub after the game, and it seems to be bad luck if we don't all go. I promise I won't be long."

"Sure, as long as you promise I'll see you later," I said.

"Of course. I'm going to give my girl a hug and watch their routine from the bleachers with my mother. Come join us." He smiled at me, then glanced at the others. "Ladies." He nodded before he turned away and gave Darcie a hug before he walked off the field.

Stephanie watched him intently. "Damn, he's got an amazing ass. I'd love to get my hands on it—and other things. He is one hell of a sexy man. A body for days, sweet, and brainy. He's the whole package."

I tried to keep the shock and disdain from my face, but I think I failed miserably.

Nora said, "You don't have feelings for Jamison, do you?"

I cocked my head. "Nora," I began. I couldn't explain why I was so irritated with these two, but my pulse raced, and I needed to get it under control. "If I did have feelings for Jamison, I sure as hell wouldn't tell you about it."

Nora laughed a shaky, not-quite-real laugh. "Yeah, well, you just got divorced. It's not like you're emotionally available now, anyway."

That was it. My blood reached its boiling point, and my pulse was going to explode through the roof.

I opened my mouth to respond, but Rose yanked on my arm. "Look, I think the girls are going to do their routine. We need to go." She pulled me so hard away from Stephanie and Nora, I had to do a stutter step to keep from falling. "Rose, what the hell?" I asked as I struggled to get my balance and keep up with her.

Rose whispered through clenched teeth. "You needed to get out of there. I did you a favor."

"What do you mean?" I asked, feigning innocence.

She shook her head and led me to the stands where our mothers were sitting. Jamison was standing on the side. "Jamison, don't leave me alone with this one," She pushed me into him. His arm went around my waist to keep me from knocking him over, "and the velociraptors again."

"Velociraptors?" Jamison said with a chuckle, his brows raised.

"Yeah, velociraptors. You know, the dinosaurs that are very territorial and work together to surround their prey?"

"Yes, I know what they are. I did see *Jurassic Park*," Jamison answered. "But who are you comparing to velociraptors?"

"Nora and Stephanie. They've always gotten under Lilly's skin, and it seems as if things haven't changed much since high school."

I put my hands up in surrender and stepped away from Jamison. "It wasn't me. They started on me. I said nothing."

"Yeah, because I pulled you away. I knew you were considering it."

"It's not my fault Stephanie is a chronic bitch, and Nora just follows her around like a lost puppy."

"Lilly, that language is unnecessary," my mother said from the stands.

"Though I'm sure much warranted," Tonya added.

"Thank you, Tonya," I said.

She winked as my mother shoved her shoulder.

"Don't be too hard on them. They've had some hard years," Rose said.

"Rosie, I love you, but stop being so softhearted. They aren't the only ones who've had hard years." I pointed at my chest.

"Alright, ladies, let's rein this in," Jamison said. He gestured with his head toward the field.

The girls were so cute in their routine. It was short, yet they had all the kicks and cheers you'd expect from cheerleaders, and at the end, some did a back flip, and others, Madeline included, did cartwheels. Hers were perfect and graceful. Not bad for being new.

As soon as they were finished, they rushed off the field and directly toward us.

"Guess what, Mommy?" Madeline had the biggest smile on her face, and her eyes were wide with excitement.

"What, honey?" I said as I crouched in front of her to get a better view of her excited little face.

"Miss Shelby, our teacher, said I was doing so good, and she's glad I joined up. I think I want to be a cheerleader like you when I get in high school." Her excitement was contagious, and a smile filled my face. "Can you still do splits and jumps and stuff like you could then?"

I thought about it. I may not be as thin as I was in high school, but I did yoga and kept up with working out as much as possible. "Yep, honey. I can do splits. I'm still pretty flexible."

"Yay. You'll have to show me," she said as she jumped and leaped with the other two.

My mother and Tonya ushered the girls out of the stadium, and Rose followed close behind. Jamison and I brought up the rear.

Jamison leaned close to my ear. "I've gotta go meet the coaches, but I'd like to see how flexible you are, too. You'll have to show me later."

The wicked grin he gave me made my heart stutter.

CHAPTER 29

JAMISON

I didn't want to be here doing any of this. But here I was, trying to make good with Lance, and he did exactly what he told me he wouldn't. He invited Jayla and Ella Raye, and they showed up as soon as the other guys left.

"Hey, y'all," Jayla said as they joined us and she placed her arm around Lance."

Ella Raye gave me a shy smile. "Hi Jamison," she said.

I puffed out a breath and took a sip of my bear as I nodded.

"Jayla and I are going to dance," Lance said as he leaned toward me. He gestured with his head. "You should dance with Ella Raye. One dance won't kill you."

I glared at him as he walked away with a smirk on his face and his arm around Jayla's waist. I reached for my phone and sent a text to Lilly to let her know our meeting was over and I'd love for her to be here.

"So, who ya texting?" Ella Raye asked.

"Lilly. Lance's sister. She should be here eventually." Being here with Lance and these two women was the last place I wanted to be. It wasn't that Jayla and Ella Raye weren't nice, or pretty—they were both—but I'd promised Lilly I'd see her later, and that's who I wanted to be with. Thinking about her made my temperature rise. If she didn't feel like coming out, I'd finish my drink and go see her.

The dance floor was full when Ella Raye grabbed my hand. "Come on. One dance. It's not like I'm going to be able to take advantage of you with all these people around." She raised her brows and pouted her lips. "Just one, and I won't bother you again if you want to go."

Her large blue eyes and dark lashes, along with those pouty lips, did me in. I wasn't attracted to her in the least, but I could tell she wasn't going to give up. I guess Lance was right. One dance wouldn't kill me. "Okay, one dance."

Ella Raye pulled me to the dance floor, and we squished ourselves next to Lance and Jayla. Ella Raye linked her arms around my neck, and we found the rhythm of the music. She sure didn't hide her moves. She gyrated up against me, her hips rubbing against my crotch. I willed my body not to react to her movements, and so far, so good.

Every time she moved, I leaned away, but she continued. I wasn't a college kid anymore, and this was a bit much. I didn't know what she thought would happen, but a one-night stand wasn't it.

The song ended, and a slow song began. I pulled my phone from my pocket to check for a message from Lilly. Nothing. Ella Raye already had her arms over my shoulders, so I took one of her hands in mine and put my other around her waist. This was better. More space and less gyrating.

"How old's your daughter?" She closed the gap and yelled in my ear so I could hear her over the music.

"Five. She starts kindergarten in a couple weeks."

"I saw her at the jamboree with the mini cheer squad. She has the most amazing auburn hair, and those curls!"

I smiled my thanks and tipped my head. Okay, Ella Raye might have been slightly annoying, but talking about my daughter was the right conversation.

Just then she closed the small gap between us and laid her head on my shoulder. I leaned away and jerked her a bit so she would lift her head.

Her eyes widened, and she leaned away a little. "Hey, it's all good," she said. Then a look I couldn't decipher crossed her gaze, and before I knew what happened, her lips were on mine.

My eyes popped wide. The shock that went through my entire body wasn't quite revulsion, but I knew it absolutely wasn't pleasure.

I pulled back quickly and looked at her. "What the hell?"

"I don't know." Her smile faded. "I had an urge, and I couldn't pass it up." She shrugged.

I shook my head. "I told you there was someone else." I went back to the table and left her alone on the dance floor.

"What was that about?" Lance asked with an annoying smirk on his face.

"What the hell, man?" I asked, seething with anger.

"What? You looked awfully comfortable on the dance floor. Maybe you should've enjoyed her kiss a bit more."

"Why can't you accept the fact that Lilly and I are together? I'm your best friend. We're as close as brothers. Why can't you be happy for me?" Anger filled my words, and my pulse pounded.

"Look," Lance said. "I'm just letting you know there are other girls to replace Carly. You don't have to waste your time on one with a broken heart like my sister."

That was it. I clenched my jaw tight. If I opened my mouth, words I wouldn't be able to take back would spew out. I was done with his bullshit.

I put my hands up to calm myself, and I felt the blood flowing through my veins. I really wanted to hit Lance. Hell, it wouldn't have been the first time. But this time, the girl was his sister.

"Watch your mouth." I stood tall. I was only about an inch taller than him, but his height never intimidated me. "That's your sister you're talking about."

He squared up to me. "Yeah, you're right. It *is* my sister I'm talking about."

We glared at each other, and neither of us was going to back down.

But suddenly a hand was on my shoulder. "Jamison, you good?" I turned my head. It was Bryson.

CHAPTER 30

LILLY

Krysty, Rose, and I were on Rose's back deck enjoying a glass of wine, while the girls watched a movie in the living room with Nolan, when Tonya, Ruth, and my mother joined us.

"Hello, ladies," Tonya said as she took a seat. "Wasn't today so much fun? Our girlies were so adorable."

"I agree," said Mom. "Seeing Madeline on the Orlinda Valley football field was exactly how it should have been. And she had so much fun. Her smile lit up her face the entire day."

"I know," I agreed. "I can't remember the last time I saw her as happy and content as she was today."

"It's so good she's here and going to grow up with our granddaughters," said Ruth. "Now, if we could get Diane and Tom to move here, and Leila and Adler to follow. Then all the kids could grow up together."

"Yeah, well, don't get your hopes up," Tonya answered. "Adler and Leila are quite happy where they are."

"Yes, they are, but we didn't come over here to talk about them," Kaye said. "We came over to get y'all out the door to have a child-free night. Go to Jerry's Pub and enjoy yourselves."

"Find someone to take your minds off things," Tonya said as she looked directly at me.

"Smooth, Tonya," I said.

"Thanks. I know you had a long night last night."

"How?" My face heated.

"He's my son. We talk."

"Yeah, well, if Lance would get his head out of his ass and stop being a jerk, it would be easier for Jamison and me," I said, irritation attached to every word. "Mom, what's his problem?"

She shook her head. "Don't know, but if he doesn't relax, I'll talk to him. He's probably just concerned about you."

"Concerned? I'm interested in his best friend. He should know Jamison's a good guy." I stood and held up my hand, to show them the discussion was over. "You know what? I think I'll go surprise Jamison. He's at the pub. Let's go, ladies." I didn't want to ruin a great night talking about my brother.

"Sounds like a plan," Ruth said. "Make sure to grab Nolan on your way out. We'll stay here with all the little princesses and babysit."

"Yep, and I'll take Maddy home with me later," my mom said.

It didn't take us long to get out the door and loaded into Nolan's truck. Once we were situated in the back seat, Kristy poured some wine.

"Seriously?" Nolan asked as he drove.

"What? It's not against the law for us to drink in the back seat," Kristy said. "It's also not the first time you've driven while we drank."

"True," I agreed. "But this is the first time he's driven, and we've drank in the back seat since being of legal age."

Kristy nodded. "True that, girlie." She tapped her red plastic cup against mine, and we drank. "I got a sip for you, Rosie," she said and took another. "It's a good night to get drunk. Who's with me?"

"Not Rose," answered Nolan. "I plan on having some fun tonight, and if you get her puking drunk, I'll be holding her hair back as she upchucks in the toilet. Not the kind of fun I want." He reached across the seat and put his hand on her neck.

"I like your kind of fun," Rose agreed.

"God you two, get a room," Kristy said. "At least I have Lilly here. She won't let me down."

"I don't know. If Jamison has his way, he might be wanting the same thing," Nolan said, making eye contact with Kristy in the rearview mirror.

"He's not lying," I said with a shrug. "Getting drunk with you or spending a hot night with Jamison? I'm picking the latter."

"I guess things are going well with you two?" Rose asked.

"So far. We both seem to have some skeletons to deal with. Trust is going to be something I struggle with for a long time."

"You don't have anything to worry about with Jamison. That's not the kind of guy he is," Kristy said. "And it's awesome you two are back together after your fling so many years ago."

I stared at Krysty. "That was really sweet of you," I acknowledged.

Rose turned to face us. "Yeah," she agreed. "How much wine have you had to drink?"

Nolan turned his head toward Rose. "What the fuck is she talking about?" He made eye contact with me in the rearview mirror. "You and Jamison had a fling? When? And why didn't I know about it?"

"First off, trash the language, and second, I just found out myself," Rose promised him.

Nolan pulled into the pub's lot and parked next to Jamison's truck. "For later, so you don't have to look for your ride home." Nolan winked, and we all got out.

"Did you send Jamison a text to let him know you decided to meet him here?" Rose asked.

"Nope. I thought I'd surprise him," I answered as I followed them through the door.

It was a typical Saturday night at Jerry's Pub. The country music floated to us from the outdoor patio, and voices were loud. The crowd was thick when we entered, and we made our way to the back patio. Kora, Darlene, and Summer were seated around a high-top table.

I gave Kora a hug. "It's so good to see you."

"It's good to see you," she said. "Are you ready for tomorrow?"

Tomorrow we're heading to Nashville to have a girls' weekend and dress shop for the wedding. October would be here all too soon. "I am," I said. "I haven't had a girl's weekend in. . . I can't think of when I've ever had a girl's weekend," I said.

"High school graduation we went to Florida," Kristy said.

I nodded. "Yep, and that was probably my last time."

Summer poured us drinks from their pitcher of margaritas, and my eyes wandered around.

"Looking for someone special?" asked Darlene. "Like maybe, my brother-in-law?"

It was dark, but I know I blushed. I could feel my face heat. My eyes rolled to the ceiling as a slow song started. I can't lie. A bit of disappointment filled me as I continued to look around for Jamison. I would have loved to feel his arms around me as we danced.

My eyes halted and my stomach churned.

I found him. On the dance floor with his arms around a woman.

"Who's Jamison dancing with?" Kristy asked.

Leave it to Kristy to understand what I was thinking.

"That's Ella Raye. A teacher from the school." Kora answered quietly.

I remembered Lance talking about her. "Lance was trying to fix Jamison up with her. He mentioned it last night at the cookout."

Just then, there was no mistake what I saw as everyone at my table's eyes went wide and Kristy's hand went to my arm.

They kissed, right there on the dance floor.

My stomach fell and twisted in a knot.

Bile rose in my throat. "I gotta go," I whispered and ran from the table, pushing my way through the crowd.

I ran out the door and around the corner of the pub away from the door and any windows. I leaned on the wall and dry heaved, but nothing came up. The last time I felt this way was when I found out about Anthony's cheating the first time, then again the second. I swore I wouldn't put myself through this again.

"Hey, you okay?" Kristy asked.

When I turned toward her, she was blurry from the tears I had yet to shed. I shook my head. I couldn't say anything. My voice wouldn't work.

"Lilly," she wrapped me in her arms.

"You want to go?" It was Nolan's deep voice. Great, just what I needed, an entire audience as my heart was torn out again.

"Talk to us, Lill," Rose said.

I sniffed and wiped my nose on the back of my hand, but refused to let the tears fall. I stared off into the darkness. "I don't know what to say. I shouldn't be upset. It's not like we ever said we were dating or exclusive or anything. It's not like he hasn't broken my heart before."

"Lilly," Rose reached out and tried to pull me toward her, but I pulled away.

I raised my hand in front of me to keep them away. "What am I doing?" I asked, as I turned my gaze to the stars. Every muscle in my body tensed as my heart pounded in my chest. "This is bull shit," I yelled. I made eye contact with Rose and Krysty. "Maybe we didn't say that we were exclusive, but we did say we liked each other and wanted to see where things went. I won't let a man get away with treating me like garbage again."

I needed to face him now. Let him know what I saw.

I pushed past them and headed toward the door. I flung it open and pushed my way through the crowd. Adrenaline pulsed through my veins and propelled me forward.

Kora hollered at me, but I ignored her. I was focused and found what I needed as my gaze fell on Jamison across the bar. Ella Raye was standing with her friend. Good for her. She doesn't need to get in my way.

"Lilly," Jamison said, concern in his voice as I approached his table.

I stared at him. His face was filled with possibly guilt and surprise, yet a smile didn't quite meet his eyes. He needed to explain what the hell it was I just witnessed.

"Hey." A hand was placed on my arm.

I turned and saw Darlene and Bryson standing there. It was Darlene's hand. "I'm okay," I told her as I brushed her hand from my arm.

I turned all my attention on Jamison. "I saw you on the floor with her." My gaze left him for a split second and fell on Ella Raye who was still with her friend, not far away. "You're an asshole." I tried to keep my voice calm, but my blood was pounding in my head, and it was getting more difficult to keep calm.

"Lilly," Jamison began as he reached toward me. "It's a misunderstanding."

His eyes begged me to listen. I gritted my teeth. I didn't want to hear anything he had to say. "What? Do you think I'm blind?" My voice was filled with bitterness and anger. "I know what I saw." I couldn't do this. I turned to leave.

"Please," Jamison said as he grabbed my arms. "Bryson and Darlene told me you saw Ella Raye kiss me, and I know it sounds ridiculous, but I didn't kiss her back." His voice pleaded with me.

I tried to ignore his words and refused to look him in the eye. My gaze fell instead on Lance. He was at the next table with Ella Raye, and the one, I guess, was Jayla, the girl he was seeing. Our gazes locked and he raised his brow. *Why doesn't he stick up for Jamison?*

Why doesn't he tell me I was mistaken? I flicked my eyes to Ella Raye. She had a smirk on her face and twirled her hair around her finger as she leaned in to talk to Jayla. *What an absolute bitch.*

I had a sudden desire to gouge out her eyes and punch that damn smirk from her face, but I wasn't that person.

"Can we please go outside and talk?" Jamison's pleading brought my attention back to him.

I closed my eyes and took a deep cleansing breath. "Fine." I turned away not waiting to see if he followed. I ignored everyone at Kora's table and the concerned voices I heard as I passed. As soon as I was outside, I walked around the corner where, just a little while ago, I thought I was going to puke. Now I just wanted to hit something.

Jamison touched my hand, but I pulled away and crossed my arms over my chest, bit my bottom lip, and leaned against the wall. *Act cool, like this is irritating and a waste of my time.*

"I sent you a text," Jamison started. He was nervous. His hands reached out to me, then he stuck them in his pockets. "But I didn't hear from you. She was bugging me to dance, and I told her I wasn't interested, but agreed to a dance. One dance turned to two. She kissed me, and I pulled away as quick as I could." He leaned over and made eye contact with me. Even though I tried to ignore him, the pull of his gaze held me, and the anger I felt lessened a bit.

Jamison continued. "She pissed me off, and I walked away. I was having words with your brother when Bryson and Darlene got to me." He grabbed my hands. "You're the only one I want, Lilly. I told you that, and I meant it."

My heart clenched. I pictured his lips on hers, and bile churned in my gut again. I swallowed down a lump of emotion. "I want to believe you, Jamison." My eyes welled up with tears and Jamison became blurry. I blinked quickly to clear my vision. "I can't. . . no, I *won't* let a man do this to me again."

I pressed my teeth together, pushed my shoulders back, and held his gaze. I had feelings for Jamison, and I believed what he said, but this was too soon, and my heart was still raw. I shook my head. "I believe you. But I don't think I'm ready to feel like this or put my heart out there again. I need more time to figure things out."

Jamison's shoulders slumped and his face fell. My heart cracked.

"Fine," Jamison said. His eyes slowly met mine, and his glistened. "If you want time, I'll give it to you, but please know, I didn't kiss her. The only mistake I made tonight was not leaving the minute the meeting was over. I should have gone straight to you, and this wouldn't be happening."

"Maybe I needed to see this, though." I held up my hand to stop his objection. "How do we know these are real feelings, and not just left over from whatever we had?"

"Because I know."

"But I'm not sure, Jamison." I squeezed his hands. "And I need to be sure." My gaze traveled over his face. His eyes filled with unshed tears, and the muscles in his jaw twitched. My heart cracked some more, and I had to will my gaze to stay on his and not look down to his lips. The hurt in his eyes made me want to give in.

A part of me needed to kiss him, but I also needed to be sure he was not only the one I wanted, but the one I needed. It wasn't just my heart on the line. I had Madeline to consider, and our families.

"Okay." He nodded. "I care for you enough to give you any time you need." Our eyes locked and he opened his mouth to speak, but then clenched his lips tightly together and walked away.

I heard his truck door close and watched as it pulled out of the parking lot. I leaned my full weight on the brick wall and covered my face with my hands.

"Lill? You okay?"

I dropped my hands and Rose and Kristy were there. I nodded.

"He didn't want her to kiss him," Rose said in a soft voice.

"I know," I nodded. "I believe him. But I told him I needed time for myself. . ." There was more I wanted to say, but my voice cracked.

Kristy wrapped her arms around me, and I cried.

I felt Rose place her arm over my shoulder. "You know what I think?"

"Yeah, we do," said Kristy, her voice uncharacteristically soft and caring. "And you might be right this time." Kristy pulled me away. "If you and Jamison are meant to be together, you will be. If the time is right, it can't be stopped."

I laughed a bit, wiped at my face, and glanced from Kristy to Rose. Rose always said those exact words and believed it with her heart. "I'm going to have to believe it, too. But now, I need to focus on me and figure out what I want and what Madeline and I need."

Chapter 31

LILLY

It was Sunday afternoon, and Kora, Summer, Darlene, Rose, and I checked into our suite in a high-class Nashville hotel. This would be our home for the next two days, and it must have cost a fortune. The living area we entered into was huge and had a small kitchenette off to the side. While Summer and Darlene checked out what I figured was one of the two bedrooms, each with its own bathroom, I opened up French doors which were on the other end of the living area and stepped out onto a balcony. I leaned on the rail and looked down onto an atrium. It was beautiful. It reminded me of a garden with walking paths, but it was all indoors. This was the perfect place to relax and clear my head.

After we all settled in, we went to dinner in one of the hotel restaurants.

"So, since you've added Lilly as a bridesmaid, your numbers aren't even. Who is Kai asking to be the other groomsmen?" asked Summer.

"He thought of asking Rowan, but Rowan wasn't sure if he'd able to get home, so he asked Nolan." Kora said as she ticked off everyone on her fingers. "I was going to have Kai's sister in the wedding also, but she wasn't sure if she could make it, so she's going to be an assistant of sorts. I'll have Rowan help her out. So my brides maids are you four, and the men are Bryson, Lance, Jamison, and Nolan."

An uncomfortable silence fell over the room. Okay, maybe it was just uncomfortable to me. I glanced around, but everyone's eyes were diverted to their plates. I did a quick couple match-up in my mind. Bryson and Darlene would walk together; they were the best man and maid of honor. It seemed obvious that Rose would walk with Nolan, which left me and Summer, Lance and Jamison. I could either walk with my brother or Jamison. I nodded. Time to address this large and looming elephant that was hanging around and sucking up all the fun.

"Alright, y'all," I said. "Let's talk about it. We need to get this Jamison thing out in the open."

"Are you sure it's the right time?" Darlene asked.

"I agree with Lilly. There's no time better than the present," Summer jumped in. "Especially when a heart is screwed, fucked, and stomped on."

I chuckled. You could always count on Summer to say things outright, with no unnecessary fluff.

"This from someone who hasn't had a decent relationship in how long?" Kora challenged; her brows raised.

Darlene looked at Kora. "So true. It's been forever. She spends all her time pining over my brother-in-law by phone but never telling him her true feelings."

Kora lifted her fork, and they both clinked forks in a cheers motion.

"And it's been going on for how long?" Kora asked.

"You're both full of shit," Summer answered them, her eyes narrowed. "I don't *pine* over Rowan. He's my best friend, and a lot nicer to me than y'all two prissy-ass bitches are sometimes." She moved her gaze away from them.

"Damn, Summer, those are some harsh words," Kora said.

"Yeah, they are. I'm a little hurt." Darlene placed her hand dramatically over her heart.

Rose and I laughed. The words might have been harsh, but Kora and Darlene were being overly dramatic.

"Whatever. You're both jealous because I say I miss him. And it's because I do, and he never says things to make me talk to him the way I'm forced to talk to you two. We have fun together."

"Fun? What kind of fun?" Darlene asked.

"Well, he hasn't been home for a while, so maybe they have phone sex," Kora said with a shit-eating grin.

"True," added Darlene. "She is uncharacteristically sweet some days. Maybe an orgasm by vibrator could explain those weird encounters."

I bit my lips to hold in the snicker that threatened to escape, and Rose hid her face in her napkin, but her shoulders shook. Summer's face was red, and her nostrils flared. If looks could kill, Kai would not be getting married to Kora in October.

Summer gently placed her fork on the table and sat up tall. "You know what? I'm not putting up with this bullshit this weekend. Y'all two can say whatever you want about this, but we need to get back to the couple who matters." She turned to me. "Lilly and Jamison."

"Look," I said. "I believe him, but right now, it's better if he and I cool off a bit."

"I know," Darlene said. "And we all support you, but he really cares for you, Lilly, and he hasn't put his heart out there since Carly's death."

My pulse sped up. I shrugged and ignored the warmth that churned in my gut. "Just give me time." My voice was soft. "My heart needs to focus on life in general. Maddy's getting ready to start kindergarten, and I'll have free time, which I've never had before. A relationship's a lot to deal with right now. I've got to focus on me and Maddie and figure out what we're doing next. I can't stay with Mom and Charles forever." I took a sip of my water. "Let's focus on Kora and Kai for the next two days. This time is about them. I can only hope my future is as amazing as theirs promises to be."

"Here, here." Summer said as she filled our wine glasses and we all toasted Kora and dug into the desserts.

Thankfully, the attention turned where it needed to be—off me and Summer's non-existent relationships—and back on Kora.

Chapter 32

Jamison

It was Sunday night, and I had been having a hard time keeping my promise to give Lilly time. I wanted to text her; hell, I wanted to call her and hear her voice, but I couldn't, so when Bryson called me and forced me to come to his house, I jumped at the offer. Now, here I was, pacing across his back deck.

"Bro, you need to have a drink and relax," Bryson said.

I shot him a hard look but continued my pacing. I had to keep moving. It felt like there were bugs crawling all over my skin, and walking was the only thing keeping them at bay.

"You should listen to him," Kai said. "You can't do anything about Lilly this second, so stop worrying."

"No shit. But it makes me feel better pacing here than being irritated at home."

Shit. None of this would have happened if I had never agreed to dance with Ella Raye.

"Bro, do what you want, but I hope you're willing to fix my deck when you wear out the boards." Bryson opened the cooler and gestured with a beer toward me. "Have a drink and relax."

Relax? Easy for him to say. He didn't do something stupid and upset Darlene.

Okay, yes, he had done stupid many times in the past, but that was different, and they always worked it out. This thing with Lilly . . . "What was I thinking?" I raked my fingers through my hair. "Why did I listen to Lance? Why did I let Ella Raye cozy up to me without putting more space between us, or better yet, why didn't I walk off the floor when the slow song started?"

"Hey, bro," Bryson said as he placed his hands on my shoulders. "You can't change the past. Seriously, you need to relax."

I looked at him and took a big breath in. I needed to calm my breathing and the churning of my stomach. The longer I went without hearing from Lilly, the sicker I felt, and it'd only been a day. She wouldn't be back until Tuesday, so I had to get used to it.

Bryson breathed in and out with me.

He did this a lot during the months after Carly died. Out of nowhere, I would get angry and basically heartbroken. My grief counselor taught me to do deep, focused breathing, and when I did it right, it helped, just like now. I felt better, too. My pulse relaxed, and my head was no longer thumping like all the blood had pooled there.

Bryson patted my arms. "There you go. You look better, like you're not going to kill the next person who pisses you off."

"Hey, shitheads. Sorry I'm late." Lance entered the backyard. The expression on his face was his usual relaxed look as if nothing ever bothered him. Which, in reality, it didn't.

My pulse began to pick up speed again. And the thumping in my head returned. *Fuck.* I pinched the bridge of my nose and sat in the chair next to Kai.

"Well, it worked for a little bit at least." Bryson said and tipped back his beer.

Lance filled the cooler with beer he brought, probably an IPA from the local brewery. "Here. It's your favorite."

He handed me one. I ignored him and turned to Kai. "Why's he here? I was hoping for a night with mature men, not an egotistical asshole thrown in."

"Sorry, man. I saw him when I was picking up food for tonight and felt like it would be wrong if I didn't invite him. He is in the wedding, and we do have things to talk about. I invited Nolan too, but he already had plans with the kids." He pulled out his phone. "So, to get started, I have a list from Kora of what we need to focus on."

Lance ignored Kai. "You're not still upset about Lilly, are you?" he asked as he sat across from me, his elbows on his knees.

I glared back at him and felt my nostrils flare with my breath. *Focus on your breathing. Relax.*

Yeah—bullshit. Won't work this time. I straightened up and pushed my shoulders back. If Lance wanted to start something, I'd make sure I finished it.

"Lance, give him a break," Kai said in his deep and calm voice.

Lance took a drink of his IPA. "What do you want me to say?" Lance asked me. "I didn't make Ella Raye kiss you. I sure as hell didn't tell you to react to it."

That's it. This fucker needs to shut his mouth. I pushed up from the chair, and Kai was right beside me with his hand on my shoulder. Bryson was quick to stand next to Lance.

"Lance. That's uncalled for," Bryson said to him.

Lance pushed away. "Look, I'm not saying anything to be an asshole. It's just what I saw." He turned toward me. "Maybe you're not ready to be in a relationship, is all I'm saying."

"Lance, what the hell's your problem?" I asked. This was ridiculous. I couldn't deal with him anymore. It'd only been a day, but I missed Lilly and was over trying to keep my best friend happy. "You do realize we're all adults, don't you? I care about Lilly, and she deserves to be treated like I want to treat her. Why do you have such a hard time with this?"

Lance stood tall. "Oh, I don't know. Maybe because my best friend is fucking my sister. And to make it worse, kept it a secret from me."

Bryson and Kai came to my side.

"Lance, dude. Come on, enough," Bryson said.

"Yeah. Let's take it down a notch," Kai added.

Kai touched Lance's arm, and Lance flicked him off. "Don't touch me, man. I'm fine". I saw Kai's jaw muscle tick. Kai was raised in a harsh environment and had raised his fist to his father many times. A fight wasn't something he'd back away from.

"Lance," Bryson cut in. "Chill, man."

Lance's nostrils flared. "Look, I'm looking out for both of you," he said to me with anger in his voice. "Just before Lilly came home, you went on a date. Remember?"

Yeah, I remembered. I did try a date, and my head wasn't in it. I thought of Carly all night. "Yeah, I do."

"Me too. You told me your heart wasn't ready to move on and had no more room for another woman. It was still filled with Carly."

"You're right." Guilt filled me and ate at the irritation. "I wasn't ready then. But it's different with Lilly."

"That was maybe two months ago." His voice raised. "How is one extra month so much different? How do I know you won't get involved with Lilly and then decide your heart doesn't have any room for her either?" He took a step closer to me. "She's doing great moving on from her divorce, but I don't think she'd be able to handle another heartbreak so soon, and I won't watch it when it could be avoided." He was in my personal space and held my gaze.

I swallowed. Part of what he said registered and hit home, but I wasn't going to back down. He needed to know how I felt. I gritted my teeth, then said, "You're right, but this is Lilly, not some stranger I just met. This is different." My voice was firm and steady, and I refused to look away.

"Exactly. It's different. She's not someone you can ignore if it doesn't work out. Our families are at stake here. You've known her your entire life. Why now?"

It was now or never to come clean. It wasn't like he could get any more pissed at me than he was. I took a deep breath through my nose, then blew it out slowly before I answered him. "It hasn't been just now." My voice was quiet and calm, and I locked my eyes to his.

Lance cocked his head and took a step back. "What do you mean?" His words were short.

Bryson made eye contact with me and raised his brow. I answered his brow raise with a quick nod.

"Jamison. What do you mean it hasn't been just now?" Lance asked again, his voice laced with outrage.

I put my hands up to keep some space between us. "Lance, do you remember the summer before our senior year of college?"

He nodded and stared off behind me. "Yeah. The summer you were always gone, and we didn't spend much time together." His eyes widened. "Why?"

"I spent the entire summer with Lilly, but we kept things from everyone. She was concerned about how to tell you."

"Wait. You fucked my sister when we were in college?" Lance curled his hands into fists, then linked his hands behind his head. "What the hell?" His voice became loud and his outrage morphed into venom. "You fucked my sister and kept it a secret all these years?"

"What did you expect me to do?" My voice rose with rage. "Tell you? It didn't matter anyway. We left things hanging, didn't promise each other anything, and when I got back to college, I met Carly, and we started dating. You know what happened then."

"And what? You threw away my little sister's heart, her feelings?"

"Lance," Bryson tried to intervene, his voice calm. "Come on."

"Don't defend him just because he's your brother," Lance pointed at Bryson.

My patience cracked, then snapped in two. "This is fucked up, Lance." I felt anger rising, but I was exhausted from hiding my feelings. "She makes me happy. I make her happy. This is why she wanted to keep us from you before and why she wanted to again this time. She knew you'd go ballistic."

"You're damn right." He yelled as he closed the space between us. "You can have any woman in this small-ass town." He was in my personal space again. "All you have to do is say the word and they would all come crawling to the almighty Jamison McKendry. Why my sister?" He demanded.

"Because I love her!" I shouted in his face.

I froze.

I didn't even realize I had those feelings until the words left my mouth. I mean, I'd thought it the other night, but I didn't think I really felt that way.

I breathed heavily, and my heart thumped out of my chest. I took a couple steps away from Lance. I had never used those words about any woman except Carly.

Could I be sure that's what I felt? I searched my thumping heart, and it calmed just a little.

Yes, I did. I loved Lilly.

"Excuse me?" he asked, his voice a bit calmer.

I took a deep breath, and when I spoke again, I was relaxed, and I knew my words were true. "I love her, man." I shrugged, and my voice calmed. "I didn't even realize it until right now. She fills the hole Carly's death caused. I'll always love Carly, but I have room for more, and I want it to be filled with Lilly."

I waited for the punch I was certain I would get in retaliation from Lance, but it never came.

"Wow," Bryson replied. "I didn't see that coming."

"How did you not?" Kai asked. "He's been swooning over her for weeks."

Bryson shrugged. "Maybe so, but it's Jamison. You didn't know him and Carly. I never thought he'd let anyone else in his heart, and the fact it's Lilly?"

He turned to Lance. "I think you need to suck it up and get over yourself. Some people never find their first love, and these two aren't getting just a first chance together, but after heartache and sadness, they found each other again and have been given a second chance."

Lance glanced at Bryson; his face scrunched up like it was in pain. "What are you? A fucking Hallmark card? That was way too sappy, especially coming from you."

"Yeah, well, what can I say? I'm a sucker for love. Especially when it's my favorite brother."

CHAPTER 33

JAMISON

I was greeted with all the smells and sounds of the salon when I walked in the door of Shear Perfection to pick up Darcie.

"Hi, Daddy," Darcie greeted me from Diane's chair.

"Hi Jamison," echoed Madeline from Kayes. They both wiggled their fingers in the air, their nails pink and glittery.

"Hey, princess." I kissed Darcie on her cheek. "Your nails look pretty."

"Thanks, Daddy. Madeline and me have the same color."

"Yeah, we're going to start kindergarten as nail twins," Madeline said.

"Nail twins? Very cool," I said to Madeline as I gave her a kiss on her head.

"Guess what, Daddy?" Darcie chimed. "It's Madeline's birthday soon, and she's going to have a *Moana* party."

"You're coming, Jamison, aren't you?" Madeline asked. "It's going to be at my grandma and grandpa's house."

I turned to Kaye, and she smiled. Yeah, I wanted to go more than anything, hopefully with Lilly, but that didn't look good. "Of course, I'll be there. Darcie can't drive herself."

The girls giggled, and I went to the kitchen to get a cup of coffee.

"I thought I heard you come in." My mother was at the small table reading a magazine, her hair in foil.

I filled a cup and sat at the table with her. "Don't you ever work?" I asked her. She worked as a secretary for the mayor of Orlinda Valley but never seemed to actually be at work.

She shrugged. "I took a couple days off to be available for you and Darcie this week in case you needed help with anything. I thought I told you yesterday."

"Nope, you only said it was Monday, and you don't work on Monday's."

"Well, I don't work Mondays or any day this week."

Madeline and Darcie came running into the kitchen. "Gramma said we can grab a snack and watch TV in the back room," Madeline said.

"Yep. So, we're going to watch *Moana*," Darcie said.

"You always watch *Moana*," I answered them. "Isn't there another movie you'd like to see?"

Madeline shook her had. "*Moana's* our favorite."

They grabbed cookies and ran into the back room, and Kaye got them settled in front of the television. I refilled my coffee and turned. I froze.

Diane, Kaye, Ruth, and my mother were all sitting at the table, and all eyes were on me. I didn't even know Ruth was here. I stared them all down and fidgeted. This wasn't a good place to be—all four of the book club with me as their focus. I placed my coffee on the counter and prepared myself for their onslaught.

I raised my brow and crossed my arms over my chest. *Play it cool.* "When is Bryson getting here? And what do y'all want?"

They all turned their gazes on each other.

"Bryson will be here soon enough." Diane was the one who finally broke the uncomfortable silence. "We need to talk with you. We talked to Kai this morning."

I puffed out a breath. They all loved Kai. When he came to Orlinda Valley last year, the book club women took him in when he was adding an addition to Shear Perfection. Since then they all treated him like he could do no wrong, and okay, he was Kai. In the short time we'd all known him, we had to agree. He could do no wrong, and he loved Kora deeply. That, in all of our minds, made him an amazing person. He was now like their adopted son—the poor boy with a bad life, who found the love of his life, and the family he always dreamed of.

With how they were all watching me, I was sure he said something about last night. But how much, and what? "What did Kai have to say?"

I looked from Diane and Ruth to my mother and Kaye.

Kaye had a tear running down her cheek and her hands over her mouth, and my mother had a silly grin on her face. *Shit. He told them everything.* My eyes studied the ceiling for a bit, and I clenched my teeth together. "So, exactly what did you hear?"

"Jamison," Ruth started. "Look at me."

Dammit, Ruth. Out of all the women my mother was friends with, she was the sweetest, most sincere person I knew. Rose was just like her. As sweet as pie and as good natured too. I did as she asked and looked at her.

"We know how you feel about Lilly, and honey, if your heart could open itself up to love again, we want you to know we support you."

"Yes, one hundred percent," Diane agreed.

"We also know Lance was being a donkey's hind end," Ruth added, then turned to Kaye. "Sorry, but that pretty much sums it up."

Kaye wiped her face and nodded. "You have such a sweet way with words, Ruth. I appreciate it."

"You're welcome, honey."

"Oh, good Lord." Diane shook her head and rolled her eyes. "We need to get back to the point. Jamison, we know you're in love with Lilly."

My mom stepped forward. "Baby boy, I'm so glad you're able to love again."

"Mom," I stepped away from her oncoming hug, "look, I don't want this to be made into a big thing. Lilly said she's not ready to move into another relationship and asked me to give her time. I haven't talked to her since Saturday night, but if she's not ready, there's nothing I can do about this, and I don't want my feelings to confuse her any more than my actions already have."

"I agree with you, Jamison," Kaye said with a sniffle. "Give her time and space if she needs it, but I know she has feelings for you. She always has."

I narrowed my eyes. "How do you know that?" I asked.

"A mother knows her daughter," Kaye answered.

"And her best friend tells her mother everything," Ruth finished.

"She can't avoid you. Your girls are besties," Diane said. "So, give her time."

"And let the book club work their magic," my mother added.

Kai and Bryson entered the kitchen as the women exited. They both had shit-eating grins on their faces. I really wanted to punch those grins.

"You're a jackass, Kai," I told him.

He shrugged. "It's all good. With the book club gossips on your side, Lilly doesn't have a chance to ignore her feelings for you."

"You know, I could figure out things with Lilly on my own."

"Sure, you could but take my word for it. Those women know what they're doing when it comes to love. I would know," Kai said, and yes, he would. He didn't think he was good enough for Kora, and the book club kept putting them together until they could no longer ignore their feelings. The rest is history.

"Whatever," I said. "What do you two want, anyway?"

"Well, we never went over Kora's list, so we're going to Jerry's Pub to complete the most important task. Beer tasting for the reception," Bryson said.

"Yep. I don't want to face her in a few hours and tell her the few things she put me in charge of aren't checked off."

I told Madeline and Darcie goodbye, and left them to watch *Moana* in the capable hands of their grandmothers. "Fine. Let's go to the pub. What exactly do we have to do?"

"We're in charge of the alcohol for the reception, so we need to go and do a tasting of the new craft brews Travis has on tap," Kai explained. "One was the IPA Lance tried to share with you last night, and there's a bit more, so it might take a while."

Now, that was something I could get behind.

"Lance is meeting us there, and we hope you two will be able to keep from bashing each other's skulls," Bryson added.

"No promises," I said.

CHAPTER 34

LILLY

I walked into my house with Rose, well Mom and Charles's. I don't think I'll ever see it as mine. Ruth had contacted Rose and said Lena and Madeline were having a visit.

"We're home," I yelled as we entered the living room, but there was no one there or in the kitchen.

"They're outside in the pool," Rose said as she went out the door.

"Mommy!" The squeals of excitement from Lena and Madeline were deafening, and to our horror, they climbed out of the pool and wrapped us in soggy hugs.

"I missed you," Madeline said as I picked her up to hug her close.

I wouldn't be able to do that much longer. I was tiny at five-four, and she already seemed almost half my size. "I missed you, too. Gosh, you're getting so big. You're almost too big for me to pick up."

She gave me a kiss on the cheek and smooshed her face into my neck. "That's okay," she said, her voice muffled. "I'll always be your baby, right?"

"You bet your brown eyes." I kissed her head and held her close. God, I loved her. She made my shitty marriage worth every second.

"Daddy, you're here!" My eyes popped open as Darcie climbed out of the pool and ran past me.

"Hey, princess," Jamison's deep and masculine voice made my heart flutter, and my breath caught.

Madeline wiggled in my arms, and I had to let her go. I watched as she ran to Jamison's arms, and he hugged her tight. "Hi, Jamison. Guess what we did today?" And the three girls pulled him to their playhouse in the corner and showed him whatever it was that had kept them occupied this afternoon.

"Well, I guess we know where we stand." Rose stood next to me and nudged my arm. "They haven't seen us in days but weren't going to show us what they did."

I nodded but didn't trust my voice. I watched Jamison with the girls. He was on his knees at the back edge of the playhouse. I could hear their voices but couldn't make out the words.

"Girls, take a seat," Kaye said. "They'll let you know what they're doing when they're ready."

"Yes. Tell us about your night and the dress you found, Lilly," Ruth said.

Rose and I sat on the couch and told the women all about our time in Nashville since Sunday. We'd had a good time once I made sure everyone understood I didn't want to think about Jamison. I felt good about my decision. I still needed to focus on Madeline, get all her supplies for school, and spend some time with her.

I planned to take Madeline to the science museum this week, the zoo, and, of course, spend a lot of time swimming with the girls. By Thursday, we should know who their teachers will be and if they will be in the same class. It would be great if all of them and James could be together, but we knew the chances of that were slim.

Jamison stood from his crouched position and whispered one more thing to the girls.

"Okay, Lilly and Rose, close your eyes; Madeline and Lena have a surprise for you," said Darcie.

Rose and I turned toward each other. She smiled. I shrugged, and we both closed our eyes. I could hear whispers around me from the women. So, whatever this was about, I was sure they were in on it.

The girls must have been in front of us, as I heard their little giggles. "Okay, open your eyes," Darcie said.

We did, and my eyes instantly started to water. Madeline was holding a black ceramic vase decorated with her handprints. It was filled with lilies with a pink bow tied around it. Lena held the same, but hers had pink roses.

"Here, Mommy," Madeline stood in front of me, her voice almost a whisper. "These are my hands, and that's the date I painted this, so you'll always remember me when I was this small."

"Same with you, Mommy," Lena said. "It was Granny's idea, and Jamison took us to buy all the stuff, and he picked out the flowers."

"Aren't they pretty?" Madeline asked. "Lilies are your favorite, and roses are Rose's favorite, and that's both your names. I love it."

I blinked rapidly and wiped away the lone tear as it fell down my cheek. "I love it, too, squirt. It's perfect."

"And when I'm away from you at school, you can remember me because you can see my hands." Madeline wiped away my tears.

I tried to smile and relax. She never did well when I cried, but yet, it was usually because Anthony did something mean or hurtful.

My mother took my vase from my hands. I smiled thanks to her.

Madeline gave me a light kiss on my cheek. "Jamison said you'd probably cry, but I shouldn't worry because they would be happy tears. He told me sometimes ladies cry when they're happy. Is that why you're crying now, Mommy?" Her voice was soft with concern.

I sniffed and glanced up at Jamison, who stood just back away from the girls, his blue eyes questioning and his expression soft. My pulse skipped. The side of his mouth ticked up just a bit. "Yeah, baby. I'm happy." I turned my gaze to her. "This was perfect and sweet and wonderful. I love them."

"Yay." She squeezed my neck again. "Now we need to go with the grandmas and make dinner. We're having tacos."

"Rose," said Tonya, "Why don't you come inside? Lena said something about you making the best tacos ever. We need you to show us your secret ingredient."

Rose snickered and wagged her brow. "I guess I need to show these old women how to open a package of taco seasoning and add it to browned ground beef." She glanced at Jamison, and I could have sworn she winked at him, then squeezed my arm.

I stood there alone in the yard with Jamison just feet away. I'd spent the past two days telling everyone I needed to give myself space and time, but now he was here in front of me, and I wasn't so sure I could wait.

Then I remembered him on the dance floor kissing Ella Raye, and my stomach clenched into a tight knot. I backed up and sat back on the couch.

"Lilly, please, can we talk?" His voice was thick with emotion.

I placed both my hands over my face and massaged my forehead, where I suddenly felt a headache brewing.

I felt the cushion next to me move, and I could smell Jamison's cologne. I sat straight as he grabbed my hands. My gaze dropped, and I watched as his thumb rubbed in circles over my knuckles. His hands were strong and much larger than mine. They filled me with warmth like they had every time he held them since I had been home and like that summer so long ago.

"Lilly," he continued. "I know my actions brought back memories of how Anthony treated you, but I'm not Anthony, and I promise I would never meaningly hurt you. You are so important to me."

My gaze jumped to his, and my pulse skipped.

"I've known you all my life. You are a part of every memory I have with this crazy extended family of ours. I started falling for you that summer."

My mouth went dry, and my pulse picked up speed.

He continued. "I won't say what ifs. I can't. I met Carly, and she became my life, but was taken from me too soon. I didn't think I'd ever be able to fill the hole in my heart her death caused. Then you came home, and there was nothing keeping me away from you. I felt an instant connection when I hugged you that first night at your mom's."

He tucked a stray strand of hair behind my ears, brushed his hand across my cheek, and pushed my chin up to meet his eyes. "And this time, when I started falling for you, I didn't stop. I fell hard, and you have filled the hole in my heart I thought would forever be empty,"

He paused for a second, and his eyes held mine. "I love you, Lilly."

He stopped talking.

I stopped breathing, and I think the world stopped spinning.

He continued. "It might be fast. I know you've only been home for a month, but these feelings have been there in hibernation for years, waiting for a reason to wake up. I think this moment is that reason."

Our gazes held, and slowly, he closed the distance between us. Days ago, I missed the warmth of his lips—the feel of his touch.

His lips brushed mine gently, and I became drugged by Jamison. He deepened the kiss, and his tongue willed my mouth to open and let him in.

I did. I desired everything this kiss gave me.

But it wasn't what I needed, not yet anyway. I pulled away and instantly became alone and empty.

"What's wrong?" he whispered.

"Jamison." I shook my head. "If this would have been us last week, I would have been there with you. I know you didn't kiss Ella Raye, but like I said outside Jerry's Pub that night, seeing you with her on the dance floor gave me a chance to reflect on my life and what I *need*." I met his gaze and the hurt I saw reflected there.

I swallowed hard and ignored my aching heart. "I told you I need time for me, Jamison. Time is something I haven't had in years. I need to figure out what I want, who I am. What Madeline and I are going to do." I took his hands in mine. "So, I'm asking you, again, to please give me time. I can't get into another relationship without knowing who I am, what I want out of life. I wouldn't be a good mother if I did, and I wouldn't be a good partner to you."

He squeezed my hands, and the muscles in his jaw twitched. "That wasn't what I wanted to hear. But I understand. I don't like it, but I understand. I've waited for you for years. I can wait a little longer."

I wrapped my arms around him and relaxed in his warmth. "Thank you. I'm sorry I couldn't give you what you wanted."

He pulled away. "You need to focus on you. Just promise me you'll let me know what you decide, no matter what it is?"

His eyes were filled with pain, and they gleamed with tears. I bit my lips to keep from kissing him and telling him I was wrong and nodded instead. I didn't trust my voice to speak.

"I'm going to go." He opened his mouth to say something but thought differently and walked into the house.

Chapter 35

Lilly

If I did what I needed to do, why did I feel so rotten? I walked to the girls' playhouse, sat on the bench next to it, leaned my elbows on my knees, and covered my face with my hands.

"Jamison just left." Rose sat next to me and wrapped her arm around my shoulder. "I guess you held strong about needing time."

I nodded, and tears flowed from my eyes. "I want to be happy, Rosie. I deserve to be happy."

"Yeah, you do. But if you feel like you need time, then you deserve to take it."

She was right, as usual. It was comforting to know that even though so many things had changed while I was gone, Rose was still the same focused and thoughtful person she had always been.

I sat up and wiped away my tears. "Jamison told me he loved me." I bit my lip and turned toward her.

"Wow," she responded. "That's huge. What did you say?"

I shrugged. "What could I say? It's what I've always wanted to hear, but I told him I needed time to figure out what I was going to do."

She grasped my hand. "And?"

"He said he's waited this long. He can wait a little longer." My heart fluttered. Jamison was willing to wait for me. *How did this happen?* I stared across the yard.

"Well, I guess you need to figure out what you want to do. You mentioned going back to school to finish your degree and become a nurse. Maybe you should."

"I know, and I'm going to look into it." I brought my gaze back to her. "But it probably won't be easy."

"If it was easy, everyone would do it," Rose said, and I laughed.

Jamison's dad used to always say those words whenever one of us mentioned something being hard or we were scared to try. Carl was such a great man. He was there for Lance and me when our dad passed away and was there for Rose and Roland, her twin brother, when their dad and mom argued. He and Nigel, Kora's father, were the rocks and surrogate fathers to our group of kids.

"Just think—Jamison told you he loves you." Rose nudged my shoulder. "I remember when you were in middle school and would daydream about Jamison kissing you and holding your hand. And how you'd mope around when he'd bring his latest girlfriend to the weekly cookouts." She squeezed my hand. "Now it's you."

"Yeah, and I turned him away. Younger me is probably screaming right now."

"Probably, but older you made a good decision."

I smiled at Rose. She really was the best, and I gave her a hard squeeze. "Thank you for understanding and always making things make sense."

She squeezed me back. "Of course. It's what I do. Now, come on. Dinner's getting cold." She pulled me up, and we linked arms as we walked across the yard.

"I almost forgot. Your amazing tacos. What's your secret?"

"I'll tell you, but don't let it go any further."

I zipped my lips.

"Love. Make everything with love, and it always tastes better."

I rolled my eyes. My heart was lighter as we walked into the kitchen. A talk with a best friend tended to do that to a person.

A hush fell over the room when we entered.

My mother came over to me and wrapped me in a hug. "You okay, sweetie?"

I nodded. "Yeah, I am." My eyes met Tonya's. She was uncharacteristically quiet, and her mouth was pinched tight.

My heart ached. Not only had I hurt Jamison, but I hurt Tonya. This was what I was afraid of. Hurting those I love.

I sat in the chair next to Tonya and picked at my fingernails. "I'm sorry I couldn't tell him what—" My voice hitched as tears swelled.

"Oh, sweet girl." Tonya pulled me toward her and squeezed me as my shoulders shuddered and tears fell. "You've been through so much."

"I didn't want to hurt him," I sobbed.

She didn't respond. Her breathing became deep, and she rocked us. "I know," she finally said. "I know."

I pulled away and searched her face. She had tears in her eyes. "I'm sorry, Tonya."

"Sh, sh, sh." She shook her head and held up her hand. "Yes, I'm upset because my son is hurting, again. But I'm glad you were honest with him. His heart is still raw, and he doesn't need another heartbreak. You take your time, and when you've made your peace with your past and are ready to move on, if Jamison's part of your plans, know you have my blessing." She grasped my arms. "But Lilly, if you realize Jamison isn't the one for you, don't feel bad or obligated. Just be honest with him and with yourself. You both have been through so much and deserve nothing but happiness."

Her look was so sincere. "Thanks."

She nodded and rose. "I gotta go and check on those damn goats and close up the chickens. Kora's staying at their house tonight." She slung her purse over her arm. "I can't wait until they have the new barn ready and move all the animals to their new home."

"Then you'll have to go there to take care of them," Diane said.

"Nonsense. Terry's staying on their property. They will be his responsibility."

Terry was Kai's father. After Kai had moved to Orlinda Valley, his father showed up. They had some major healing of their own to do, and over the past year, Terry got sober, and they had mended some fences.

"You'll miss those goats," said Ruth, "and you'll be lonely on all your property with no one else around."

"I still hope Jamison will build on his plot someday, and maybe Rowan will come home."

"It would be so nice to see Rowan. Maybe he'll make it for Kora and Kai's wedding," Rose said.

I sat with a plate of the best tacos ever and listened to the talk about Kora and Kai's wedding. I took my first bite and had to admit, they were pretty amazing.

Soon after I finished eating, everyone left, and Rose took Madeline with her. I started to clean the kitchen and became lost in the familiarity of washing dishes and scrubbing pans.

Once the kitchen sparkled, I grabbed a book and cuddled on the couch under a blanket and started to read. Mom and Charles had already gone to their room, so I had the living room to myself.

"Hey, sis, what you doing?"

"Shit, Lance." I jumped and placed my hand over my racing heart.

"Sorry." He chuckled a little.

"Why are you here so late, and how did you get in so quietly?"

Lance took a seat next to me, and I scooted over to give him space. "I just talked with Jamison and thought I should come check on you."

I searched his blank expression. I couldn't tell if he was being helpful or hurtful. You never could with Lance. He had a perfect poker face. Always neutral.

He continued. "I was being selfish, and I'm sorry."

I studied his features and bit my lip as I tried to figure out if he was sincere.

The only expression he had on his face was a small smirk. That's as sincere as I'd get from him. "It's okay. I didn't make this decision because of you. I need to decide what I'm going to do. I have to put me and Maddy first for now."

He relaxed into the cushions. "What are you thinking?"

I took a deep breath. It was time to be vocal about what I want with people other than Rose and Kristy, see if anyone thinks I'm crazy. And who better to start with than my older brother? "Maybe I'd go back to school. I have some college under my belt. I'm thinking I should see what it would take to finish my nursing degree. I always wanted to be a nurse, and I still do. Even if it's just part time or on call."

"I think that's a good idea, but would you really go through with it?"

I narrowed my eyes. "Why wouldn't I?"

"I don't know," he said. "Sometimes I think you don't want to be successful. It's like you're scared to try and fail, but you need to try, anyway."

I cocked my head and stared at him. Again, his face was blank. I couldn't figure him out. "You know, Lance, sometimes you're so much like Anthony."

He moved back like I slapped him. "You're not serious. When was the last time Anthony encouraged you to do anything? I didn't know him at all, but I know he was controlling. You're saying *I* am?"

"I'm sorry. Maybe I was a bit harsh, but you're always in people's faces and in their business. When they're happy, you have to go and screw it up, and then you flip sides and support them. It's like you want people to do things your way and let you lead them, just like in high school when you were co-captain of the football team. You were a leader, and everyone listened to you." I placed my hand on his knee. "But it's not high school anymore. Maybe you need to see that sometimes people don't need to do things your way, and you don't have to be in charge all the time."

He grasped my hand. "I know. You're right. I do like to be in charge, but I was wrong about you and Jamison, and I've screwed up. I had no clue you two ever had feelings for each other, and now I find out my best friend is in love with you. I was jealous and a little hurt that neither of you trusted me enough to talk to me about any of this."

"And you think it would've worked out well if we had told you about us all those years ago? Look how you reacted now."

He sighed and raked his fingers through his hair. "Look, sis, I'll tell you what I told him tonight. You should totally ignore me and my sorry ass. You've both been through more than most people should ever go through in a lifetime. I don't know what you want, but if it's Jamison, please don't let me get in your way. You're both my favorite people. I love you guys."

My brother could be a giant turd at times, but he had a big heart once he let people see it. I gave him a hug. "Thank you, Lance. That means a lot. But I still need to focus on me and Madeline first, and I hope Jamison still wants me by the time I figure my shit out."

Chapter 36

Jamison

"What's wrong, princess?" Darcie had been sitting at the kitchen counter for at least fifteen minutes and hadn't even touched her peanut butter toast. She just kept picking at the crust. "You need to eat. We have to leave in a few minutes."

"I know," she said as she continued picking at the crust.

It was the first day of kindergarten. She had been excited all summer for this day to come, and now that it was here, she looked forlorn. It broke my heart.

"Hey, you know I'll be there as soon as school's out, and we're going with James and Uncle Bryson for ice cream."

She nodded.

"What's wrong? Talk to me, princess."

"What if Madeline and Lena find new friends and don't talk to me anymore?"

I breathed out, relieved that was the only issue.

"Princess, all three of you are in the same class. You're best friends. I'm know it will all be just fine. It's the other girls who will be wanting to be friends with the three of you." I pushed her peanut butter toast closer to her. "Now hurry up and eat. We're leaving in five minutes." I wiped the counter and straightened up the kitchen. I was anxious to get going. It'd been almost a week since I'd seen Lilly. She hadn't gone to the Friday night barbecue, and I hadn't seen her around town.

If I got to the school early enough, she wouldn't be able to avoid me.

I zipped Darcie's lunch box and placed it in her backpack. "Gotta go."

She drank her milk and wiped her mouth on her napkin as I opened the door and rushed her into the garage.

The drive to the school was quiet, and soon, I pulled into the parking lot. I parked, as we were allowed to walk them in on the first day and glanced around. No sign of Lilly's car. It was 7:30. The doors had just opened for drop off, so I hadn't missed her.

I hopped out and opened Darcie's door. "Ready?"

She nodded and climbed out, her face pensive—or as pensive as a five-year-old could be. She grabbed my hand as we walked across the parking lot and up the walk toward the main entrance.

Katrina Bloggins, a second-grade teacher and someone I knew from my high school years, opened the door when we approached. "Hi, Jamison." She greeted us with a big, toothy smile.

"Good morning, Katrina," I responded. Katrina and I dated very briefly in high school. She'd gotten divorced after a short marriage stint and had been hitting on me ever since Carly's death. No matter what I said to her, she never took the hint that I wasn't interested.

She brushed her hair behind her shoulder before she crouched and addressed Darcie. "Hi there, Darcie. Are you excited to start kindergarten?"

Darcie shrugged and looked behind her.

Katrina stood. "I'm sure she'll have a great first day."

"Madeline!" Darcie's sour demeanor evaporated instantly, and my heart skipped a few beats as Madeline and Lilly joined us in the doorway.

"Good morning, Lilly." Katrina's sweet-as-pie voice gained an edge of bitterness. I lifted a brow, but she didn't notice as we entered the school.

Darcie grabbed Madeline's hand. "I'm glad you're here." She got close to her ear. "I was nervous," she attempted to whisper, though we all heard her.

"Good morning." I smiled at Lilly and caught a whiff of her perfume. I itched to reach out and touch her. Well, I really itched to kiss her soft, plump lips, but I'd have to pass. "How are you holding up so far?"

She shrugged one shoulder and tilted her head briefly. "I'm getting by." Her smile lit up her face. "It's good to see you."

Those words lifted my spirits instantly. "You too."

"Daddy, we gotta go." Darcie was hopping from one foot to another.

"Yeah, Mommy. Come on." The girls started down the hall leading to the lower grades, and we followed.

"Lilly, Jamison." Rose caught up to us, and Lena met the girls. They all entered the room together and found their cubbies easily.

It didn't take long until Darcie and Lena were settled and on the carpet. All nerves were gone from Darcie, though Madeline had a hard time separating from Lilly.

"Hey, Maddie," I said to her as I gently peeled her arms from Lilly's neck. "You're going to have so much fun today, and if it's okay with your mommy, you can go get ice cream after school with Darcie and James and tell us all about your day. What do you think?"

Her large brown eyes were bloodshot, but she bravely wiped away the tears with the back of her hands as she nodded. Darcie and Lena came to their friend's rescue. "Good, I'll see you after school. Why don't you wave goodbye to Mommy and go sit with Darcie and Lena. I know you're going to have a great day."

She looked at me from behind her long lashes and gave my waist a hug, then gave Lilly another long hug, and finally went off with the girls.

I turned to Lilly, whose eyes were glistening with unshed tears, and did the only thing I knew to do. "Come on." I took her hand in mine and led her to the privacy of the hallway and pulled her into a hug. I wasn't sure how she'd react, but I relaxed when her arms locked around my neck and her head lay gently on my shoulder.

"It looks like someone's having a hard time." It was Bryson. Lilly pulled away and sniffed.

Darlene dabbed at her eyes with a tissue and handed one to Lilly.

"Don't worry," Bryson said. "You're not the only one having a difficult time with separation anxiety." Bryson pulled Darlene to his side. "And this one needs to gather herself and get to her classroom."

Darlene gave him a quick kiss. "I do need to go. I'll check on them later and let y'all know how they're doing." Darlene said her goodbyes and walked to her classroom at the other end of the small building.

"Well, I gotta run as well. High school doesn't stop for anyone." He squeezed Lilly's arm. "Hang in there, Lill. They'll be graduating soon."

"Oh, goodness, Bryson," Rose said to his retreating back.

"Thanks, y'all, for everything," Lilly said as we walked down the hall and out the door.

"Call me if you need to talk," Rose said. "I've got to go." She held Lilly's gaze and glanced at me quickly, then back to Lilly. "You good?"

Lilly nodded with a small smile.

"K. Love you."

"Love you back," Lilly answered.

We walked in silence to Lilly's car. I put my hands in my pocket because I wasn't sure if she wanted any more physical touch. At her car, I opened the door for her.

She sighed and looked up at me, her eyes clearer than they were earlier. "Thank you, Jamison." She put her hand on my chest, and a shock went straight to my heart. She must have felt something, too, because she picked her hand up almost instantly and climbed into her car.

As soon as she started it, desperation flowed through me. I didn't want her to go so quickly, so I knocked on her window, and she rolled it down. "Would you like to go to Orlinda Valley Drugs and grab a quick breakfast or at least a cup of coffee?" I knew she might say no, but I had to try.

It felt like forever before she nodded, and when she did, I let out a breath.

Thank you, Lord.

It wasn't an admission of love, but I'd take it.

CHAPTER 37

LILLY

"I'll take an orange juice and biscuits," I said. "Do you have strawberry jelly and honey?"

"Of course. I'll put your orders in and be right back with your coffee." The server, Gloria, left, and I fiddled with the knife and fork on the table.

I couldn't tell if I was so jittery because I'd left Madeline at kindergarten or if it was because Jamison was sitting across from me. Finally, I rested my elbows on the table and wrapped my hands around my neck and gave my chin a place to rest.

My gaze met his. I couldn't read any emotion in his eyes like I'm sure he could in mine. I bet mine radiated nerves and insecurity, which was absolutely ludicrous. I was sitting across from Jamison. He wasn't judging me at all. Hell, just a week ago, he'd told me he loved me. I searched his eyes long and hard. Jamison loved me. My heart skittered a bit before it got back to its normal rhythm.

Gloria returned with our drinks, and I immediately took a big sip of the sweet, yet tangy juice.

"I guess you're still not into eating oranges even though you're an adult."

I laughed lightly. "Nope. I still think it's too much work to peel one when I can drink it."

"See, you haven't changed much." His smile filled his face and made him look years younger, not that he even looked his thirty-six years. "Lance told me you were thinking of going back to college and finishing your nursing degree."

I sighed heavily and rubbed my hands over my face. "I thought about it, but I don't know if I should."

"Why not? You've wanted to be a nurse since we were kids. I remember how you waited impatiently for Lance or me to fall off our bikes or out of a tree so you could bandage our knees."

"Not quite," I said as I bit the inside of my cheek.

His brows went up.

"I just wanted you to get hurt so I could nurse you back to health." I felt the blush creep up my neck and cover my face.

Jamison rubbed his chin with a smirk. "Really?"

I pursed my lips and nodded when Gloria came back with our food. I got a brief reprise as we prepared our plates and ate in silence for a bit.

"Seriously, what's keeping you from going back to school?" he asked between bites.

I shrugged one shoulder and thought about a good answer as I chewed my biscuit with strawberry jelly and honey on it. My favorite. "Madeline needs me right now."

"Yes, she does, but she also needs you to be happy and your best self."

His look was focused on me and held my gaze. Challenging me.

"It'll cost money. I have it, but I should put it away for her education."

"With what you'll make as a nurse, you can replace it. She's only five—well, soon to be."

Okay, he was right again. "People will think I'm crazy going back to school."

"Lots of people in their thirties and older go back to school." He placed his hand over mine on the table. "Stop making excuses and be honest with me. What's the real reason?"

I stared at his hand on mine and focused my attention on the heat radiating from him into my skin. My nerves seemed to calm and my heartbeat slowed. I raised my gaze to meet his. I could tell Jamison anything and I knew without a doubt he would listen, really listen to what I said. I took a deep breath. "What if I fail? I could fail." My voice was soft.

He grabbed both of my hands in his and leaned on the table. "Are those your words or Anthony's?"

I held his gaze and swallowed down the lump which had formed in my throat. "But I could fail. Then what would people think?" My heart thumped hard against my chest, and my eyes dropped to the table.

"Look at me, Lilly-Pad."

His words calmed my heart, and I cautiously lifted my gaze.

"I believe you can do whatever you set your mind to. If you want to be a nurse, go. Do it. Will it be easy? Hell no. But you know what my dad used to say."

I smiled and nodded. "If it was easy, everyone would do it."

"Damn straight." Jamison got up from his side of the table and moved next to me. He grabbed my hands again. "I want you to know

I believe in you, and I will help you with anything you need. And so will everyone else. We will all help you. We all . . ." He hesitated. ". . . want you happy."

I had a feeling he wanted to say something else but was glad he didn't. "Thank you, Jamison. I'll look into it."

"No time like the present. I have the day off. If you want, we can go to my house and hop online—or the library if you'd rather."

"The library?" I chuckled. "When was the last time you stepped foot in a library? Do you even know where the Orlinda Valley library is?"

"Hey." He nudged my shoulder and leaned over to pull his plate to him. "I've taken Darcie to story hour at the library lots of times."

We got quiet as we finished our breakfast. The quiet gave me time to contemplate going back to school and try to talk myself out of it, but no matter how hard I tried, it didn't work. I wanted to do it.

"So, what do you say?" he asked as we left the pharmacy a while later. "Want to look at classes now?"

"Sure," I answered without thinking. "How about my house? My mom's at home for the morning, and I think it's better that way."

"Not sure you can trust yourself alone with me?" His grin was mischievous.

"I'm not going to answer that." I couldn't without either lying or telling the truth. Neither of which would be a good idea. Not if I really wanted time to figure out what I wanted to do.

Of course, when we got to my house, my mother wasn't alone. Tonya's car was in the driveway.

"Good choice. Now *my* mother will be in on this. You sure you don't want to sneak around behind everyone's back and go to my house instead?" he asked with a grin.

"Nope. I'm done sneaking around." I pulled on his arm, and he followed me up the walk.

"Well, look who it is," Tonya said when we walked into the kitchen. She hugged me first, then Jamison. "Did the girls do okay at school?"

As soon as the question was asked, my heart broke for Madeline, and I felt those damn tears well up in my eyes again. I blinked them back as Jamison placed a reassuring arm around my waist.

"Maddy and this one here had a bit of a hard time separating, but I bet after today, all the separation anxiety will be one-sided." Jamison squeezed me tighter.

I glanced at him through blurry vision and wiped my face. "I hope so. It will be easier for me to leave her if she's happy. I'll have to deal with my own loneliness."

"You'll be fine." My mom said. "Can I get you something to eat? Coffee or water?"

"No thank you. We just ate, Kaye." Jamison answered for both of us.

"So, what are you two planning on doing today?" My mom asked.

I couldn't tell if it was an honest question or if she was prying. It didn't matter. She was good at doing both, but I wasn't ready to let others know about my thoughts about school. Not even my mother.

"Lilly was thinking about passing her time by going back to college and finishing her nursing degree."

So much for keeping my thoughts to myself. I rolled my eyes and walked to the table.

"Lilly, that's a great idea," Tonya said.

"Oh, baby. It is. You need to focus on yourself. You've always wanted to be a nurse," my mom agreed.

"I know. I'm just going to look into it and see what steps I would need to take. It doesn't mean I'll do it." I turned to Jamison. "Go ahead and get comfortable. I'll grab my computer."

By the time I got back to the kitchen, our mothers had left, and I didn't ask where they went. As long as they weren't going to stay in our business was all I cared about. I booted up my computer and sat in the chair next to Jamison.

Jamison and I spent the next couple hours going through the colleges within driving distance. This was a perfect time to look because classes started at the end of August. I'd be able to hop in at the start of the fall semester if I decided to go through with it. It didn't give me much time to overthink what I was doing, which was probably for the best.

I decided to go to the community college not too far from home, then transfer to a four-year college after I graduate. Chunking college into two-year increments seemed more attainable than looking at a four-year college. Jamison and I had been searching online for over an hour when our mothers came into the kitchen, their purses over their shoulders.

"We're heading out," my mom said with a sheepish look on her face. "We're picking up Ruth and going to Diane's for the day. Charles will be home later."

Tonya pushed her to the door. "You two be good." She winked and they left.

Jamison grinned. "Looks like it's just us."

My heart fluttered, and I had to wipe my palms on my shorts before I touched my computer again. "Yep. Let's get back to this." I needed to keep us on track. It was about me right now.

Jamison helped me understand the online requirements. Since it had been so long since I attended school, I would have to take some tests to make sure my math and writing skills were up to par; then it should be pretty simple. I filled out the admission forms and made an appointment for later in the week to meet with a counselor.

I sat back and puffed out a breath. I did it. I was enrolled in college. Excitement rolled through my stomach and made it churn. I turned to Jamison and wrapped my arms around his neck. "Thank you so much, Jamison." I was on cloud nine. I'd made a decision to better myself and get my life on track. This was a good first step.

He hugged my waist. "I'm proud of you. This is huge, and you're going for it."

Doubt hit me like a brick. I backed away. "What if I'm not ready? What if I don't have time for work and studying and Maddy and all the things I need to do for her? Am I being selfish?" My eyes locked on his. My hands became clammy, and my gut churned as fear took refuge inside it right next to its best friend doubt.

Jamison grabbed the side of my face. "Stop. I'm here, and I'll help you with whatever you need. Your mother will help, too. You have family and extended family. Rose and Kristy. You're not alone anymore."

His blue eyes were sincere and wrapped me in warmth, and I relaxed. He rubbed my cheeks and the back of my neck gently. I concentrated on the feeling, and without realizing what I was doing, my lips met his. He hesitated for a split second, but I pulled him closer and deepened the kiss. Our tongues met, and he leaned in. The kiss was warm, gentle, and forgiving—exactly what I needed.

My life had been shit for so long, and I forgot what it was like to have someone want the best for me. Being home awoke the part of me that had been hibernating for so many years. I deserved to be happy. I deserved Jamison.

My heart exploded and I pulled away just a bit.

I didn't just deserve Jamison, I needed him. Yes, I needed to be independent and have a purpose, and I needed to go back to school to make that a reality...but I also needed Jamison.

I broke the kiss and held his gaze. The corners of my mouth crept up. The man I'd loved in private for so long was here helping me start a new life back home in Orlinda Valley. Jamison McKendry wanted to be mine.

Suddenly, everything seemed possible. Everything seemed right.

Chapter 38

Jamison

Lilly pulled me into a tight embrace. "Thank you for everything, Jamison."

I leaned away and lost myself in her eyes. Those big brown orbs that always pulled me in and held me tight. "I only supported you in your decision. I didn't do anything exciting."

She shook her head. "I don't mean just helping me with school. I mean *everything*." Her eyes filled with tears, and they slid down her cheeks. She wiped them away. "I'm sorry," she said in a sob.

I pulled her to me and held her as she cried on my shoulder. I rubbed her back until her sobs subsided a bit. "You have nothing to be sorry for. But talk to me. What's wrong?" I leaned back, and her gaze met mine.

She slid her hand across my cheek and caressed my face. "Nothing's wrong. I'm just an emotional nightmare." She pulled in a shaky breath, wiped away her tears, and grabbed my hands. "If this is where we were meant to be, why did it take us so long?"

"I've wondered the same thing," I said. "And thought long and hard about it. All I can come up with was that we weren't meant to be together before. We both had to grow and bring amazing little people into the world. We came back together when we were both hurting and both empty. I'm the aspirin you need to relieve your pain, and you're the Band-Aid to heal my heart."

Lilly nodded. "I agree with you, partially."

Her voice was so sure. So final. It frightened me. "What do you mean?"

She brushed her fingers over my lips to quiet them. "We came back together now to give each other a second chance, to heal our hearts and find love again."

My eyes popped, and I held my breath.

"I wasn't sure what I wanted," she continued. "I was scared we were rushing into a relationship. But my heart never had to force itself to have feelings for you. You always had a part of it, and until recently, it was never filled. But you fill my heart to the brim."

She paused, and her eyes glistened. "And I love you, Jamison McKendry."

A smile erupted across my face, and a lightness filled my chest. I blew out the breath I had been holding. "You do?"

She nodded. "I always have."

She placed her lips on mine, and this time the kiss was deep and hot. Our tongues met and tangled. My insides went numb.

She pulled away. "I want you, Jamison." Her gaze was filled with desire. "I want to be with you." She rubbed her hands up my chest and laced her fingers behind my neck. She licked her lips, and her breath was heavy. "Can we?"

Lilly's lips were glistening and rosy. Her eyes glittered with desire. I wasn't sure how we got back here, but I did know she made me feel things I haven't felt in years. "You don't ever need to ask. If you want to, I am one hundred percent on board."

The corners of her lips matched her eyes, which glittered with mischief. That was the look that had thrown me over the ledge many times during our summer together, and desire erupted throughout my body.

"Follow me," she said.

That wasn't hard to do. She pulled me through the living room and down the hall to her bedroom. Her ass swayed and her hips looked absolutely delicious. As soon as we were in her room, she pushed me against the door and shucked my shirt above my head like I was an ear of corn.

Mmm. She moaned as her hands roamed up my chest and caressed my nipples. I sucked in a breath between my teeth and reached out to her.

She shook her head and stepped seductively away.

"Woman, don't tease me."

"I'm not teasing you." Her voice was sultry. "It's called seducing." Her eyes traveled slowly up my body and stopped on my lips.

I licked them slowly and got the response I wanted.

Hers devoured mine, and a deep moan escaped my throat. I tried to wrap my arms around her to pull her to me, but she pulled my arms from around her waist and cut off our connection.

Fuck. Air deflated from my lungs. I needed her. She was driving me crazy. My head fell back against the door with a thump. "Lilly, what are you doing to me?"

Her hand pushed against my chest. "It's been so long since I've wanted a man like I want you."

She kissed my chest and licked my hard nipple.

"Fuck," I said in a breath.

"It's been so long since my body has throbbed with desire like it is now." She pulled her top off and stood in front of me in a lacy black bra.

Blood rushed through my body. I wanted her so badly it hurt—literally.

I reached out, desperate to touch her, but she brushed away my hand and cupped my hardness through my pants.

I moaned, and my eyes closed. It sounded like I was in pain, and I was. My cock was throbbing, and my heart was pounding.

She started rubbing up and down, and I thought I might come undone right then.

"You want me, don't you?" she asked in a seductive whisper, her eyes on mine.

"What the hell do you think?" I took in a deep breath and found courage I didn't know I still possessed, and my eyes held hers. "You know, I should walk away. What if I don't want to be taken advantage of?" I tried to joke.

"Go ahead," she whispered as she jerked my pants down and got on her knees. "Leave if you want." She pushed my pants down my legs, caressing my skin as she went. I slowly stepped out of them.

She stroked her hand up and down my erection. "But I don't think you want to."

Her tongue touched the head, and she licked all the way down and back up.

"Dammit." The feeling was amazing. "I'm not going anywhere," I whispered—I think—I'm not sure if my voice actually worked, because just as I said the words, she wrapped her mouth around me and sucked.

Holy hell.

It was too much, and it felt so good; I knew I was going to explode soon, and though I didn't want to, I needed her to stop. "Lilly." I pulled her to her feet and tried to catch my breath. Her lips were wet and swollen, and when she licked them, I was done, as if I wasn't already.

Two could play this game. I pushed her back and onto her bed and pulled her pants off. I about came immediately when I saw the matching black lace panties she had on.

She lay there like a goddess with her arm over her head and "come fuck me" eyes.

I dragged my hand softly over her breasts, and a shiver shook her body slightly. I continued my hands down her body, and pulled her panties off.

I wanted her as much as she wanted me. Shit, I doubt it. I'm sure I wanted her more. I kissed her stomach and traveled down and licked the sensitive area between her legs.

She moaned and thrust her hips upward, but I held her still. "Jamison."

The high-pitched whisper of her voice about drove me over the edge again, but I kept up what I was doing until she let out a high-pitched groan and yelled my name. I knew she had reached her peak. I was hard, and she was wet.

I kissed my way up her body, and my mouth found her nipples and sucked them, then finally met her mouth.

Our kiss was deep, and we both moaned when I pushed my hardness inside her. Her hands immediately left my neck and cupped my ass. She pulled me deeper into her, and I was more than willing to oblige. Our lips met again, and I leaned on my elbows while I thrust slow yet hard. I brushed her hair from her face. I wanted to see her expression when she came.

Her eyes closed tight, and she wrapped her legs around my waist. "Jamison, yes."

"Lilly." I thrust one more time and exploded in her as her warmth wrapped around me and she let out a moan of ecstasy.

She lay on my chest when we finished, and I held her close. My heart thumped hard. I'd just made love with Lilly. It wasn't just sex this time, and it would never be again. I had no doubt our time together was now. I kissed her head tenderly. The smile she gave me when she tipped her head up made me feel complete.

"I love you," I whispered as I kissed her lips.

"I love you," she said as she cuddled tightly into my side.

A very insistent buzzing sound woke us from a nap. "I don't think they, whoever they are, are going to go away," I said lazily as I got out of bed and fumbled through my jeans pocket for my phone. "It's not mine."

"Shoot," Lilly said as she got out of bed and found her phone in the pocket of her pants. I enjoyed watching her naked in front of me. "You're beautiful."

"Jamison . . ." She grabbed for her T-shirt, but I jumped up and pinned her arms.

I shook my head. "Don't cover yourself. You are absolutely perfect. Everything about you." I kissed her tenderly and felt myself grow hard.

She giggled. "Thank you, but that was my mom. They want us to meet them for lunch. In like thirty minutes. We don't have time for anything else."

I shrugged. "So, we're a little late." I grabbed her and threw her on her bed, and we went for round two.

We walked into Jerry's Pub hand in hand. Our mother's faces were ecstatic. My mother squealed loud enough for people in the next county to hear. "Holy hell, what do we have here?" She squeezed me so tight, I thought my ribs were going to explode.

"Mom . . ."

She thumped me a bit hard on the back and turned to Lilly. "Well, someone has an after-sex glow about her." She held Lilly at arm's length.

"Oh, my God," Lilly said as she turned as red as her tank top.

"Mom, really?" I saved Lilly from any more embarrassment, pulling her to the other side of the table so she could sit by Rose.

"So, I'm guessing all went well with the colleges?" Kaye asked.

I looked blankly at Kaye for a second before it hit me what she meant. I'd totally forgotten Lilly and I had been looking at schools for her to attend.

"It did," Lilly said, and she filled them in on what we'd found out. "So, I hope to be starting in a few weeks.

I placed my arm around her shoulders. "See. It looks like everything worked out and everyone has your back, just like I told you."

"Yep. You were totally right." Her smile lit up her face, and she turned to everyone. "Thank you for supporting me and welcoming me home. This past month and a half has been the best time I've had in . . . well, let's just say a long time." She turned to me. "And now it's gotten even better."

Chapter 39

Lilly

It was two thirty Friday afternoon, and I pulled into an already crazy-long pickup line at Orlinda Valley Elementary School. I put the car in park and rolled down the windows. It was a beautiful afternoon, still warm enough to enjoy the waning summer days but with a little less humidity so the heat wasn't squelching.

I glanced through the statistics book I'd picked up earlier at the community college library after I registered for my classes. I was starting with statistics and biology on Mondays and Wednesdays, and on Fridays I had a math lab—since my entrance exam scores were a little low—and my biology lab. My classes were all at eight o'clock in the morning through lunch; then my plan was to stay on campus and study in the library until it was time to pick up Madeline.

I waved to Brenda, another mother whose daughter was in the same class as the girls, as she pulled up in the line next to me and rolled down her passenger side window. She leaned across the seat and spoke out of the window toward me. "Zyanna and Zeek are excited about tomorrow. Do you think they'll be able to swim?"

I leaned my arm on the window and leaned out a bit so she could hear me better as well. "They sure will. The pool is still nice. So, make sure they wear their swimsuits." Tomorrow was Madeline's birthday, and we were having her *Moana* party at my mother's. Along with the Hawaiian theme, they were going to swim.

"Great. I'll drop them off at one."

"Perfect. I'm glad they'll be there, and James will be excited to have another boy to hang with," I answered.

We said our goodbyes as the doors to the school opened, and little people burst forth. I spotted Madeline, Darcie, and Lena immediately. They were standing with Zyanna and some of their new friends. Madeline's face was lit up with excitement. I was so thankful that she was happy and settling in.

Finally, it was my turn, and all three girls climbed into my car. Rose had started a part-time job at the doctor's office in town this week, so I picked up the girls most days. This worked perfectly. It gave me time I loved with some of my favorite little people, and I always knew at some point I'd get to see Jamison. Today, though, was Friday, and we were stopping at Shear Perfection.

"Who wants to stop by Frosty Freeze and get milkshakes before we go to the salon?"

My question was met with highly enthusiastic me's and squeals, which woke up every cell in me that might have possibly been exhausted. We drove the short drive—everything in Orlinda Valley was a short drive—to Frosty Freeze, waited in line with what seemed like every other kindergarten parent, and ordered milkshakes. Two strawberries, and one vanilla for Lena, then it was off to Shear Perfection.

The grandmothers were waiting for the girls with open arms. They had planned a celebration for the completion of the first week of school and the beginning of birthday weekend. To say my mother was going overboard for Madeline's fifth birthday was an understatement. I couldn't argue with her, though, as this was her first birthday to celebrate with Maddy in person.

I followed Summer as she got the girls situated at the pedicure stations. They continued sipping their milkshakes.

"Your hair's pretty, Summer," I said. The woman who was always doing something out there with her hair for as long as I could remember had suddenly started coloring it more normal colors, and now it looked as close as ever to her original light brown I remembered from high school.

"Thanks," she answered. "I decided it was time to start growing up a bit. I'm over crazy hair color, for now, anyway. We'll see how long before I get an itch to try something new." She turned her attention to the girls. "So what colors are we going to do on these, little women?"

I stood back and watched as the girls chose their colors, and Diane and my mother came and joined Summer. Spa day had officially started, and I was in the way. I needed coffee and went into the kitchen to roast a Keurig pod.

"So, you made it through the first week of your baby in kindergarten," Tonya commented as she took a seat at the table with a can of Diet Coke in her hand.

I nodded and sat with her. "I did." That's all I said. She wasn't just in here to chit-chat about the girls' week. She was fishing for information about me and Jamison. Since Monday's day of college searches and admissions of love and desire for each other, the week had been fun. I'd cleaned his house again on Tuesday, and to my surprise, he came home from work at noon, and we had each other for lunch *and* dessert. Wednesday, we had pizza night with the girls and stole kisses and touches without the girls noticing.

Tonight, we are having a date night and shopping for some last-minute things for tomorrow's party. The kids were having their weekly camp out this week at Tonya's, and I was looking forward to a camp out of my own in Jamison's bed, which was what Tonya was fishing for—where I was going to spend my night and with whom.

"Did you get your college classes set up?" she asked.

Again, I nodded. "I did."

She narrowed her eyes and studied me intently. "You're being very unforthcoming with your explanations."

"Not true at all," I said as I sat up tall and smirked at her. "I'm just answering your questions directly."

"Fine, then." She sat tall to meet my eyes. "Then I will ask a direct question and stop dillydallying. What are your plans for tonight since the girls will be out of the house? Are you planning a sleepover of your own?"

"Don't answer that, Lilly-Pad." Jamison's deep voice and footsteps filled my ears, and my heart flipped in my chest. He leaned down and kissed me lightly and held my gaze. "What you do on your child-free night is none of my nosy mother's business."

"Nosy mother? Is that a respectful way to talk about the woman who was in hard labor for forty-eight hours and gave birth to you?"

"Oh, please, Mom. Don't try to guilt me with how much trouble I gave you during childbirth and how long it took you to recover. If it was so bad, you wouldn't have had any more children."

"Well, it was bad. Your dad and I planned on having three babies back-to-back, but you traumatized me so much, I had to wait two years before I could think of pushing another watermelon out my hoo-ha."

I about spit out my coffee and choked on it.

"Seriously, Mom?" He pulled me out of my chair, and I got control of my choking. I don't know why Tonya surprised me. She didn't say anything out of the ordinary. "Come on. I want to say hi to the girls and get you out of here. I want to hear all about your day."

Our fingers intertwined, and I smiled into his soft blue eyes. "Sounds great to me."

He let go of my hands long enough to kiss Tonya's cheek. "Love you, Mom. Sorry, I gave you such a hard time thirty-six years ago."

"Oh, baby boy, I've forgiven you. Don't you worry your handsome little self about it anymore."

I laughed as Jamison rolled his eyes.

The girls were getting manicures when we found them. "Daddy!" Darcie wiggled her fingers toward his face.

"Beautiful, princess." He kissed her head.

Madeline and Lena wiggled their fingers at him in the same way.

"Y'all have the same color."

"It's princess pink, and we wanted to match for my birthday," Madeline told him.

"And we're all going to wear our same swimsuit tomorrow," Lena said.

"Yep. We need everyone to know we're princess sisters. Princess Lena, Princess Madeline, and Princess Darcie."

"Princess sisters, huh?" I said, my hands on my hips.

"Yep," Madeline answered. "We don't have flower names like you and Rose, but we wanted names the same so we could be sisters just like you."

Jamison shook his head. "God help Orlinda Valley," he said with his eyes to the ceiling. "Do me a favor," he said as he crouched in front of them, all three sets of eyes on him. "Be sweet cheerleaders and not the terrors of the town."

"What?" I squealed and slapped him. "We were not terrors."

"That's not what I remember," he teased.

"Well, if you want to go shopping with me tonight, I suggest you stop this conversation now," I warned.

"And if you want to keep things under wraps," Summer said. "I suggest you two get out of here as soon as possible. We need to finish the princesses' nails, and you're bothering me—Seriously." She shooed us away.

"Bye, girls," I said as I backed away with a chuckle. She was right. We needed to leave. We said our goodbyes and decided to go on our shopping trip in his truck. I climbed in, he pulled out of the parking lot, then pulled into the Dollar General parking lot down the street.

"Jamison, what the . . ." I didn't finish my sentence. He had the car in park, my seatbelt unbuckled, and pulled me to him in the hottest kiss of my memory. It went on for a while and was so hot and deep that a moan escaped from my throat.

Finally, he pulled away but lingered close. "I couldn't wait any longer and didn't want little eyes to see."

"That's fine, but maybe shopping can wait." I dragged my nails up his chest to his neck. "Maybe a quick tryst in bed would cool us both down."

He moaned as my hand slid down his body toward the waist of his jeans. "Woman," he clasped my hand and stopped its descent, "that sounds amazing, but I think we better get shopping. I've been fantasizing about tonight all day, and with what I have planned for you, we won't be leaving my bed till morning."

I smiled wickedly as I moved over and buckled my seat belt. "Then let's get shopping over with. I want to know what you have planned. It sounds exciting."

CHAPTER 40

JAMISON

I woke with the sun peeking through the slits in the blinds the next morning. A smile filled my face when a soft moan reached my ears. I turned over, wrapped my arms around Lilly's naked body, and kissed her neck.

Her sexy, sleepy moan got a little louder and woke up all parts of me. I cuddled into her back to feel her heat and skin as close to me as possible. I kissed her neck again, then traveled down to her shoulder. I slipped my hands around her body and laid them to rest on her soft, firm breasts and kneaded them until her nipples hardened.

She scooted her bottom up against my hard-on and lifted her leg around my lower body and situated me at her opening. "God, Lilly." She was as wet as I was hard.

"You're not the only one wanting something this morning," she said, her voice groggy. Her hands traveled down to my ass, and she pushed me against her and moved herself until I slid easily inside her. "Jamison."

Her voice threw me over the edge. The arm that was under her cupped her breast, while my other hand found its way down her stomach to the sensitive area between her legs. While we moved together, I fondled her. I wanted to feel her come apart while I was inside her. From this position, I could push deeper into her and feel her most sensitive areas, which was exactly what I did until we both exploded at the same time. I slowed our rhythm and caressed her skin.

Lilly rolled over and faced me, and our lips met in a small, gentle kiss.

"Now, that was the perfect way to say good morning," I whispered against her lips.

I felt her smile. "Yes, it was. Do you think the girls will want to spend the night with the grandmas every night?"

"We could see, but first, we've got to get up and get our day started. I feel like we need a shower."

I pulled her from the bed, and not long after an amazing shower, we were dressed and heading to pick up the balloons, cupcakes, and cake. With everyone getting to the house at one, we had four hours to do everything, and from what Lilly described as her vision, she'd probably need every bit of those hours.

"Is it just me, or does it look like a bottle of Pepto Bismol exploded all over a Hawaiian beach?" Lance asked as he joined Bryson, Adler, Kai, and me at a table far away from the screams and splashes from at least fifteen kindergartners.

He wasn't wrong.

You could tell the book club women, led, of course, by Kaye, were making up for all Madeline's birthdays they'd missed. The party was a combination of princess and Hawaiian themes. There was a pink princess castle bounce house in one corner of the yard, and food tables covered in pink tablecloths with luau grass table skirts wrapped around each one. Food was piled high on the food tables. Cookies in the shape of castles and crowns, cupcakes with princess-themed picks and Hawaiian picks, and a ridiculously large princess castle cake that sat in the middle of what seemed to be a beach.

I had no idea who was going to eat all this sugar, but everyone better take something home or we will be eating it for the rest of our lives.

The girls were running around with crowns on their heads and hula skirts around their waists. They even attempted to force the few boys in attendance to wear them also, but James made his thoughts known early on, and the boys became knights and saved the girls from the make-believe dragon that lived on the tropical island.

Lance placed a well-camouflaged cooler on the table. "It's okay, you old men can thank me later. I come bearing gifts." He opened the cooler. "I stopped by Jerry's Pub and loaded up on Raging River IPA and SunnyDays Lager. Take your pick."

It wasn't hard to get us on his side. "You do realize you're older than me, right?" Bryson asked as he grabbed a can of IPA.

"And me," agreed Adler.

Lance narrowed his eyes at Adler, "I think you're one month younger than me, and anyway, it's not age that makes y'all old. You're married and fathers. I'm single, childless, and available. Parenthood ages you. It's a scientific fact."

"Scientific fact?" Adler asked. "Well, it's another scientific fact that regular sex keeps you young."

"If that's the truth, I must be a teenager," Bryson said with a grin.

"I'm there with ya, man." Adler lifted his beer can. "To our beautiful women and them keeping us young."

"Where am I in all this?" asked Kai. "I'm not married yet but get regular sex."

Lance glanced at him over his beer bottle. "You're on your way out. You better enjoy your young years for the couple months you have left. It's all downhill from here."

"It's no wonder you're single." I jumped into this conversation. Lance and his negative attitude on relationships was getting old.

"So, where do you fall in this, big brother?" Bryson said with a raise of his brows.

I glanced around the table. Kai and Adler had shit-eating grins on their faces, and Bryson was still challenging me to answer. Lance, though, was messing with the label on his bottle, and his cheek was sucked in. I knew that look. He was irritated and refused to meet my gaze. This was my chance to stick up for Lilly and me, let them all know where we stand, or back off and give Lance what he desired.

Sorry, Lance. I was tired of doing the "right" thing for my friend. It was time to think of what was best for Lilly and me. Maybe I cared more about Lilly than my friendship with Lance. "Looks like I'm on the same team as Kai. Not married but have a beautiful woman, and the sex is amazing." As soon as the words were out of my mouth, I relaxed.

Kai raised his beer. "That's what I'm talking about. To Lilly and Jamison." He and I clinked beer bottles.

Bryson pounded me on the back. "I'm proud of you. You and Lilly deserve each other, finally."

"Did I hear my name?" I turned and Lilly, Kora, Darlene, and Leila were there. "I don't remember allowing alcohol at my daughter's five-year birthday," Lilly said as she made herself comfortable on my lap. I wrapped my arm around her waist and held her tight.

Just the simple act of sitting on my lap in front of our family and friends put my pulse in overdrive. This beautiful woman was mine and would be as long as possible. "Well, if it makes you feel any better, I didn't bring it. Lance did."

"Thanks for throwing me under the bus. No one forced you to take one," Lance said.

"Well, you sort of did. You called us old," Kai said as Kora sat on his lap.

"Yeah, you did, and then we started talking about what keeps us young," Bryson responded.

"And what was your answer?" Darlene asked as she sat on his lap and took a sip from his beer.

"Just you, baby," Bryson answered as he kissed her. Her arms wound around his neck.

"How do you two not have a million kids?" I asked. "You're both always all over each other."

Bryson and Darlene stared at each other, and Darlene shrugged.

"I don't know that a million would be possible, but two would be perfect," Bryson said, his eyes still on Darlene.

"What?" Kora squealed.

"Yep. Baby number two is due in April," Darlene said, her face radiant.

"But we were supposed to be pregnant together," Kora whined.

"I guess we better get busy then, babe," answered Kai. "I don't think anyone would be offended if you were pregnant for the wedding." Kai glanced around. "Anyone?"

"Go for it, man," Adler said. "Then the grandmas would each be happy."

"What do you mean?" asked Lilly.

Leila's sweet face lit up, and her shoulders met her ears. "We're finally pregnant."

"What?" Was the question of the day.

"We told Diane and my dad last weekend," Leila answered.

Leila and Adler had been trying to get pregnant soon after they were married but were having trouble, and Leila had a miscarriage earlier in the year. This was fabulous news.

"We're already four months along," Leila said. "I'm due in February."

"Is that the appointment you had to go to a few weeks ago?" Lilly asked.

She nodded, and Adler's face radiated happiness.

"Great," Lance said. "Looks like next year is going to be busy. Just what this group needs is more babies."

"Someone really needs to get laid," I joked.

His glare was harsh.

"Dude, relax," I said.

"No, seriously, don't worry about me. I'm good. Jayla's keeping me busy," Lance said. He took a drink but didn't take his eyes off Lilly and me. "And all joking aside. I'm happy for you two. It will take a bit to get used to, but who better to be with my sister than my best friend? At least it will be easy to kick your ass if you hurt her. I've done it before."

I laughed. "Well, good thing for me, I don't have to worry about that happening. I won't hurt your sister." The mood around the table changed and became serious. I could feel all eyes on us. I fixed my gaze on Lilly's and picked up a lock of hair. "I love her and promise I will always keep her safe."

Lilly's smile filled her face, and she leaned in and kissed me. It was a gentle kiss. I cupped the side of her face and kissed her longer when she went to pull away. I loved the feeling of warmth that appeared deep in my gut every time she kissed me. It calmed me and made everything right.

"Umm, y'all . . ." Bryson's concerned voice alerted us.

"Daddy, why are you kissing Lilly?" It was Darcie.

I held Lilly's gaze for a beat. Her eyes were wide, and my heart thumped against my chest.

We had an audience. Darcie and Madeline, along with Lena, Skylar, and a couple other princess' and hula-dressed little girls, stood there watching us.

Darcie's expression was clear, but Madeline's was shrouded.

Lilly got off my lap and kneeled on the ground in front of Madeline, and she climbed on her lap.

Darcie came to me at the chair. "Daddy, do you love Lilly?"

To have the simplistic look on life that most five-year-olds do. It was easy to see why. Everyone whom Darcie knew who cuddled and kissed loved each other. I glanced around. She grew up with all of these people.

I looked at the group of grandparents on the deck, all eyes on us. Love was everywhere.

I was lucky. We were lucky. "Yes, princess. I love Lilly."

Darcie's eyes lit up. Madeline's face was confused. "Maddie, is it okay for me to love your mommy?" I needed Madeline to be okay with this. If she wasn't, I wasn't sure Lilly would see us through. Hurting Madeline more than she had already been hurt was not in the cards.

Darcie placed her arm around Madeline. "This is good, Madeline. Your mommy makes my daddy happy, and you said your mommy is happy for once. That's what it's like when people love each other. They make each other happy."

Madeline looked at Darcie, then at me, her large brown eyes red with unshed tears. Lilly pulled her chin up so their eyes met. "Darcie's right. Love is a good thing, Maddy, and I love Jamison with all my heart, and he loves me."

I got out of my chair and kneeled on the grass next to Lilly. "Maddy, hon, I love your mom, but I also love you, and I hope you will be okay with me loving both of you and spending more time with you."

Madeline's lips pinched together, and her large brown eyes became thoughtful. Her gaze passed over all three of us, and when it met Darcie's, it lit up. "Does this mean Princess Darcie and me are going to be sisters?"

The girls wrapped their arms around each other and jumped around in a circle.

Lilly laughed and got the excitement under control as nerves coiled inside my gut like a bunch of snakes. "Girls, one step at a time. Let's just spend more time together and start there," she said.

The girls stopped jumping.

"So, are you good with this, Maddy?" I asked her.

She smiled and jumped into my arms. When her arms linked around my neck, the snakes in my gut disappeared. She pulled away and looked deep into my eyes. "You love my mommy, Jamison?" Her expression was serious.

"I do. Very much."

"Good. My mommy needs someone to love her." Madeline pulled Lilly's arm to me. "You can hold her hand and be part of our family."

Lilly and I smiled at each other. Everything was going to be all right. I kissed her, and the girls giggled. Little arms wrapped us in a group hug.

I looked between both girls. "So, it's okay for Lilly and me to date each other?" Dating sounded immature for what I felt for her, but it was an easy word for the girls to understand.

"Yes," Madeline answered with a nod and a wide smile.

I looked at Darcie. Her look was thoughtful, and she placed both her hands on my cheeks and looked thoughtfully into my eyes. "You're happy now, Daddy." She turned to Lilly and smiled. "Thank you for making my daddy happy."

"Oh, sweet girl," Lilly said as a tear rolled down her face.

I pulled them in for another hug. My heart was full, and the hole that had been in it for so long was filled with love for my girls.

Epilogue:

Ten Months Later– Lilly

Jamison and I were married in a small, simple ceremony in February at Orlinda Valley Methodist Church. Rowan and Bryson were the groomsmen, and Kristy and Rose were the bridesmaids. James was the ring bearer, and our girls were the flower girls. It was for family and close friends only, which meant almost all of Orlinda Valley was there.

After a small reception in the basement, we took a quick honeymoon out west at Adler's family's ranch in Texas. Hundreds of acres, a beautiful house, and nothing to do but ride horses and enjoy each other, and that's exactly what we did.

It was early June when we came to Jamison's property to check on the progress of the house we were having built. We were living in Jamison's house in town for now, but we'd just sold it and were hoping to move into our home by the end of August.

Jamison and I walked hand in hand, and the girls skipped along ahead of us. Becca ran and barked, zigzagging through the pasture, back to the girls, and circled around us. She loved the open space and her freedom to run.

The property was beautiful. The front acre was wide open and flat. A perfect spot for a large house, which was where we were having our home built. The back was old pastureland, which Jamison was having cleared. We were going to have goats and chickens also. Yes, I fell in love with Kora's animals, and so did Madeline. Since they were no longer around, it was quiet without the crow of a rooster and the bleats of goats when we visited Tonya's.

We continued our walk down a mowed path. Jamison wanted to show us the area he and the guys had been clearing.

"This is beautiful, Jamison," I said. The trail we were on opened up to slight rolling hills. You could tell where the river was, as there was a line of trees in the distance.

"What's your favorite tree, Lilly?" Darcie asked as we walked to the back portion of the property.

"I know what she likes. Mommy, what are those trees with the pretty white flowers that we would always see in the park?"

I became thoughtful, as Jamison wrapped his arm around my waist. "You mean the dogwoods, Maddy?" I turned to Jamison. "We loved the dogwoods that bloomed in Central Park. Some have pink flowers and others white. You would love them, Darcie."

"Can we plant one of those, Daddy?" Darcie asked.

"I just finished clearing a section. I took everything down but a few trees. Take a look," Jamison said and gestured with his head.

"That's mommy's tree," Darcie said, and she and Madeline took off in a sprint toward the weeping willow that stood in the middle of a few large oaks.

"Mommy, look," Maddie said. On the other side of the oaks were two flowering dogwoods. The flowers were at the end of the season, but the trees were lush and healthy.

"Jamison." I looked at him with wide eyes.

He shrugged. "When we were clearing, we noticed these. I knew you'd mentioned dogwoods, so we kept them. Kai knows a person who owns a tree removal company. He's going to come out here and take down the oaks so the willow and dogwoods will thrive. I thought this would be a perfect place to build a pavilion so we can enjoy the river, the trees, and our family."

The weeping willow was tall, with flowing boughs hanging to the ground. The girls sat under them with laughter in their voices.

The dogwoods had thick trunks with deep green leaves and a few flowers that were still hanging on in the heat of the early summer. It was quiet back here. You could hear the soft rush of the river and birds as they sang in the trees.

"It's a perfect place for us to come and enjoy the water and be a family," I said as I wrapped my arms around Jamison. I kissed him gently, and he brushed my hair behind my neck.

"I'm glad you think so. I have big plans." His face lit up with joy.

I had no doubt. Everything he did for us was more than it needed to be. He was a perfect boyfriend, an amazing fiancé, and now he was absolutely the best husband imaginable, and spoiled each of us rotten with love.

"Daddy, I think we need to plant mommy's lilies under the dogwood tree. That way, my real mommy and my new mommy will always be together, and we will be one big family."

"Darcie," I said as I bent down to look her in the face. "I want you to know that we will always celebrate your mommy, sweet girl. Without Carly, we wouldn't have you, and you are my most favorite redhead ever."

I sat in the grass, and the girls sat down with me. Becca joined us and relaxed in the sun.

"And without you," Darcie said to me, "I wouldn't have a sister, and my daddy wouldn't be happy."

Jamison joined us, and both girls climbed into his lap. "And without any of you girls, I wouldn't be complete. You three are my life." Jamison gave both girls a kiss on their heads.

Everything was perfect. I had the man of my dreams—literally—a beautiful biological daughter and an amazing bonus daughter.

It was almost impossible to believe that this time last year, I had no clue what life was going to throw my way when I came home. But here we are. Madeline had finished her first year of school, she had amazing friends, and we had a life I was so thankful for.

Best of all, Jamison and I had each other and a secret we hadn't told anyone yet.

Jamison lifted both girls off his lap, and they sat facing us. "We know you both love being each other's sisters, but do you think you two would like to be big sisters?"

I looked at Jamison, my eyes wide. We weren't sure when to tell the girls our news. "Are you sure?" I asked him.

He nodded.

"We talk about being big sisters all the time," Madeline said.

"Yeah, but I already am," Darcie replied.

Madeline's brows lowered. "You aren't that much older than me."

"But I still am."

This was the only time they squabbled. Our news might be what put an end to it, for a little while anyway. I took a big breath. "We're going to have a baby," I said.

The girls' mouths both dropped.

"Well?" I was nervous, but like Jamison assured me, I didn't have to be.

"Will she be a princess like us?" Darcie asked.

Jamison chuckled, "Well, maybe. Unless it's a boy, then *he* could be a prince."

"We're having a brother?" Madeline asked with disgust in her voice.

Again, I was nervous. "We don't know yet, but we need you to be prepared either way."

The girls looked at each other and leaned toward each other and whispered. They did this a lot. Talked among themselves, so we couldn't hear it.

"Okay, a boy wouldn't be that bad," Darcie said.

"Yeah," Madeline agreed. "Skylar has a brother, so they can play together."

"He won't be alone like James. That would be good," Darcie agreed.

"Well, you're both being very mature," Jamison said.

"What's mach . . . that word you said, Jamison?" asked Madeline.

"It means you made a decision that someone older than you would make," Jamison explained.

"Oh, okay, and one boy won't be too bad," Darcie said, with her face scrunched up.

"Well," I looked at Jamison for support. I was still getting used to our news and we weren't sure how the girls would take it. "We aren't having one baby. There will be two."

"At one time?" Darcie asked, grimacing even worse than before.

I nodded. "We're having twins."

"Two brothers?" Madeline asked.

"Or two sisters," I said hoping to reassure them both a little.

"Just think of all the princesses if we had two more sisters," Darcie said, the grimace suddenly gone and replaced with wide eyes and a huge smile. The girls jumped up and ran off, chatting excitedly amongst themselves. Words like princess and castle are all we heard.

I watched them and laughed as I moved to lean on Jamison. "Hey." I nudged him. He was staring off into oblivion. "What's wrong?"

He turned slowly toward me. "I never thought until this moment that it could be two girls." He shook his head. "God help us if we have two more girls."

As I kissed his lips, my smile was wide. "If we do, you will be perfect. You're an amazing girl dad. If we have boys, well, it's a good thing I'll be a nurse. We'll save money on medical bills if they're as crazy as their father was."

He grabbed me, and I squealed with laughter as he laid me down on the grass. "Remember, you loved me even when I was crazy and accident prone."

Young Jamison was always breaking a bone or getting stitches. I held his face and stared into his blue eyes. "I loved the *idea* of you. Now I love the *real* you. Every single thing about you."

"You are amazing, Mrs. McKendry." He kissed me lightly. "I love you more than all the grass on our property and the stars in the sky. He brushed hair out of my face and placed a soft kiss on my forehead. "You drive me wild Lilly-Pad."

My heart fluttered as it often did when he looked at me like that. I kissed his lips and became lost, as usual, in all things Jamison.

Our kiss was interrupted by the screaming of two little princesses as they jumped on Jamison's back.

He laughed and wrestled with them in the grass.

I placed my hand on the small pooch that was our babies.

It didn't matter if they were boys or girls, because I had no doubt they would pull our family closer together.

I might have dreamed of Jamison when I was younger, but reality is better than dreams any day, and in five months, there will be two little beings running around who were a perfect mixture of my family, no matter if they are two boys or two more amazing little girls.

Notes to the Reader

Thank you for taking your time and reading *No Love Like Yours*. I hope you enjoyed reading it as much as I enjoyed writing it.

If you loved the story and characters, I would be so grateful to you if you would take the time and leave a review wherever you purchased the book. Reviews help authors and are so appreciated. I hope you come back to Orlinda Valley again. The third book *No Place Like Home* will be out in 2025.

I would love to hear from my readers, so please connect with me, on Instagram and Facebook—Donna R. Madden Writer, or email me at drmaddenauthor@outlook.com or scan the QR code to join my newsletter and find my books everywhere.

www.ingramcontent.com/pod-product-compliance
Lightning Source LLC
Chambersburg PA
CBHW030151310726
48970CB00005B/1690